An Extraordinary Union

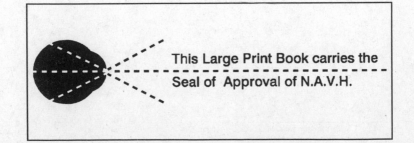
This Large Print Book carries the
Seal of Approval of N.A.V.H.

THE LOYAL LEAGUE

An Extraordinary Union

Alyssa Cole

THORNDIKE PRESS

A part of Gale, Cengage Learning

GALE
CENGAGE Learning·

Farmington Hills, Mich • San Francisco • New York • Waterville, Maine
Meriden, Conn • Mason, Ohio • Chicago

GALE
CENGAGE Learning®

Thorndike Press® Large Print African-American.
The text of this Large Print edition is unabridged.
Other aspects of the book may vary from the original edition.
Set in 16 pt. Plantin.

LIBRARY OF CONGRESS CATALOGING-IN-PUBLICATION DATA

Names: Cole, Alyssa, author.
Title: An extraordinary union / by Alyssa Cole.
Description: Waterville, Maine : Thorndike Press, 2017. | Series: The Loyal League |
    Series: Thorndike Press large print African-American
Identifiers: LCCN 2017004717| ISBN 9781410497901 (hardcover) | ISBN 1410497909
    (hardcover)
Subjects: LCSH: African American women—Fiction. | Women spies—Fiction. |
    Pinkerton's National Detective Agency—Fiction. | United States—History—Civil
    War, 1861–1865—Fiction. | Large type books. | GSAFD: Historical fiction. | Spy
    stories. | Love stories.
Classification: LCC PS3603.O427 E97 2017 | DDC 813/.6—dc23
LC record available at https://lccn.loc.gov/2017004717

Published in 2017 by arrangement with Kensington Books, an imprint
of Kensington Publishing Corp.

Printed in the United States of America
1 2 3 4 5 6 7 21 20 19 18 17

For Isabell, the last enslaved person and the first emancipated person in my family's history

PROLOGUE

April 1861
Baltimore, Maryland
"It will be an easy assignment, a simple pass-
ing on of information. One that even a girl
such as yourself should be able to handle."

Elle suppressed a bitter laugh as she recalled her Loyal League master LaValle's briefing from a few days before.

Easy?

Either her superior had dreadfully under-estimated the Southern male's love of an opportunity to do violence, or he'd purposely set her in the middle of danger. She doubted it was the latter, but the man *was* unduly annoyed at her for having the gall to aid her country without virtue of a certain appendage hanging between her thighs. As if a penis would somehow prove more use-ful to the Cause than her peculiar "gift." From what Elle had discerned over the last few months, whatever supposed benefits the organ conferred were canceled out by mulishness and a propensity for tomfoolery. The scene around her proved that well enough.

Her skin prickled with unease as she watched men stream into Baltimore's Bolton Street Station, egging each other on as they awaited the train carrying those first brave souls to answer Lincoln's call for volunteers after the abomination at Fort Sumter. Hats were pulled low and the rumble of deep voices plotting mischief filled the air. The crowd continued to grow, filling with plug uglies and longshoremen and aristocrats alike, until the air was thick with the smell of tobacco and unwashed bodies. The possibility of an *easy* assignment had been trodden under the boots of these scoundrels with hate in their hearts and excitement in their eyes.

Elle pressed her back to the wall and hoped the dingy gray frock and head wrap common to slave women would help her blend into the shadows.

"Gonna give these Yankee bastards a taste of my prick," a homely man a few feet away from her said, tossing a small, sharp knife from hand to hand.

Something akin to fear shivered down Elle's spine — but true fear was rooted in

8

the unknown. The secessionists of Baltimore had already ripped up the railroad tracks and torn down the telegraph lines, cutting off the city from the Capital and showing that they meant every threat they uttered. They were plotting death and discord. Elle knew exactly what would happen if any of them suspected the black woman in the corner was in possession of ciphers that, once decoded, would bring many of their ilk before the justice of the Army of the Potomac. Baltimore had a secessionist problem, and Elle was there to solve it — if she wasn't found out first.

Her stomach lurched as a man brushed past her, and she chastised herself. She'd survived weeks on the stormy seas during her ill-conceived voyage to and from Liberia the year before; she should be able to gird her loins a damned sight better than that. Hell, she'd lost Daniel and survived that, too. She felt a wash of heat at her eyes and pushed away thoughts of her best friend and the rejection in his spun-honey gaze the last time she'd seen him. That was the past. She'd experienced a sight more danger than seasickness and men's broken hearts in the last few months.

She was a Loyal League woman now. Her gift had gained her entrance into the society of blacks, freed and enslaved alike, with networks across the country funneling as much information to the North as they could gather. It was her quick wit — and quick draw — that had ensured her place as a detective, working to prevent utter chaos across the country as it slipped further into disunion. The nation was now embroiled in a war that would either see her people freed or forsaken. Whether LaValle had downplayed the Baltimore situation was unimportant; this was her first solo assignment and she refused to give anyone, Union or Confederate, the pleasure of her failure.

Elle looked at the large clock face in the central hall of the train station, willing the minute hand to move faster and the train bearing the regiments to arrive. Her target was the Washington Artillery out of Pottsville, Pennsylvania; she sought their manservant, Nick Biddle. While Biddle was seen as a capable aide to the company's captain, like many of her brethren he was much more than that. He was another who had sworn the Four L's: Loyalty, Legacy, Life, and Lincoln.

There was a sudden commotion from the swath of men closest to the tunnel. The realization of impending action throbbed through the crowd from one end to the other just before the train whistle cried out, announcing its arrival. The men all around Elle surged forward, as if the train emitted some magnetic force on them, drawing hatred to righteousness. Elle's stomach twisted again and she closed her eyes against the ugly scene before her.

Men shouted and showered the train with garbage and rocks. Animal entrails and other waste slammed against the impervious metal with little effect, but inside there were men made of flesh and bone who would have to march though this madness.

Why must it be like this? Elle suddenly felt small and insignificant in the face of the pure hatred filling the air around her. She missed her home. She missed her parents. What was her purpose in this fight in which neither side could truly be trusted?

She closed her eyes and focused her thoughts inward, taking a deep breath to quell her racing thoughts. She *would* reach Biddle and relay the message, crowd be damned. She was no simpering miss. She was Ellen Burns, and she was going to help destroy the Confederacy.

She lifted her skirts to move toward the train, but a man stepped in front of her. He was taller and broader than the ragtag group who had occupied the space before him.

11

He, too, exuded a kind of magnetism, drawing Elle's gaze to him when she should be looking away. His clothing, tight britches and a rough-hewn coat, suggested he was a dock worker. The odor of fish further supported her supposition.

The men around him seethed, becoming more riled as they watched the actions of those already attempting to storm the train, and he joined them in their anti-Union rants. "Jeff Davis is the true President!" he cawed over his companion's heads. He shifted position, allowing her a better view of him. Most of his face was obscured by a heavy black beard that needed trimming, but his eyes were visible. Unlike the other men around him, whose gazes were dark with a kind of feverish mania, his intense blue eyes were clear and attentive as he surveyed the crowd. He seemed of them but not one of them, something Elle could pinpoint with accuracy since she had spent a good portion of her life in just such a position.

His head swiveled a bit more and his gaze locked on hers. She froze like some creeping thing that hopes if it doesn't move it can go undetected by that which would prey on it. Their gazes held for an infinite moment, and the roar of the crowd faded into the background. A disquiet she'd never known gripped her; the man didn't leer or hurl abuse or look right through her. He *saw* her, and that was the most dangerous turn of events that could have befallen her.

Their staredown was broken when he was jostled by another surge of the crowd, which was slowly but resolutely pushing toward the door of the station. Everything came back into focus and Elle released the breath that had been caught in her gullet. The soldiers had disembarked and were marching from the station toward the street now, and the angry men searching for targets followed right along. The majority of the regiments who'd arrived were heading to Fort McHenry, save Biddle's, which was heading to the Capital. Elle held many ciphers in her head; the ones she needed to get to Biddle were only a small portion. She couldn't risk passing such information by post, and telegraph lines were down or unsecured. Biddle was the only man present who had sworn the same oath as she, and thus he was the only man she trusted to get her information to the Capital.

Elle slipped out of the station through a side door and pressed along buildings behind the seething crowd as she tried to follow the path of the regiments. Biddle should have been easy to find, being the only Negro, but in the midst of the unruly mob hurling invectives and the police officers halfheartedly trying to protect soldiers, it was hard to make him out. The crowd did her work for her. As a group of men split off from the other Penn regiments, she heard one voice and then another shout "Nigger! Nigger in a uniform!"

All hell broke loose then, with the barely restrained mob converging on both the regiment and their own city police officers. Fists began to fly, as did bottles, bricks, and anything the incensed men could get their hands on.

Elle froze for a moment, fear robbing her of her purpose; then she remembered her first night of training with the Loyal League. LaValle had shoved a small book entitled *The Art of War* at her with the command, "Read this tonight. You'll recite it to me word for word in the morning or you'll return to the North where a woman like you belongs." That he'd thought it a difficult task showed his limitations, not Elle's. In the end, the ancient strategies had proven more useful than anything LaValle had tried to impress on her. As the rioting men whipped themselves up into a fervor, it was Sun Tzu's words that spurred her forward:

"In the midst of chaos, there is also opportunity."

She scurried into the mass of people, her small stature allowing her to slip through the roiling crowd like a sleek catfish through the river grass. Biddle was in her sights, and she aimed straight for him. He turned just as she skidded to a halt in front of him. Elle was shocked to discover the man was older than her father. "I see you have traveled far," she said.

His reply was quick, given with just a hint of paternal indulgence that should have annoyed her but comforted her instead. "I have, and it has been a lonesome road, my child."

Elle felt relief splinter through her. The task was almost complete.

"Remember this, and pass it on to those who would aid our cause when you reach Washington: Eight to sixteen as the crow flies. Thirty to forty-five as the sun sets," she rushed out, then took his hand and bade him repeat it. She didn't think it took a spectacular memory to remember two short ciphers, but she had no personal reference point given her own stupendous ability. She hoped she was right.

"I will see that this gets to Pinkerton's

ears," he said, then turned and continued on with his regiment. As he walked away, Elle's knees began to shake with relief. She had waited days to complete a mission that had taken perhaps thirty seconds.

Biddle was walking ahead of her, then suddenly he wasn't. He was flat on the ground, a deep gash on the side of his head. He'd been felled by one of the bricks that were still being hurled by the secessionist bastards as they rioted. The fear that had stalked Elle her entire mission pounced then, crushing her under its weight as she looked at Biddle's prone form in disbelief. For a moment she thought he must be dead, surely he must. But then he staggered to his feet, looking back at her with dazed eyes before being hustled off by members of his regiment.

She snaked her way back into the crowd, heart thumping and lungs finally filling with air.

Success. Something akin to a smile tugged at her mouth, but it was just a physical response to the adrenaline and pride that coursed through her veins.

She spied an opening in the melee, an alley used by slaves as a shortcut while running errands. It would lead her out to a street that would be free of the vile men who surrounded her now. She'd almost made it to the alley's opening when a man's grip closed around her arm, tightening like a vise. She tried to pull away, but she could not escape the strength of his grasp.

"Why did you run to that man?" The accent was a strange mélange of country boy and foreigner — German? — the same as so many lower-class men as to be unexceptional. She turned and her breath caught in her throat — again. It was the blasted dock worker from the train station.

How was it that she was invisible to men like him, except in the exact moments it would cause her the most trouble?

"I ran because walking isn't prudent when in the midst of a mob, you fool. Now release me at once," she demanded before she could stop herself, then growled in agitation. She was supposed to be meek and unassuming if accosted, but her natural inclination got the better of her. It wouldn't be the first time, and if LaValle got wind of it he wouldn't be pleased. She modulated her tone to pleading, her accent to one that matched her clothing. "Please let me go, sah."

His eyebrows rose, but his expression was one of amusement, not anger. "Not until you answer me. Either you're an uncommon hussy, hoping to circumvent your competition, or you sought that regiment out with some specific purpose. You can tell me now, or I can ask those fellows knocking skulls over yonder for their opinion."

Humiliation scalded Elle to her toes. It wasn't that no one had ever spoken to her that way before — plenty of people had belittled her in her lifetime — but the insinuating smirk on his face was too much to countenance. She kept her gaze locked with his, but she let it soften just a bit to throw him off kilter. It worked, in her favor not his. The moment she felt his hold give slightly, she jabbed a fist forward, connecting with his side, near the kidney. Hitting a white man was dangerous, but no more so than her mission being discovered if she was arrested.

He released her in that first split second of surprise, and that was all she needed. She turned and took off. She would outrun him. She would make it back to her safe house.

She'd gotten a few feet away when pain exploded at the base of her throat, the tender hollow where neck meets clavicle. Sharp, slicing heat and then a jagged chunk of brick tumbled down the front of her dress, edged in red. She couldn't breathe,

18

and when she brought her hand to her neck, blood flowed over her fingers.

No.

Elle prided herself on having never fainted, but the world started to go dim around the edges, and although it was a cool spring afternoon she was sweating like it was midday on the plantation in Georgia.

"You dagnabbed wench. Why didn't you just answer the question?" a deep, rich voice asked. Then her feet were no longer touching the ground and she couldn't tell if it was because she had passed out or been pushed over. Everything was growing hazy, even the pain at her throat. For a moment she floated in nothingness and then she was crushed against something warm and solid and scented with the tang of the sea. After that, darkness edged in and consumed all. . . .

When Elle awoke, she didn't know where she was or how much time had passed. She was in a dark room, lit by the dimmest candle, and she supposed that some would call the hard surface she lay on a bed. There was something at her throat that smelled of hospice. She groaned.

LaValle's face appeared above hers, and although she knew she often vexed him something awful, his relief upon seeing her awaken was clear.

He brought a cup of water to her mouth, and although she wanted to drink like a horse at the trough, he only allowed her a trickle. When she tried to swallow, she was thankful for it.

"You aren't to speak," he said before she could ask what had happened and how she'd ended up in this small chirurgery. "Doctor's orders, and a blessing for me. What I need from you requires only a nod or a shake, girl. Did you pass the information to Biddle?"

She nodded, her chin pressing into a poultice that rested on her neck. She kept her gaze averted from his, unable to talk and not wanting to see his disappointment, his judgment.

"Excellent," LaValle said, taking her chin and lifting her face in his direction. His gaze was speculative as he regarded her. "I had my doubts, but you just might prove useful to the Cause after all."

CHAPTER 1

January 1862
Richmond, Virginia
"No man can put a chain about the ankle of his fellow man without at last finding the other end fastened about his own neck."

The tract of text popped into Elle's mind as she tried to remain calm in the face of yet another indignity. She surely hoped Mr. Douglass was right; she had to believe he was, or else she would give in to the angry fantasies that plagued her every time she was forced into the presence of her mistress. She still had half a mind to dump the steaming cup of tea in her hands directly onto Susie Caffrey's damned head, but that wouldn't have been acceptable even when she was a freedwoman. Besides, as much as Susie chafed her hide, she was a sight less painful to deal with than the sting of a leather strap.

Still, it was mighty tempting, especially as

the young woman lounged on the chaise in the mansion's parlor, issuing orders like a tyrant and flipping through a scandal sheet detailing the goings-on of the Richmond elite. The gossip rags were Susie's obsession, as if the fact that her father was a newly elected Confederate senator and war raged on their very doorstep weren't excitement enough. She read them in the guise of doing her duty for the Richmond Vigilance Committee, a group that played at spy hunting but relied on belligerence and wild guesses to control their fellow citizens.

Elle briefly allowed herself the fantasy of the dark brew dripping down over the chit's ridiculous frilly hat, savored the possibility of destroying Susie's perfectly set curls and staining the beautiful blue silk gown she wore. It would almost be worth it, just for the memory. Remembering everything that she saw and heard was Elle's specialty, and there were a rare few things caught in the steel trap of her mind that brought her pleasure of late.

A pair of pale fingers snapped in front of her face, pulling her from her reverie.

"You're dumb, but I know you're not deaf," Susie drawled. "Now I see how the tea went cold in the first place, with you lolly-gagging about like you don't have work to do. I *said* take it away." Susie's eyes were a warm hazel that could have been kind, but she narrowed them like a grimalkin at Elle before returning her attention to her frivolous newspaper.

You're a slave now, Elle reminded herself of LaValle's words as she turned and marched out of the parlor and down the high-ceilinged hallway lined with marble statuary and exquisite paintings. The two cornrowed plaits she used to tame her thick curls bounced against her shoulders, propelled by the force of her stride. *You'll do as you're told and you won't give them any sass. Too much depends on this.* That command stuck in her craw, though. Instead, she thought of Sun Tzu's advice for luring an enemy into defeat: *"Be extremely subtle, even to the point of formlessness. Be extremely mysterious, even to the point of soundlessness. Thereby you can be the director of the opponent's fate."*

Yes, that was much more to her liking.

Elle repeated the words as she took the "cold" tea that Susie had rejected and returned to the kitchen, nearly scalding herself when it slopped over the rim of the delicate china cup and onto her hand. She bit back an exclamation — it wouldn't do for her to be shouting in the kitchen, or for

23

her to make any noise at all. She had a role to play.

She slowed her angry pace — it wouldn't do to break any dishes, either. The last thing she needed was to call attention to herself. Despite her sour mood, she gave a friendly nod to Mary, the head of the household slaves, as she entered the hot kitchen. Mary's small, rounded nose and wide cheekbones marked her as a slave, although her skin was barely darker than Susie's — the color of fresh milk with the slightest dash of rich cocoa added for taste.

"She sent it back again?" Mary asked, glancing in the direction of the parlor before rolling her eyes. "Lord, Li'l Bit. Not that Miss Susie was an angel before, but she been pure devil since you showed up. She always finding something to get on you about! I shoulda warned you she was in a mood today."

Elle couldn't help but smile when Mary addressed her by her nickname. It made her feel like she belonged, despite the fact that she was at the mansion under false pretenses. *"You a li'l bit too small and a li'l bit too dark, but you still pretty all the same,"* Mary had told her when she first arrived. *"Best be careful around Marse Caffrey and his friends."*

Mary moved around the kitchen, deftly

navigating between the chaos of cooks and liveried slaves preparing for the arrival of Senator Caffrey and his guests. Elle followed close behind her, like Mary's noontime shadow — shorter, darker, and totally silent. Although she paid attention to everything Mary said, she was also observing the other slaves, listening to snippets of their conversations in case someone shared something they'd overheard from the Caffreys and their guests.

Despite her heavy workload, Mary had taken Elle under her wing upon her arrival. The other slaves had quickly grown tired of having to explain things to the mute woman who seemed unable to do the simplest tasks with efficiency, but Mary had worked with Elle until she grew accustomed to her place in the household. And if Mary found it strange that Elle always wanted to do work that kept her in the presence of Senator Caffrey and his compatriots, or in his office while he was away from it, she didn't say anything about it.

"As if tea come cheap these days," Mary continued, taking the cup from Elle's hands. She blew carefully and then took a quick sip. "The stuff is scarce as hen's teeth! Men risk their necks smuggling past the Yank blockade, and this little fool think nothing of throwing it out like the wash water. I swear, that girl ain't worth more than a fart in a whirlwind."

Mary took Susie's laissez-faire attitude about the blockade personally. Her husband, Robert, was a slave, too, and a respected river pilot who was sought after by every captain on the James. He was hired out to different men, getting to keep a sliver of each fee paid to his master. During their short visits, he told Mary the particulars of how the upper classes were obtaining smuggled luxuries like tea and sugar, despite the Union blockade, while most struggled to get the bare essentials. Occasionally, he'd been forced to smuggle the goods himself. It galled him to help sustain those who fought for the continuation of slavery, but a slave, especially a hired-out slave with a wife working in a senator's mansion, was in no position to turn down a demand from Davis's army. Besides, every coin he earned brought him and Mary closer to buying their freedom.

Mary stormed over to the cask that had been filled to the brim with coffee beans when Elle arrived but was now perilously close to empty. "Oh, good Lord, and coffee is even worse than tea. Nearly fifty-five cents a pound! Missus is going to have my head.

Maybe I should try that chicory mix folk been using. . . ." Mary receded into her thoughts, obviously calculating where and how and from whom she could obtain what product at what price, and what would be lost in the bargain. With the war waging all around them, supplies were tight and tempers were short. Yet Mary had to keep the house running like there wasn't a blockade, or face the repercussions.

"I know it's dead wrong, but when the missus get on me about how stringy the roast is or how the potatoes is spoiled, I wish Abe would just recall his navy and lift the blockade," Mary confided, her dark eyes weary. "Ain't that a shame? They say the man's thinking of freeing us and all I can worry about is what missus gonna hound me about next."

Elle gave the woman's shoulder a reassuring squeeze, and Mary patted Elle's hand in thanks before grabbing a pile of napkins to fold. "As for Susie, she's all a tizzy because her daddy's bringing home some Reb come down from Maryland. Said he's carrying news from them sneaky Baltimore secesh, who smile in Lincoln's face and then plot against him behind closed doors."

Elle's hand went to her throat at the mention of Baltimore, but she caught herself before she touched the thick scar there. What mattered was that she'd recovered from the injury, although her inability to talk after her injury had given LaValle the brilliant idea of having her pose as mute. It would keep her sharp tongue from ruining the sensitive arrangement of working in a target's home; if she couldn't talk, she couldn't place herself and other operatives in danger. She understood that there was a kernel of punishment in the order, too; payback for one terse rejoinder too many. Her mama always did say her smart mouth would get her into trouble one day.

Mary continued. "Marse got stuck waiting for a ferry with the fella and think he's the best thing since Moses parted the Red Sea. He been lonely since we moved out here for the Congress, you know. Funny, since there are so many more people here than back on the plantation."

It was amazing how much information, both business and personal, people bandied about freely in front of their slaves. Elle didn't know why it still surprised her — after all, it was why she had been assigned that particular mission — but each fresh realization incited a confusing mixture of both glee and contempt. She felt a flicker of excitement, too, this time. This new friend of the senator's might be useful. New sources of information always meant the possibility of learning something that could help stamp out the rebellion for good.

Mary prattled on about the goings-on in the house, unaware that Elle was pondering things like the fate of their nation. "This fella better be careful, though — Miss Susie ain't had a beau with the men all going off to fight, and she's ready to sink her claws into anybody. He could be a dried-up old prune, long as he's not married, and maybe even if he is."

Elle nearly opened her mouth to concur, then shut it tightly, instead giving Mary a wry smile and rolling her eyes. Being a slave again after so many years of freedom in the North was hard enough, even if it was just an act; the additional subterfuge of being a *mute* slave was an added difficulty.

Damned LaValle and his ridiculous ideas.

"Go on and make sure the table is set right," Mary said as she turned back to her work. "Last thing I need is the missus hounding me about a soup spoon or bread plate out of place. You remember how the settings go?"

Elle nodded. Remembering minutiae was her raison d'être, but of course Mary wouldn't be privy to that.

She headed into the dining room to double-check the place settings. As she worked, she wondered what news this Reb brought with him from Baltimore. Plenty of secessionists had remained in the city instead of fleeing south, and they used their connections to garner information for the Confederacy. The information she'd provided to Biddle had taken down a politician and his underlings; further proof that treachery within the Union reached to its very highest levels. If this new man was carrying information from Baltimore that could supplement the information already preserved in Elle's memory, this stranger could prove to be very valuable, indeed.

Sunlight streamed into the dining room, highlighting the finery — the satin finish of the patterned wallpaper, the large walnut table that had been polished until it shone. Light glinted off of the silverware, accenting the fine china at each setting. Elle thought of her own dwelling in Richmond: one tiny, shabby room in a home for hired-out slaves with a bed barely fit for a barn animal. And it was a damned luxury compared to what other slaves, the ones who worked the land from morning to night with no reward, called home. And this was what the South fought to maintain.

Elle darted out a hand to adjust a small plate that hung precariously on the edge of the table, but her angry musings turned what should have been a gentle prod into a forceful nudge. The plate flew off of the edge of the table, hovering in the air for a moment suspended in time before her hand shot out and caught it. She gripped the plate to her chest, surprised that her wildly beating heart didn't tap out a tune on the ceramic. A broken plate was a punishable offense — Missus Caffrey was very particular about her household, and Elle didn't want to invite her wrath in addition to Susie's constant harassment. She laid the plate down, gently this time.

"You move quicker than a spring-loaded cat." It was a masculine voice that made the ridiculous observation, deep and smooth and tinged with a lilt that spoke of shores far from Richmond somewhere in its past. There was something familiar in the voice that slipped around Elle like the velvet lining of her favorite cloak on a cold New England day.

She whirled and found herself facing an expanse of gray: a Rebel uniform stretched over a wide chest. Broad shoulders and strong arms filled the rest of the jacket, and

31

when she looked up, warm gray eyes stared down into hers. Not gray — a stunning silvery blue that would have been enhanced by the uniform of whichever side he had chosen in this terrible war. Jet-black hair hung over his ears, complemented by side-burns that were just a bit overlong and shot through with streaks of silver. His face was smooth and unlined, except for the crow's feet that creased the corners of his eyes.

"You put those boys doing drills down at the Central Fairgrounds to shame. Most of them can't even walk straight," he said, his vivid gaze locked on her. "And not a one of them is half as pretty as you."

Heat rushed to her cheeks, unbidden and unwanted. Now that he had spoken more than a few words, Elle could detect the trace of a Scottish accent. She'd heard the accent often enough back home in Massachusetts, and in her current dealings with the grocer MacTavish and his clan of Richmond aboli-tionists, but it had never made her face heat like a cauldron over a flame. She wasn't sure any man's voice ever had. She was poleaxed, and by a man whose every marking screamed *ENEMY!*

His rosy lips curved up into a grin as she stared at him, as if their situation were normal. As if he weren't making conversation with a slave, and insinuating conversation at that.

That's when realization set in for Elle. She was alone in a room with a man in a Rebel uniform, and he was smiling at her. Maybe if it had been an innocent grin she would have been less alarmed, but it was the smile of a man who was used to getting his way. She backed away from him, watching his smile recede as quickly as her feet did. After only a few steps, she found herself pressed against the dining table.

He wouldn't . . . he couldn't in the dining room, could he? Surely he wouldn't be so brazen? Elle had known that there would be a risk of this, of being taken advantage of by a man who saw her merely as a vessel in which to slake his desire. It could happen anywhere, really, North or South, but in these parts it was something of an institution. The slaves who were barely darker than their masters, like Mary, were proof enough of that.

Her fingers itched to grab one of the sharp utensils behind her, but if she fought him she'd surely be beaten and likely removed from the house. Her compatriots would lose a vital source of information and all might be lost if Senator Caffrey searched too deeply into how she had come to work in his household.

Elle's stomach gave a vicious tumble and she inhaled sharply, as if fresh air could blow away the sickness building in her belly.

Anything for the Union. The rallying cry rang hollow, but she had pledged to serve her country. Elle squared her shoulders and looked the man in the eye, hoping he couldn't see her fear. If he were going to try to ravage her, he'd have to acknowledge her first, dammit. His brows rose in confusion as she held his gaze and then it was he who stepped back, a frown pulling at his mouth as comprehension dawned on him.

"No," he choked out. His jaw was tight and the playful light had gone from his strange, dual-tone eyes. "I would never."

His words were brittle, and it was instantly clear that she had mistaken his intentions. His reaction intrigued her, even as her heart raced from the fright he'd given her. Despite the atrocities they committed against her people, she knew that a Southern man was just as human as she; they were the ones who had trouble coming to terms with that reality. But the deference in the man's tone and the guilt on his face were something she hadn't experienced since arriving in Richmond, and she couldn't help but wonder at it.

"My apologies if I frightened you, lass. I only meant to tease, but these aren't exactly teasing times, are they?" he asked, stepping out of her path. "Please forgive my boldness."

Elle realized that her hands had been clenched into fists, and his apology only made her ball her hands more tightly. She couldn't have spoken if she wanted to, and was glad that she wouldn't have to thanks to her subterfuge. She pushed past him and made for the door just as Senator Caffrey and his wife swept in. They didn't spare her a second glance, but she could feel the strange man's gaze on her as she fled. It was a weight at her back, pushing her to get away from him and the confusing reaction he had stirred within her as fast as she could.

She was usually so careful, had even been called graceful, but as she rushed through the door she bumped right into Susie, who had been pompously gliding into the room like a debutante entering her cotillion. It was the barest of impacts, but the young woman somehow ended up flat on her back, legs pumping the air indignantly.

"Help! Mother!" Susie's hoops still valiantly performed their duty, which was unfortunate given her horizontal position.

At least her petticoats were clean; many Southern women had already been reduced to old, frayed things as they used their fine fabrics to sew Rebel uniforms and other army necessities at their sewing circles.

Senator Caffrey and his wife gasped and looked away. The stranger took a sudden interest in the silverware Elle had thought to skewer him with, but his face was red as a tomato, except for where his lips pressed into a pale line.

And here I thought breaking a plate would be the worst I could do today, Elle thought. Shocked laughter tickled her throat, but she swallowed against it and collected herself. This was no laughing matter. She was supposed to be a prized operative, but she had drawn more attention to herself in the last few minutes than would have been advisable, ever. Susie had already taken an instant dislike to her, and now she was sure to be out for vengeance. Showing the handsome stranger her drawers was likely Susie's end game, of course, but Elle imagined that the woman had probably planned to do so on her own terms.

Elle forced her expression into one of contrition and leaned forward to help the woman up, but Susie pushed her away viciously, causing her to stumble back.

For someone who can't seem to pick them-selves up, she sure is strong.

"Get away from me, you clumsy thing," Susie spat, her face contorted by fury. "Mute, stupid, and now it seems she's blind, too? Because if she's not, then that means she knocked me over on purpose."

Elle's gaze veered toward the elder Caffreys. An accusation of intentional violence against one's owner was not one that was taken lightly. They looked at each other, her brows raised, his drawn.

The blue-eyed man sauntered past Elle and knelt at Susie's side.

"Now come, Miss Caffrey," he said. His voice was soothing and drew Susie's attention, just as it had Elle's. "It was an accident. I told her to fetch me some water and be quick about it, and she must have seen how parched I was because she flew out of here like the devil himself was after her! Sometimes people do the stupidest things without meaning to." His glance flew up to Elle's, lingering for a moment before returning to the prone Susie.

He sounds different, Elle thought, ignoring his pointed look and the fact that he was defending her. She focused on the details she needed to remember. Details were use-ful. Details were safe. His burr was softer and his Southern accent more pronounced. *Like he's purposely trying to sound more like them. . . .*

Senator Caffrey and his wife chuckled uncomfortably, but Susie wouldn't be appeased, even as the handsome man pulled her to her feet and held her hand in his.

"This is the second time today she's harassed me," Susie said. "Earlier I told her never to bring me cold tea again unless she wanted to be out in the fields where an animal like her belongs, and she gave me a *look.* Now she's knocked me to the ground. We treat our darkies like family here, but something about this girl just ain't right."

"You know she's simple, dear," Mrs. Caffrey said patiently. "A regular darkie isn't very smart, what do you expect from a simple one? Remember what Reverend Mills said in last week's sermon. *'We must treat our slaves as we treat our children, for they know no more than a babe.'* Do you get mad when Brutus knocks you over?"

Brutus was the neighbor's dog. He was an ill-behaved, slobbering mess, yet Mistress Caffrey thought Elle was of the same class as he. Heat suffused Elle's face and tears pricked at her eyes, embarrassing her more than if she'd been the one to show her drawers. She hated being the center of attention, hated the feeling of everyone watching her like she was a creature on display instead of a human being. She'd had enough of that for a lifetime. Mostly, she hated the way the blue-eyed man observed her with his keen gaze. It took her back to all those years spent on the abolitionist circuit, where she had been expected to recite prose, spell difficult words, and generally serve as a shining example that negritude did not have to equal idiocy.

I can recite the entire works of Shakespeare, you damned ignorant girl! What can you do besides simper and cry? Elle wanted to scream, to shout the words of Scott, or Keats, or Donne. But that would be foolish. It would undermine everything she and the others who fought for the Union were working toward, and in the end they'd still think her a slave, just one who could perform a special trick. She'd be a source of amusement for their guests, like a beast that could dance on its hind legs. Even people who considered themselves her friends had treated her as such, and Elle never wanted to be anyone's parlor act again. But she didn't mind putting on another type of performance.

She let the angry tears come, and dropped to her knees in front of Susie, shaking her head repentantly.

They want simple, they'll get it, she thought viciously as she grabbed at Susie's skirt, wringing the fine material in her hands. Ugly noises worked in her throat, and she hoped that such sounds were something truly within a mute's range, or that no one would be the wiser if they weren't.

Susie glared at her with revulsion, and Senator Caffrey and his wife looked at her with impassive disdain, waiting for her demonstration to be over. But the stranger looked at her with something in his eyes that wasn't disgust or pity. There was something knowing in his look, and there seemed to be a bit of mischief, too.

Susie kicked at Elle's hands, and Elle jumped back to her feet. She kept her head down so no one could discern the fury behind her tears.

"Look at how sorry she is that she hurt her mistress," the Rebel soldier said. "Anyone can see that the fool doesn't know any better, with that gibbering and crying. You know these darkies can't do nothing unless they're told, so don't worry yourself about her clumsiness. Come now, your papa promised me good conversation with a pretty young woman. Was that a lie?"

Susie's face was returning to its regular

peachy hues from the angry mottling of just a few moments earlier. Just like that, she didn't even seem to remember Elle existed.

"Papa never lies," she cooed up at the man, and Elle wished she could push the chit down again.

"Good," he said with a smile, then turned to Elle with that inscrutable look. "Get on now. And stay outta here so you don't upset your mistress again."

"I see you know how to handle them," Senator Caffrey said approvingly as Elle made her exit, this time walking slowly with her head bowed subserviently. She shook with anger at her dismissal, at having to bow and scrape for these people who wouldn't know common sense or hard work if it hit them like scattershot.

She returned to the kitchen, masking her anger as she hurried through the long hallway, nodding her head deferentially at the newly arrived guests as they filed past her. She began cleaning up after the other servants as they prepared the platters of food, but her mind kept going back to the man in gray.

Why did she care that he had been upset about scaring her? Did he deserve some special citation for being human enough to realize that a slave woman might be scared of rape? And why had he lied to Susie about asking her to fetch him some water? Did he mean to hold it over her?

Elle stormed over to the wash basin and began scrubbing pans, ignoring Timothy the cook as he hovered over the stove, stirring a delicious-smelling sauce. She didn't bother asking what it was — none of the slaves would get a taste of it.

The only thing that mattered about the man in the dining room was the color of his uniform, Elle told herself. That said everything about what he thought of her, his chagrin be damned. Despite his attempts to spare her any trouble, he'd made a point of ordering her out like a simpleton. Now she wouldn't be able to hear what was discussed during the meal, or to learn what information the man had brought.

She scrubbed at an exceptionally filthy pan and then dashed it into the basin.

"Who worked you into such a fine froth, Miss Elle?"

Elle turned to find Timothy watching her with a look that hovered between amusement and concern. Timothy was the only person who knew who she was, who she really was, but she couldn't risk anyone hearing her speak to him. Not being able to talk was one thing, but not being able to vent one's frustrations was well and truly isolating. She growled with frustration instead.

Timothy gave a high-pitched chuckle; the sound fit his slight stature. He was barely a head taller than Elle. His light, even-toned voice was a comfort to her frayed nerves.

"Later, Elle. There's a package coming in tonight, by the way. Something that could be mighty useful to us. Should be delivered to the bluff around dusk, if you're able to pick it up."

Excitement pulsed through her. He was talking Loyal League business.

"I'd pick it up myself, but I gotta do extra work because Jack the kitchen boy took sick with that fever going round." His expression darkened. "And I'm barely gonna sleep tonight — I gotta get up tomorrow early to go pick up the slave they bought this past week. He's younger than Jack, even."

The Caffreys were still adding to their household it seemed. *At least it's not so bad here. They don't whip easily and —*

She placed a hand to her stomach to quell the nausea the idea induced. Was a few weeks all it took to start losing yourself, then? To start rationalizing away the abomination of slavery so that she could think of people like the Caffreys as "not so bad"?

They were buying a child — likely breaking up a family. They were beasts.

"I know," Timothy said quietly. Then he sighed and tried to imbue his voice with good cheer again. "Can you do me this favor, traveler?" he asked with a smile.

Elle nodded, waiting for him to give her more information about the package. When he didn't, she raised her eyebrows at him, milling her hand in front of her to indicate that he should tell her more.

"Can't talk now," he said with a wink. "Next course got to be plated and ready to go in twenty minutes. The shipment time okay? You fine with going alone and giving me the details tomorrow?"

She gave him a decisive nod. Her bad mood had seeped away, replaced by excitement. She didn't believe in supernatural hogwash, but her instinct was reliable and it told her that something momentous was being put into motion. She so badly wanted to help the Union win this war, and whatever awaited her tonight was going to help her do it.

She just knew it.

CHAPTER 2

Malcolm was sure to look appropriately smitten as Susie batted her lashes and giggled behind her hand, but no amount of faked gentility could hide the ugliness he'd seen spew from her earlier. The fact that the recipient of her outburst had been fleeing from *him* when the accident occurred didn't make the situation any better.

He'd been trying to read a correspondence that had been slipped to him upon his arrival; that was why he'd ducked into the dining room, how he'd stumbled upon the woman he shouldn't have spoken to from the start. He'd never been one for segregation, be it by race or by class, and his work ensured that he had friends and contacts in every strata of society. Still, he didn't know what had driven him to speak to her in such familiar terms. Perhaps the idea that he could use her as a source if need be? No, that was ex post facto. He knew why he'd kept at it, though — when she'd turned, her full Cupid's bow lips had been on the verge of forming a smile and her wide brown eyes had shone with vital energy. Her thick hair had been plaited into two girlish braids, but there was no doubt that she was a grown woman: the plain cotton dress she wore highlighted her slim waist and ample bosom. But it was the moment that knocked any trace of lust right out of him that had fixed her in his thoughts for the remainder of the evening.

The way she'd stared him down when she thought . . . He suppressed a shudder at what she'd thought him capable of. She had every reason to, especially given his current outfitting and their current location, but the mere idea triggered unbidden memories that made the rich dinner rise in his gorge.

She'd been defiant, though. The way she'd squared off with him filled him with both admiration and a terrible rage that he'd made her feel she had no other option.

"Do tell us more about Baltimore," Susie prodded. "It's been so boring here. Even Christmas was a sad affair — no tinsel, no presents, just injured soldiers and paltry cakes and horrid snow and cold. Thus, you must warm me with your stories." She stared at him, one brow lifted. "Is it true

46

that it's very dangerous to be a Rebel in Maryland, and that you escaped the authorities by outwitting them? Did you help destroy the railways?"

Admiration flashed in her eyes, along with a hint of desire. He'd seduced seditious women for information before, and this one was passing fair, but the "treating human beings as chattel" aspect of her personality was too front and center to make the task enjoyable for him. But just because he didn't plan on bedding her didn't mean he wouldn't string her along.

All's fair in love and secession, he thought bitterly.

Across the table from him, a barrel-chested young man with rough-hewn features and a thick red beard stared at him, the envy on his face practically scrawled in India ink.

"Ah, it isn't too hard to outwit a Northern man," Malcolm said, lowering his voice so Susie had to lean in closer to him. "You just distract them with some stories about the poor little darkies being whipped or some such and they're too busy bawling to pay mind to much else."

The words galled him, but they needed to be said. He'd traveled all over the States in the past year as a detective for Mr. Allan

47

Pinkerton's Secret Service, most recently finding and infiltrating pockets of Rebels in Baltimore City, and he'd learned the fastest way to form a bosom friendship with a man was to ridicule his enemy.

Laughter rang out around the table, along with a few congenial hoots of support, proving him right.

"You know it don't take but one Southron to destroy ten Northern men," said a mustachioed man farther down the table. He looked like the only fight he'd ever had was with his barber, which might explain his terribly uneven facial hair, but still he spoke like he'd been at Sumter, Bull Run, and Nashville.

Malcolm smiled in admiration like the man was Hercules himself. "That's just exactly right."

Mustachio flushed with pleasure at the acknowledgment and tipped his glass in cheers, and Malcolm felt the fisherman's pure pleasure at reeling in a catch.

Gotcha. Malcolm could always discern the moment when someone decided to be at ease with him, to give him some degree of trust. There was a subtle shift in the air, a strengthening of some invisible bond. Trust was a funny thing in that people thought they guarded it closely but were often willing to hand it over at the slightest sign of camaraderie. Malcolm was accustomed to being alone, and generally preferred it when he wasn't on assignment, but he was glad for others' innate need for connection that made his difficult work at least a bit easier, even if he didn't understand it.

The jealous man across the table ran a hand through his fiery beard and spoke loudly in Susie's direction.

"The last Northern man I met had a very short acquaintance with the long end of my bayonet," he said, the art of subtlety apparently not in his wheelhouse.

"Rufus, please don't speak of such things at the table," Susie huffed, then turned back to Malcolm. "Don't mind Ruf. We grew up together. He's always following me around now telling me his disgusting war stories, but I prefer a man who knows what a woman wants to hear."

"It seems all of the men have stories to tell," Malcolm said, gesturing around the table.

Some of the other men present were talking big about the Union men they'd captured, or skirmishes they'd routed them at. A few of them had been at Manassas. Malcolm wasn't egotistical enough to doubt that the soldiers had seen battle and that some were damned good at it, but most of them didn't even know why they fought.

His present career had led him to many a conversation with Southern men, and not a one of them knew what they were *really* fighting for. Pride, or states' rights, or to show them Northmen what for were the reasons generally provided to him in some form or another, but as he watched the slaves bustle around the table unacknowledged, he knew the real reason. And that was why he wouldn't rest until the abomination was routed from the country he now called home. His family had fled from Scotland after those in the aristocracy had stolen their land and their bodies and their lives. He wouldn't sit idly by while it happened here, too.

"What about you, Mr. McCall, do you have any titillating stories?" Susie asked, batting her lashes up at him again.

Malcolm had bluffed, berated, and bamboozled information out of Rebels from Sarasota to Susquehanna, in ways more varied than most folk could imagine. There was the band of ruffians he'd infiltrated in New Orleans, dead set on assassinating President Lincoln and with the means to do so. Malcolm had helped prevent that. Never had a man gained Malcolm's respect more quickly than Lincoln with his quiet, heart-breaking acceptance that his countrymen, the people he was trying to save from themselves, wished him dead. Malcolm believed that was the night the president finally understood there could be no compromise, and that bitter battle would rend the nation he'd sworn to protect in two.

Malcolm had always been for the Union, even before self-serving secession had forced its birth; but after that night in a solemn presidential train car, he was for Lincoln as well. If it hadn't been a bizarre notion in this young country, he would have pledged fealty like the Scottish clansmen of old. But this was the New World: Spying was his fealty, his wit his sword.

"I've seen a thing or two in my time," Malcolm said, knowing that vague bon mots would only increase his worth in Susie's eyes. "I'll do whatever it takes to defend my country, but the things I've seen aren't appropriate for the present company."

Across the table, Rufus growled in annoyance. Malcolm grinned at him.

"Our Susie does so much to help with the war. She's the leader of the local sewing circle," Mrs. Caffrey supplied helpfully, while Susie preened. "The North didn't know just how skilled our ladies are. They

51

can stop the fabric from coming in, but they can't stop our needles from flying. Uniforms, tents — whatever our boys need, our ladies can supply it."

Susie held out her hands, showing him her bruised red fingertips as if they were badges of honor.

"I'm also a volunteer with the Vigilance Committee," she said. Her chin was held high, awaiting praise for her bravery.

"Well, one thing's for certain: The South can never lose with women such as you supporting us." Malcolm grazed her finger-tips with his, quickly, and Susie curled her fingers as if trying to hold on.

"She's helped ferret out at least two suspected spies," Mrs. Caffrey added. "Our Rufus here took them down to Castle Thunder himself. They won't be getting out of that prison anytime soon."

"Not ever, if the hangman gets to them," Susie said blithely.

The women tittered, as if they were discussing recipes and not death. Susie's hobby would have worried him more if Vigilance Committees weren't a bunch of bunk. Asking every stranger in town "Where're you from?" and "Where're you going?" and "Do you need a good hanging?" wasn't spycraft — it was lunacy. Still, he flashed Susie his most charming smile and said, "I hope I'm not under suspicion."

He began to prepare himself to go on a subtle defensive if necessary. In the many times he had passed through the city, Malcolm had shared both his whiskey and his anti-Northern sentiments with men who would swear on a stack of Bibles that he was Reb through and through.

"I'll admit, I almost had you pegged as a soft heart when you defended that pickaninny who knocked me to the ground," Susie said, a trace of bitterness in her tone. Here she sat, living the high life while the blockade starved her people and men fought and died, and she was jealous of the stingiest attention he'd bestowed upon her slave. Incredible.

Malcolm thought of the glint in the slave woman's eyes before she'd thrown herself prostrate at Susie's feet. Just as she'd looked upon him with unflinching acceptance, there had been defiance in the way she had begged forgiveness. That lass was far from simple, even if she couldn't speak. There was intelligence in her dark eyes that would not be disguised, although most of the people in this household probably couldn't deign to acknowledge it.

"Defend? I saw that she'd upset you, and

just wanted to get her out before she could do you any further harm. And because I wanted to have your attentions for myself." He smiled through his disgust, showing his teeth. It made him feel feral, but Susie blushed and blinked up at him.

His response had been satisfactory.

"Tell me more about yourself, Mr. Mc-Call," she demanded, used to bestowing orders with her sweet-tea tones. Malcolm found himself dwelling on the mute slave again. He didn't know why, but it bothered him that she couldn't speak. It was selfish, and odd, but he couldn't help but guess at what her voice would sound like.

Susie cleared her throat expectantly.

He tried to look abashed. "I hate talking about myself, but I'll make an exception for you. When I get back to the table. If you'll excuse me for just a moment . . ."

Malcolm stood and left the table. He needed to read the note he'd been given, and it couldn't wait until Susie stopped thrusting her bosoms in his face. He meandered down the hall and asked a slave for directions to the privy, wanting to ensure his leaving the table didn't arouse suspicion.

The small room was cramped and dim, but he managed to remove the note from his jacket pocket. *Iverson's bluff. edge of woods. dusk.* The words were scrawled hastily in a loopy cursive. A simple map was sketched underneath, indicating a meeting point in one of the wooded, less populated areas of town. Beneath the map were the words *many one.* He wondered at their meaning, but knew the longer he took the more ruffled Susie's feathers would be. There was no time to puzzle the extraneous words just then.

He'd ascertained that there was at least one other operative already stationed in the vicinity, but he didn't think it was the stable boy who had slipped him the note. Perhaps the butler, who had hovered over the table through supper? Or the mulatto woman who had taken his coat when he walked in?

He walked back to the dining room slower than he should have, and he knew the reason for his delay; he wanted to see the woman from earlier. He knew that desire and detective work didn't mix, and desire and slavery were another set of knots entirely, and one he had neither the skill nor inclination to untangle. However, he wouldn't be visiting this place again after today, and something within him demanded that he make amends.

But she was nowhere to be found, and he returned to the dining room just as Mrs.

Caffrey was making an announcement to the other guests.

"Mr. McCall, you're just in time," she said as he took his seat. "We were just discussing holding a ball here in a week or so to celebrate the New Year. Things were so dismal that we hardly celebrated the holidays, but I think it would lift everyone's spirits in these trying times. I'd like to think it's an early celebration of our impending victory as well. I'm not suggesting you take French leave from your regiment, but we'd be so happy if you could attend."

He gave the woman an ingratiating smile and was about to turn her down when Senator Caffrey cut in. "Some of the staunchest supporters of the Confederacy will be in attendance. The women can have their dancing and other such nonsense, but we men will be talking business. You have a good head on your shoulders, and your opinion would be valued."

Malcolm paused. He was due back in Washington in four days. He'd planned to leave immediately and make a few stops along the way, but plans changed. Right now, Senator Caffrey was looking at him like a man who needed an ally, and Malcolm was happy to serve in that position. If he were a few days late but returned with use-

56

ful information, Pinkerton wouldn't complain much.

"Well, I'm sure my commander won't mind me extending my furlough a bit, especially if I'm here at the esteemed senator's behest," he said. Malcolm realized that something more was expected of him, and quickly added, "I'd be delighted if Miss Caffrey would save the first dance for me."

The woman fairly beamed with pleasure, as did her mother. "Why, of course, Mr. McCall, although I do intend to see you often before then."

Rufus again made an inarticulate sound and then sputtered, "You promised the first dance at the next ball to me, Susie."

The young woman eyed him, obviously relishing his jealousy. "Now you shall have the second, Ruf."

"I'll take my leave then," Malcolm said, rising in his seat.

"So soon?" the lady of the house said with obvious dismay. He guessed he was supposed to be so smitten by their daughter that he'd have to be dragged away.

"I have business to attend to," he said gently. "As much as I dislike it, this war won't resolve itself, and there's always something that can be done for the Confederacy. May I call on you tomorrow?"

He let his gaze linger on Susie.

"Yes, of course you can," Senator Caffrey said, standing to shake Malcolm's hand and walk him to the door. "Anselm, get this man his coat," he said to a lean, gray-haired slave as they stepped into the hallway. The man hurried away, and when Malcolm's gaze followed him he was met with a sight that made his heart thump out of sync.

The slave woman stood with her back to them, polishing the wooden banister of the grand staircase outside the dining room as if it were the most important task in the world.

"Elle, what are you still doing here, girl?" Senator Caffrey asked. "Get on back to town before you set Susie off again. And if your master asks why you've been docked a half-day's wages, mayhap I won't tell him it's because you nearly killed my daughter."

Elle, Malcolm thought as she nodded and walked toward the kitchens, her gaze trained on the floor. Malcolm knew that slaves weren't paid, but that she'd be forced to report back on wages she would never have seen anyway — and punished for their loss — seemed even more despicable.

"She doesn't live here?" Malcolm asked.

"No, she lives in a colored rooming house on the other side of town, where some of the hired-out darkies stay. I send her wages to her master," Caffrey said. The practice always surprised him. There had been a time when he wondered why slaves didn't just run away once they were out of their master's view, but he knew now that family ties, fear of the unknown, and harsh runaway slave laws made it all but impossible for most slaves to make the attempt. Caffrey continued. "We're renting her while we're in town since we left most of our help back at our plantation, but my wife doesn't like to keep the pretty ones around at night, lest I go a-wandering."

Senator Caffrey elbowed him congenially, as if they were old friends, raising his chin in Elle's direction. "Can you imagine having that under you, and her not able to make a sound?"

Malcolm feigned amusement and elbowed Caffrey back, perhaps slightly harder than was acceptable. Anselm's arrival with his overcoat saved him from answering the despicable question. "I'll see you tomorrow, Senator."

He left the man leering down the hallway and went to the stable. He paced as the boy prepared his horse, a strange melancholy hanging over him. When Malcolm rode off, his mind was whirling with emotions he needed to categorize and file away, lest they undo him. He was behind enemy lines and trying to ingratiate himself to as many of the Confederate establishment as he could. Getting angry over everyday occurrences like a downtrodden slave and a master who lusted after her wouldn't help anything.

But he couldn't reason away the raw frustration at the way Caffrey had so blithely mentioned taking advantage of the woman. Malcolm didn't think Elle was simple, but Senator Caffrey and his family did, and still the man dreamt of forcing himself on her. Rape was a sin, as was subjugating other humans. Malcolm's mind got muddled with anger thinking of how, in these lands, institutionalized sin was seen as a way of life that needed defending.

"Leave me be! Or at least have the decency to send my boy away!"

A plaintive voice from years gone by and leagues away rang in his mind. That the gang of English dogs had followed the second request but ignored the first had changed the course of Malcolm's life. The act of violence had planted a seed of malevolence that had eventually grown to rip his family apart. It was one of many injustices that wouldn't allow him to stand idly by in this war.

He was about to push his horse into a gallop to outrace the unwanted memory when he saw a figure walking up ahead along the dusty, rutted road, a too-thin cloak draped about her shoulders as she hunched through the cool wintry evening. There was no question of who it was, or of whether speaking to her was the exact opposite of what he should do. Still, he slowed as he approached her.

"Miss Elle?"

Her name on his lips felt familiar and right.

Her head whipped up, but her face was unreadable. The late-day sun highlighted her cheekbones and the smooth darkness of her skin. It reminded of him of the newly tilled soil after a spring rain, fresh and sweet. Her eyebrows rose and he realized he was delaying her from wherever she was going. Maybe she had a husband waiting at the rooming house for her or visiting from a plantation. To Malcolm's consternation, he found that possibility didn't sit well with him at all.

"I just wanted to give my apologies again for today," he said. "I'd fall on my sword before hurting a woman in that way. Any woman."

Her lips parted in surprise, sending a rush

61

of want through him even as he was apologizing for it. But Malcolm had experienced lascivious thoughts before, and that wasn't what this woman inspired in him. He prided himself on his careful deliberation, but words were spilling out before he realized his mouth was moving. "I won't lie: I teased you earlier because I think you're beautiful. Maybe the loveliest woman I've ever clapped eyes on. But it was wrong of me to frighten you. I'll be coming and going at the house over the next few days" — he saw the wariness creep into her eyes, and raised a hand to allay her suspicions — "and I want you to know that you're safe in my presence."

Senator Caffrey's leering gaze cropped up in his mind's eye.

"And you're safe from any other unwanted advances, too, if you see fit to let me know. No one will harm you while I'm here. It's not much of an offer, but I'll do what I can. Good day, Miss Elle."

And with that he rode off toward his hotel, leaving her standing on the side of the road with a shocked expression on her face. His heart was nearly beating out of his chest, as if she were the first woman he'd ever spoken to. It was a risk to speak so to a slave, but for reasons he couldn't quite understand, he'd needed her to know he'd protect her if he had to. Nearly every aspect of his life was a lie — his job changed from town to town, as did his hair color, social status, accent, and loyalty — but that was one thing he needed to be true, and perhaps not just for her benefit. If someone understood that bit of truth about Malcolm McCall, maybe he wouldn't fade away into the mist as the roles he played became ever larger and more dangerous. If he died in Richmond, there would be one person who'd know he wasn't exactly who he seemed to be, and her name was Elle. He was glad of that.

In any event, she was mute; it wasn't as if she could tell anyone if she found him strange.

CHAPTER 3

As Elle made her way to the meeting point, buffeted by the crisp evening breeze, the stranger's words whirled about her head like the long-fallen leaves that crunched beneath her thin-soled shoes. Malcolm, Senator Caffrey had called him in the foyer, and Susie had called him Mr. McCall as Elle eavesdropped from the hallway.

And he'd called Elle "Miss," which he had to know was an honorific that showed respect for its recipient.

What was this Malcolm McCall about? Lying to Susie in the dining room. Stopping to talk to a slave woman to put her at ease, to offer her his protection from the very thing she'd feared from him, all while wearing that damned Confederate gray — what could it mean? Elle cursed her special talent heartily. She was one of the very few people who couldn't fool themselves into forgetting what someone had said. Her

64

mind preserved his exact words, as well as the look on his face as he'd delivered them. Wildly earnest, as if he hadn't understood what was driving him to speak to her, either.

It wasn't any easier to push away the feelings that had leapt to the forefront of her mind at his vow. It had been a long time since anyone had considered her safety their priority. Her parents hadn't meant to do her harm, but forcing her to exhibit her talent to strangers when they had first moved up North had made her feel like something unnatural. Memorize this; recite that. It'd felt like even those who wanted nothing but the best for her saw her as more parlor trick than person.

Even with years gone by, with her skill tucked away and used only for her own enrichment and that of her students, Elle still felt a strange sort of shame and anger when she thought of how she'd been treated. She'd been the Venus Hottentot of the abolitionist crowd, with the exception that it was her cerebral lobes that had been of interest to the gawkers. Still, when rumblings of secession began, Elle had realized her trick could be useful to the Cause. Most people had agreed without hesitation — so what if it necessitated placing her at the heart of the danger? Those who had opposed her hadn't done so out of fear for her safety; it had been simple patriarchal reflex. Even those naysayers had relented when her usefulness had become obvious.

Elle wasn't afraid of danger, and it had been drilled into her how rare her talent was — her gift from above had to have some purpose. When the North made concessions with the Fugitive Slave Act and half of her small town uprooted and fled to Canada, Elle had begun to form a hazy idea of how her skills could be of service. Her Daniel being captured by slavers — Daniel, who was born free and unfamiliar with the true horrors of the South — had brought into deadly clarity just how her skills could be used.

Daniel.

It felt like a sin to think of her friend, captured by men who looked like McCall, while her cheeks still burned at the bastard's kind words. His actions were befuddling, but her body's response to him was infuriatingly easy to decipher. She'd been annoyed that he would risk drawing attention to her again, but her body had heated as she stared up at him. She'd felt a stirring low in her belly, a sensation she hadn't experienced since she and Daniel had been together those few times. Before he'd decided that she must choose between him and her ambitions. And now here she was betraying him again.

And to think he'd scoffed when she'd told him she couldn't be a good wife to him.

Malcolm had stirred up something dark and definitively forbidden within her and then gone and called her beautiful. What *was* he playing at? Whatever it was, she needn't ever find out. If she didn't steer clear of him, he'd bring a heap of trouble and drop it at her doorstep. She didn't need her instinct to tell her that; it was just common sense.

Elle reached the meeting point, a secluded bluff overlooking the James. The setting sun stretched its fingers down the length of the river, its fiery caress tinting the waves with dabs of orange and gold.

Elle admired the water as it churned by, powerful enough to break free of nearly any restraint, and she was envious. She pulled her cloak closer and shivered in the river breeze as a familiar weariness descended upon her. She pushed through it, fighting the undertow of exhaustion that tugged at her skirts and her eyelids. There was a time for fatigue, and that was when the infernal war was over. She'd be a lot more tired working a field all day if the Union were to fall, that was certain.

A twig snapped behind her and she whirled.

Standing before her, once again, was Malcolm McCall. The last rays of winter sunlight glinted off of the buttons of his jacket, like a warning flashed from afar. Had he followed her? Perhaps his earlier deference had been a misdirection.

"Miss Elle? What the devil are you doing here?" he asked, his voice low. Something in that voice made her warm where she should have been cold, the very last thing she should be feeling. It also sparked a memory, one that hovered just out of reach. She wasn't used to the sensation of wracking her mind for something and coming up empty. Why did he have this effect on her?

"Are you here for a rendezvous?" he asked. He took a step toward her, and she tried to discern if he had been tipped off about her meeting, and whether she could reach the blade in her garter quickly enough. If he rushed her, she could give him a quick jab and redirect his momentum and use it to send him over the edge of the cliff —

Malcolm's incredulous bark of laughter cut off her scheming. He shook his head and regarded her much too appreciatively. "I'm here because I received a missive from an associate, but that couldn't be you," he said. "Could it?"

Elle felt a sting of indignation alongside her confusion. Was Malcolm McCall really the package Timothy had arranged for her to pick up? This man who couldn't fathom that she could possibly be the operative he was supposed to meet? If he was, she wasn't going to cut him any slack. There were protocols, and if he was truly supposed to be meeting her he'd have to abide by them. She crossed her arms and looked off into the distance, pretending to ignore his presence.

When she glanced at him from the corner of her eye, he seemed to understand that she was waiting for something.

"Well, I guess I have to give you some kind of sign," he murmured, stroking the evening stubble on his chin. Elle tore her eyes away from the rhythmic movement. "Is there a password? Is it 'many one'?"

That was close to the most recent Loyal League password, but she would take no chances. Besides, she enjoyed seeing him outside of his comfort zone. She was distinctly outside of hers, and why should she be the only one?

"This is ridiculous. That's what the paper said. Many. One. Am I supposed to pull the password out of my —"

She glanced at him sharply, and he paused, assessing her body language.

"Out of . . . many, one?" He chuckled. "Of course. E pluribus unum."

Elle nodded and was rewarded with his brilliant smile.

"So you're a friend of Abe, not an admirer stalking me through the woods," she said, her voice husky from disuse. "I suppose I should be relieved, although I'm not certain what help you can provide us." His eyes went wide, and she prepared for him to give her the same boring diatribe about women working in the field that she'd come to expect.

"You can talk," he said. He raised his hand toward her and moved it in a quick circle. "Well? Keep at it."

"Pardon?" Elle asked, crossing her arms even more tightly. For a moment, she was back on the stage of a small theater, a sea of white faces staring at her expectantly. She hated that he could make her feel that way. Thus far, every interaction with McCall had left her at a disadvantage. She thought she understood people and their motivations better than most, but she couldn't guess at

70

what he was doing — or why.

An amused grin lightened his features as he advanced, giving Elle a glimpse of the mischievous boy he must have been. He pushed his hat back and rubbed his forehead with his fingertips, like a student tasked with long division.

"I'm sorry. It's just . . . I shouldn't admit this, but I've spent a good part of the afternoon wondering what your voice would sound like if you could talk. And now you can, and it's prettier than anything my weak imagination could come up with."

Elle wanted to be furious at his forwardness, especially in light of their first meeting, but something about the man was just pure engaging. She could see why he'd make a good detective. In order to be successful, she had to be quiet and unseen, but Malcolm had a different kind of talent. Something about him was naturally attractive, made you want to sidle up next to him and hear every tall tale he spit out and then tell him your own. There was some relief in the realization that his magnetic pull was part of his skill set, that it was natural for her to be affected by him.

She scowled at him. Just because it was natural didn't mean she had to like it.

"If you're an operative, then we should

update each other on what intelligence we've gathered," she said. "That's the only reason you need hear my voice."

"That's not the only reason, but I'll take it. I'm sure old Pinkerton wouldn't mind me doing my job, either."

Elle allowed herself to be a little impressed. Pinkerton only took on the best detectives the country had to offer, recruiting them to join the network that fed information to the government's newly established Secret Service. He was also smart enough to admit that the most valuable information to the Union was usually provided by Negroes. She trusted the man's common sense for that fact alone and decided to extend just a bit of that trust to Malcolm, whom he'd obviously seen as fit to join his ranks.

Malcolm sat down on the grass, stretching his long legs out in front of him, and then patted the ground next to him.

"I know you're tired, running around after those people all day. Come. Rest."

Elle sighed. She hated it, but he was right. Every part of her ached; she wondered how the people who toiled in the fields managed to survive and then reminded herself that her parents had done exactly that for half their lives. She lifted her chin to show her reluctance and then flopped down in the grass next to him, a safe distance away from his outstretched hand.

"Romantic, isn't it?" He inclined his head in the direction of the setting sun. "Now all we need are some flowers and a few pretty lines of poetry." He reached over and plucked what had been a vibrant wildflower before the winter frost robbed it of its hue. Elle would've found it charming if they weren't supposed to be discussing matters of import. And if he weren't a white man in Confederate gray.

She crossed her arms over her chest and harrumphed, reciting the verse that came to mind as she stared at the ridiculous man in his dangerous uniform with his tiny, fragile flower. " 'O, what a tangled web we weave, when we practice to deceive,' " she said wryly.

"You know the work of Scott?" he asked, the surprise in his voice plain.

"I have that unfortunate honor," she said archly, downplaying her memory. It was easier than explaining that she could recall most of his canon at the drop of a hat.

Malcolm's brows drew so tightly that Elle marveled his ears weren't dragged onto his cheeks.

"What's this?" He leaned toward her. It

73

wasn't menacing, simply a motion of curious disbelief. "I'll not have you impugning the name of a great son of Scotland, Miss Elle. My mother used to make me recite his poems after Sunday dinner. I have a few memorized," he said, as if that was something impressive.

She gave him an indulgent smile. She was tempted to ask him how many, or to recite something from a more obscure work just to show him up, but realized she had nothing to prove. It was hard to remember that sometimes, since she'd spent so much of her life being used as a human trump card.

"It's even more surprising that you fight for the Union then," she said instead. "Here, I'll regale you with the words of a *real* writer: 'But for the Sir Walter disease, the character of the Southerner . . . would be wholly modern, in place of modern and medieval mixed, and the South would be fully a generation further advanced than it is.' "

Malcolm gave a shout of surprised laughter. "What codswallop is that?"

Elle lifted an arm from her chest and regarded the cracked and broken state of her fingernails like an old wise woman. "Those astute words belong to one Mr. Mark Twain. I can recommend a title for

74

you since you seem quite unacquainted with quality literature."

She didn't know why she felt this urge to poke at him. They should have already been discussing business. She didn't care for men like McCall, who seemed to think that a handsome face and charming words could get them whatever they wanted; it galled her all the more because it was true. McCall got to parade about as a Rebel hero while the only role she could play was that of a slave.

"What business do you have with me, McCall?" The words came out harsher than she intended, but her patience was wearing thin. Maybe it was the way he stared at her, like she was something that could be had, too. Or perhaps it was the small part of her that didn't mind his bold examination.

"How'd you become a detective?" he asked bluntly, ignoring her question in favor of his unabashed interest in her. "How did you secure a position in Senator Caffrey's house? And how have you been relaying information?"

"You sure you work for Mr. Pinkerton?" Elle ran her gaze over him doubtfully. "Subtlety doesn't seem to be one of your strong points."

"Rest assured, I do," he said. "And I'm

damned good at playing a role, too. I've never forgotten myself while undercover, but today I almost did."

Elle cringed, waiting for a leering reminiscence of their encounter in the dining room. Instead, he made a sound she'd sometimes heard from her class when her back was turned to the students. A smothered laugh.

Malcolm shook his head. "I was ungodly close to losing my composure when you knocked Miss Susie on her rear end. I know it's not amusing to you, since you have to deal with the wench every day. But the look on her face! The way she was kicking her legs like to and fro! I half expected to find a pot of butter on the floor beside her the way she was churning."

He stood and reenacted Susie's magnificent tumble and subsequent conniption; then he laughed full out, a hiccupping sound that was so ridiculous Elle had to join him. She was surprised to feel the warm, giddy sweetness of mirth stealing through her tired limbs. Earlier in the day, that moment had been a nightmare, the biggest mistake of her career, but now Malcolm had turned it into a joke. One that only the two of them could possibly share. Malcolm's hat fell off of his head as he shook with laughter, and that sent them into another round of hysterics.

Her stomach muscles were cramped from her exertion; she couldn't remember the last time she'd laughed so freely. She'd forgotten how such a simple act could lighten the heavy burdens of daily life. She wanted to remain aloof with McCall, but there was something about sharing a moment of lightness in the midst of horror that resisted formality. Their eyes met as their laughter tapered off, and she realized that despite their unfortunate first encounter there was a sense of ease between them. That wasn't something that happened often, and for it to happen with him of all people was unsettling.

Elle wiped at her eyes and drew herself up. She hadn't trained to giggle on a bluff with a handsome detective. "You're the one wearing gray, so you can tell me about yourself first," she said carefully. "Have you really mustered with the Confederate army?"

A smile lingered on his lips as he stared out straight ahead of him. He plucked a piece of grass and twirled it between his long, square fingertips. Elle could already discern that he was a man who liked to keep his hands occupied.

Do not even think it, she warned herself.

"I have, in a way," he said, and she returned her gaze to his face. "I've spent time with a few regiments, but I've never fought for the South. I gather information for a few days and then skedaddle. Even if it weren't out of the question, my brother is doing his own work for the Union that keeps him on the road. I never pegged him for a soldier, but it turns out he has a knack for counterintelligence. I'm not interested in trying out that brother-against-brother nonsense the papers keep playing up. I'm an emissary of Pinkerton's Secret Service above all, no matter the vile things I have to say to get these Rebels to trust me." His voice hardened as he spoke, and Elle again glimpsed the serious man who hid beneath jokes and innuendo.

"Why?" she asked abruptly.

"Why do I want them to trust me?"

"Why are you doing this?" She ran her hand over the grass beside her skirt, the spikey greenery tickling her palm. "I know why I'm doing it, I know why the other Negros in the Loyal League do it, but why do you?"

Many of the abolitionists Elle had encountered during her time on the anti-slavery circuit had been kind people, but just as many hadn't viewed her any more highly than a slave master would. Slavery was a cause to them, a crusade, and they couldn't be bothered to care about the spoils of war. Some of them only objected on the basis that slavery led to the corruption of the white race, and could give two figs what would happen to the slaves once the institution was demolished. Although any help was better than none, her chest tightened at the possibility that Malcolm fell into that category.

"That's a reasonable question," he said, glancing at her from the corner of his eye. "You wonder if I'm some holy roller, or if I want to ship the slaves back to Africa. I'm a foolish man, but not enough to doubt my own eyes. There isn't anything inferior about you or your people in the slightest."

The strange feeling in her chest coiled tighter. That wasn't what she'd expected at all. How did he know just the right thing to say?

He's a damned good detective, that's how. Just like you. Remember that.

"I thought you'd say you're in it for the adventure." She fidgeted with her skirts.

"Do I strike you as the trifling sort, then?" His tone was mock wounded, but with an edge. She'd hit a nerve.

"Come, McCall. You're the sort of man

the adventure stories are made for. Tall, broad, charming, and quite well aware of all of those things." She thought he would laugh at her assessment, but he looked away from her instead.

"My family is from Scotland," he said. The furrow between his brow hinted at some distressing memory. "Many Scots didn't come here by choice, you know. The English aristocrats had been beating us down, measure by measure, since the Jacobite rebellion, and finally they decided they wanted more land. For sheep grazing, of all things." He glanced over at her. "You can stop me if you're familiar with the details."

It took Elle a moment to register that he thought she already knew about the fight to restore the throne to the House of Stuart. That assumption usually cut the other way; it was strange not having to prove it to him. She didn't recite from Donelly's *History of Scotland and Her People* in response. Instead, she said, "I've read a bit about the Clearances and the rebellion."

He gave her a grim smile, as if it pleased him that he didn't have to explain further. "They took away our weapons, they taxed away our earnings, and finally, they came for our land. The places our families had lived and died for generations. They'd arrive with no warning and tell you to clear out, usually passing the message along with the heel of their boot or the swing of a club. For the women, it was much worse than that." The fine lines at the corners of his eyes grew deeper. "They destroyed families and took everything that was ours, and then forced us onto boats departing for America so they wouldn't have to look upon their own shame."

He continued. "I fight for the Union because America is supposed to be a land where people can be free from tyranny, where families aren't ripped apart to make a profit, where men aren't whipped for speaking their mind and women aren't abused worse than brood mares."

Elle had been holding her breath, drawn in by the hypnotic lilt of his voice, his brogue drawn to the fore by the vehemence of his anger. He looked at her, those blue-gray eyes like the sea before a storm. They were mesmerizing . . . and familiar, some-how.

"I was a lad when we were forced onto those stinking ships and pushed out to sea without a care for our survival. There was aught I could do then, but I'm a man now, and God help the Rebel who tries to stop me."

The stalk of grass had been crushed in Malcolm's grip and he stared out at the river, his mouth tight.

Elle had heard similar stories from the grocer MacTavish and some of the other abolitionists, mostly Scots and Germans who met in the storeroom behind the grocery store. Man's inhumanity to man wasn't solely regulated by skin color, although it did allow its practitioners to choose their targets more easily.

"I've lived up North most of my life, nigh on twenty years," Elle said finally. "I'm a free woman; that is, I have papers that say I am. My master freed my mother and father and me after he inherited us from his father. I remember everything from before we were free, though. Sitting at my mother's knee in the hot fields and trying to help with picking the tobacco. How hungry we always were. The vermin in the slave quarters, and what happened when a woman named Dancy was too tired to work anymore."

Elle shut her eyes. She hadn't thought of those things in a long while, and the sensations briefly overwhelmed her — the smell of sweat, the songs the slaves sang in the fields.

Malcolm cleared his throat. "What did your family do once freed?"

"My parents did the same as yours when they arrived here, I imagine. Tried to make the best life they could for us from the second chance we'd been lucky enough to snatch up. We settled in Massachusetts. It was far enough North that my parents could feel a sense of security. Plus, we were well situated to help folks who had to take their own freedom when it wasn't given, as ours was. We sometimes hid travelers to Canada in our cellar and arranged rides up through New Hampshire and over the border. I taught at the local colored school, eventually, and my daddy worked as a waiter at one of the hotels. Mama cleaned people's houses until her arthritis got too bad. It was . . . nice."

She missed that life so much. The life after she'd begged to stop being carted around on the abolitionist circuit. Coming home to the smell of mama's cooking and the stories her daddy would tell about the people who stayed at the hotel. There had been whole stretches of time when they could live their lives in some semblance of peace. And then everything changed.

"When the Fugitive Slave Act passed, my free papers were just so much trash on the roadside. Slave catchers were given free rein to start snatching up black folk and bringing them down South, and they got paid finely for their trouble. My father wanted to leave for Canada, taking the same routes we had pointed escaped slaves toward over the years, but mama said she was too tired to run."

She thought of the fear on her mother's face when Elle had returned from her visit to Liberia. How her voice had broken as she hugged Elle and groaned, "They've taken Daniel." Her heart ached at the memory, and at the knowledge that she might never know what had become of her friend. It was unspeakable, but the most jaded part of her hoped he was dead. That would be better than whatever horrors awaited him, a proud freedman all his life, in the Deep South.

"Did you agree with your father?" Malcolm asked. "Did you want to leave?

She cleared her throat and hoped he didn't see the moisture that glossed her eyes. "I tried leaving — I'd gone to Liberia to see if repatriation was something that appealed to me."

"Since you're here with me, I gather it didn't?"

She didn't like that, *with me,* but she didn't address it.

"I knew on the way there that I'd made a

mistake," she said. "And it grew more apparent with each passing day once I'd arrived. Everyone I met was perfectly nice, but just because you're surrounded by folk who look like you doesn't make a place your home. I want to change things *here,* in my own country, and there's a way that I especially can be helpful."

She paused. She almost didn't want to tell him. Sitting in the cool evening air talking with Malcolm made her feel normal, and people always treated her as anything but once they learned about her talent. But the man was a Pinkerton, so he'd find out eventually. Best to do it on her terms.

"What is this talent? Leaving people in frightful suspense?" He gazed at her with an interest that brought heat to her face, although she was all too used to being stared at.

"My mind works in a funny way," she said, fixing her gaze on the ground. "I can remember everything I read and see, and most of what I hear. I remember it and it doesn't go away. And when this rebellion started and I heard talk of slaves getting information to the Union to help them defeat the Confederates, I just knew I could be of service."

She darted her gaze in his direction and

then wished she hadn't. It would have been better if he'd looked at her as if she'd grown another head, or if he said it was the devil's work. She was used to that. Instead, his eyes fairly glowed with admiration.

"Funny is not the right way to describe this skill, Elle. Extraordinary. Wondrous. Magnificent." His voice was deep and rich, and each of his words sloughed away a layer of her defensiveness.

Oh dear Lord, she thought, then looked away at the darkening sky to avoid those eyes of his. She'd seen that there were specks of gold in their depths, flashing at her like a lure trying to reel in a curious fish.

He gave a short, sudden laugh and she stiffened at the derision she picked up in the sound. Perhaps she'd judged him too soon and now he would show he was just like the rest of them. A memory of being onstage in a stifling room in a too-warm dress flashed in her head. *Ellen, recite the first chapter of Mrs. Stowe's wonderful novel for the audience.*

"What?" she asked, chin rising haughtily of its own accord.

He sighed deeply. "I thought to impress you with mention of the paltry sum of poems I've memorized. You probably have hundreds in that pretty little head of yours, an unimaginable multitude."

Elle felt that peculiar relief he kept inspiring in her. "You're quite correct. I'm sorry, Mr. McCall, but you'll have to find another way to impress me," she said.

Where did those words come from?

She realized she was sitting loose-kneed beside him, leaning across that invisible line that represented a safe distance from a man. She drew her knees up to her chest and wrapped her arms around them.

If he noticed her withdrawal, it did nothing to dim the brightness in his eyes as he regarded her. "I've been told I have a knack for accomplishing the impossible, so be quite careful what challenges you lay before me, Miss Elle."

The air around them suddenly seemed heavy, like a humid July evening instead of the crisp cold of January. Elle stared at him, unsure of what to say and why she was wondering just how he'd approach such a challenge. Malcolm was looking at her, too; then the grin she was learning to steel herself against pulled at his lips.

"A detective who remembers everything," he said, pivoting back to her revelation. "Well, this just verifies what I knew when I first saw you."

"What's that?" she asked.

"That you're something special."

Elle's heart sped up at his words, although she kept her face expressionless. Blank. Few people had ever considered her on her own merit. Most of the abolitionists she'd worked with saw her as a creature to be pitied or an oddity to be put on display. Even Daniel, love him as she did, had eventually only seen her as a prize that should have been his. Now this man strode in relaxed as you please, making her feel like she was something more than a morality tale or a sentient recording device.

It wasn't fair.

"That's how I came to be a detective," she said after clearing her throat and steeling her reserve. She would not acknowledge such a compliment. She couldn't. "This has been my most important mission thus far. I've been sending what information I can through the grocer MacTavish and his crew, who has ties to the Loyal League. The head of the League recommended me personally for this job and I nearly bungled it today."

She cut her eyes at him. He had been the one to make her lose her wits in the dining room earlier.

"Because of me," he acknowledged. He had the grace to look shamefaced.

She nodded. "Because of you."

"They'll forget," he said confidently. "I'll make them forget."

"How?" she asked.

"They'll be too busy focusing on charming old Malcolm McCall," he said. He spoke the words with a confidence that wasn't misplaced. After all, there she was sitting on the grass with him and sharing stories as if they were old friends.

"What information have you gotten since you arrived in Richmond, Malcolm?" she asked, trying to change the topic back to what was important. "I mean, Mr. McCall."

"How is it that I'm calling you Elle but you think you should call me mister? We can't have that."

Elle rolled her eyes.

"Can you focus on the task at hand for more than thirty seconds?" she asked in exasperation.

The thrashing of footsteps approaching through the high grass sounded from down the hill.

"Someone's coming," he said in a low voice, jumping to his feet and grabbing her hand to pull her behind him.

"The master detective at work," she muttered, as he sprinted ahead of her into the more heavily wooded area. He dove behind a stand of thick bushes and dragged her with him just as two men stepped onto the bluff. They seemed to be surveying the wide expanse of river. Elle was so focused on the men that it took her a moment to realize how Malcolm held her.

She'd been pulled into his lap as they crouched. He snaked one arm around her waist just under her bosom, holding her close against his chest. The other hand rested on his revolver. His thighs surrounded her on either side, hard as the uncomfortable chairs in the Caffrey parlor but much more pleasant to perch on, though both were forbidden to her. He smelled of leather and horse and sweat. The sweat of a hard day's work, not the stale scent of someone who'd gone ripe while being waited on all the day. There was a difference, Elle had learned.

The sculpted planes of his chest made their outlines known to her back, and the beat of his heart was like a soft, insistent knock that she could not answer. Would not. Her own was hammering harder than a blacksmith at a forge.

She risked a glance up at him and her breath caught; the encroaching men had best fear taking a step too close to them. Malcolm's jaw was tight and his gaze was narrowed like a hawk's. Behind his smiles and jokes, McCall was a man to be reckoned with. She didn't know why this made heat race up the back of her neck, but it did.

She wanted to position herself away from the overpowering heat and scent of him, but the noisy crinkling of her skirt could attract attention. She rested her hands on his thighs to balance herself, ignoring the play of hard muscle beneath her palms, and focused on eavesdropping. That was her sole purpose for being in Richmond, and she'd do well not to forget it.

"I think we can move the last of the materials over the river by night without being seen. We can station a lookout here to signal when we arrive," the man with the skinny legs and short torso said.

"I don't know," said the second man, taking off his hat to scratch his bald head.

"We don't have time for dawdling, dagnabbit! The Yanks will choke this country to death like a snake in the crib while you're busy thinking. Just give me the go-ahead!"

Smugglers? Elle wondered. *Why would they be meeting here of all places?* Thanks to Mary's talks, she knew which routes were deemed best and which were considered too dangerous for the small, swift boats that slipped in with goods for the highest bidder.

Malcolm shifted just the slightest bit, but Elle wore no hoops in her skirt to keep her a respectable distance from him, and the raising of his knees caused her to slide farther down into his lap. Her bottom shifted over his groin and he exhaled sharply, his breath tickling the curls at the nape of her neck.

She tried to put Malcolm out of her mind as she listened to the men, but a sweet warmth was spreading in her belly, and the sensation spiked when his large hand gripped her waist even harder. She could feel the strength of him through the thin cotton dress and the chemise beneath it as his fingers pressed into her. She couldn't tell if he was pulling her closer or trying to preserve her modesty by holding her away, but his touch felt much too good either way.

The dawdling man finally spoke. "All right. Let's tell Caffrey that the plan should be set in motion. The final word on the matter will arrive soon enough and then we'll see whose war this is."

They turned and walked away, but neither Elle nor Malcolm moved, lest one of the men circle back for some reason. The dusk deepened as they waited, each moment feeling like an eternity. Through her skirts, Elle felt something warm and solid press into her behind. She'd felt that seductive pressure before, during her brief romance with Daniel, and her core pulsed at the remembered pleasure that had followed.

Her quickened breath was audible, and she was sure he could feel the heat radiating from her, especially from the part of her that was pressed against him.

"I should get up," she said finally.

He should have moved his hand from her waist, but he didn't. "Maybe you should. But do you want to? That's another thing entirely, isn't it?"

His mouth was near her ear, and the deep vibration of his voice made her shiver. His lips brushed against the shell of her ear as he spoke, and Elle let out a soft gasp from the unexpected goodness of it. His manhood surged against her bottom once again.

"Malcolm, we should leave this instant," she said more firmly, although she didn't move, either. She knew if she turned around she would see the kind of person she'd been told to avoid intimacy with all her life. But sitting like this, he was just a man. A warm, solid man who stirred something inside her that went against everything she thought she knew of herself.

His breath rasped in her ear as he released the hold on his gun. His hand moved slowly, the drag of his fingertips across her collarbone raining sparks of pleasure in their wake. Elle had read about doctors who applied electrical currents to their patients as treatment, and she wondered if it was anything like the feeling Malcolm's touch inspired in her. She was all sensation beneath this barest caress of his hand. The sound of rushing water drowned out everything else, making Elle feel as if they were alone on an island of infinite possibilities even as the logical part of her protested.

His fingertips caressed her throat. When his hand slid over the raised scar, he paused abruptly. "What happened here?" His lips grazed her ear as he spoke, sending a burst of sensation through her.

"An agitator in Baltimore —" She froze. Those gray-blue eyes . . . they were suddenly all too familiar.

She leapt out of his embrace, stumbling away on shaky legs. Her body fairly cried out in displeasure at the loss, but she couldn't allow this to happen. He was a man used to getting what he wanted, so his ignorance was understandable, but she knew well enough what could happen to her if she succumbed to his advances. On top of that, he'd nearly cost her mission twice now, it seemed.

"You were the dock worker who chased me," she said, pointing a finger at him. Her cheeks had already been heated by his proximity, but now scalding humiliation raced up her neck to join the arousal. There she'd sat boasting of her powerful memory — to a man she should have recognized on sight. Perhaps LaValle, and Daniel, had been right to doubt her.

"I was the detective posing as a dock worker who rushed you to a doctor as you bled," he countered. He rose to his feet, hands raised. He regarded her with narrowed eyes, and she knew that he, too, was pulling up memories of that day and trying to match her face to the raggedy slave woman he'd encountered. "You ruined my best workman's shirt that day."

Elle was struck. *He* was the one who had saved her? That realization was crowded out by the memory of what he'd insinuated that chaotic day: that she was a woman who could be had cheaply. A hussy.

She adjusted the neckline of her dress and pulled her cloak closed. Beneath it, her skin still tingled where he'd traced paths with his fingertips.

"We may disagree on whether you drove

95

me into danger or saved me from it, but on one thing we cannot. Nothing good lies down this path," she said, adjusting her skirt and hoping the rustling of fabric hid the shake in her voice. "It doesn't matter whether you're Union or Reb — I won't be used as a plaything to satisfy your curiosity. If you must know, I'll tell you straight out that I've got the same thing beneath my skirt as any of the white misses you've bedded. Just a few shades darker."

Malcolm rose to his feet with a grim laugh and a shake of his head. It was full dark now, but the starry night sky provided enough light for her to see him by. He took her hands in his, rubbing his thumbs over the backs of them and sending unbidden desire racing through her at his touch.

"Elle, I won't lie and say that I'm not curious. It's your eyes . . . there are depths there that make a man itch to know you better. Your wit is quick and your tongue sharp. Is it so hard to believe I have no ulterior motives?"

She snorted.

"There are always ulterior motives," she said. That was one thing she'd learned in this life. Everyone who had offered her anything — abolitionists, missionaries, and even Daniel — had all wanted something in return.

Elle lowered her face so she wouldn't have to acknowledge the way Malcolm looked at her, like she was a tome that he wanted to curl up with for days on end, savoring every word. She was quiet for a long while, struggling against her warring emotions. Their brief contact had felt good, and somehow right, but anything further was out of the question. It was simple as that. It angered her that he could speak of the possibility of more so casually. But of course he could; for men like him, an infatuation with a black woman would be seen as a lark. But the ways it could ruin her were endless.

She pulled her hands from his. "How quickly you've forgotten your offer of protection, Mr. McCall. Does Mr. Pinkerton know that he's sending men who are too busy trying to bed a house slave to do their damned jobs? You haven't provided me with one iota of information, but you found time to seduce me in the underbrush. How does that help the Union? How does that help my people gain their freedom?"

She said the words more for herself than for him, but she saw that they had an impact. He folded his arms behind his back, as if that was the only way he could keep from reaching out for her.

"You're not really a slave," he reminded her, his voice low.

"Correct. If I were, you could have your way with me without this pretense of seduction." Her face was warm and she was perilously close to tears. Why?

"Elle —"

"What? Nothing you can say changes the essential fact that I will not have you. Even if I would, I'm certainly not someone you would bring home to Ma and Pa, am I?" she asked. He didn't say anything, but his long silence was answer enough for her.

She drew herself up and turned to walk down the hill, pretending her heart didn't hurt because a man she barely knew couldn't even pretend to lay claim to her.

"Wait here a stretch before you come down in case there are people about. Couldn't have word spreading that you were seen up here with a darkie," she said.

"Elle —" he began, but she cut him off.

"It wouldn't do either of our investigations any good if we were thought to be fraternizing, Mr. McCall," she said, all business.

With that she began picking her way back down the hill, hoping to save at least a few shreds of dignity after letting him grope her like she was an adventuress.

"It's not safe for you to walk alone," he said, starting after her.

"Anything is safer than walking with you, Mr. McCall," she said bluntly, holding up a hand to stay him. "Good night."

She stumbled down the hill hoping that a good night's sleep would rid her of the awful feeling lodged in her chest. She'd been right to be wary of Malcolm McCall. She was well acquainted with being correct, but never had she so sorely regretted it.

Chapter 4

The hullabaloo of downtown Richmond swirled around him, but the clatter of carriages and cries of vendors trying to hawk their meager wares may well have emanated from the moon for all Malcolm noticed. He kept his eyes and ears open, although he couldn't stop thinking of how perfectly Elle had fit in his arms the evening before, and of the stinging rejection that had washed over him as she marched down the hill. He wasn't overfamiliar with that emotion and found he didn't like it one bit.

The discovery that she was the woman he'd encountered in Baltimore was both a shock and completely unsurprising. There, too, his eye had been relentlessly drawn to her, even in the chaos that had surrounded them. It'd been reckless to chase after her, demanding answers in the midst of a riot. When she'd gone down bleeding and choking, he'd let his cover slip completely, gathering her up from the street and hustling her to a doctor he knew treated Negro patients. He'd had to slip out of town immediately after, and his persona of a German dock worker had been lost to him, but he'd often wondered what had become of her. Now he wished he'd never found out because he was sure Elle Burns was going to be his downfall.

Even as she warned him off, eyes blazing, all he'd wanted to do was pull her close and let the insanity of the war fall away. But it was that very insanity that made it impossible for them to be together.

Guilt had gnawed at him all night, along with worry over how Elle had fared after leaving him on the bluff. He was no ruffian, and he tried to be kind even to women who were simply another component of his missions, but he'd long ago decided on the path he would take in this life, and getting twisted up over a woman was nowhere on the map. He'd seen what caring too much could do to a man, and his various careers had always conveniently allowed him to avoid such entanglements. But something about the dad-blamed Loyal League detective had hooked him, and good.

He regretted having taken liberties with her, but he could still feel how the pulse at her throat had raced under his fingertips. The heat of her body against his in the cold winter evening had been a brand. She was a bold woman, Elle, not the mute shadow she playacted in Caffrey's household. He knew a thing or two about playing roles, but it galled him that Elle's effectiveness was partially rooted in society inherently seeing her as inferior. Because of that, she'd never believe that he actually felt something for her. And if she did believe it, if she reciprocated it, what then? What could become of the way her sharp words made him feel lucky to be at the receiving end of them?

Nothing, that's what.

Not for the first time, but for the most selfish of reasons, he cursed the institution of slavery to hell.

As he walked, he scanned the shop fronts for the name Bitnam, the cousin of a lawyer who had kindly introduced Malcolm into many prominent Baltimore secessionist circles. His original reason for visiting Richmond had been to deliver correspondence from Maryland and to glean what he could from their recipients, and that was something he intended to make good on. He'd opened and read the letters of course, and any important information was jotted down; making good on the deliveries kept up appearances. There was no need to burn bridges unless absolutely necessary.

He stopped in front of a fabric shop with the name he sought painted onto the glass window. As he stared at the satin, lace, and tulle beyond the glass, his eyes adjusted to the dimness inside and a movement grabbed his attention. A hoop skirt wide enough for three bustled up to the counter, and its owner pointed to an ornately beaded fabric behind the counter.

Susie Caffrey.

Malcolm walked into the shop in time to hear her say in a voice sweeter than pecan pie, "That price is absurd, Mr. Bitnam. Extortionate. I doubt a true Southern gentleman would charge his sister-in-arms such a terrible price. That seems like something a Yankee would do, and I'm sure my fellow members of the Vigilance Committee would agree."

She ran a fingertip over the pearl-festooned fabric, and Bitnam looked up, the worry lines creasing his forehead remaining even as he smiled at Malcolm.

"Good day, sir," Malcolm said. "I have a letter from Baltimore for Mr. John Bitnam. Am I correct in assuming you're he?"

"You are correct," Bitnam said, his smile widening as he moved toward the counter.

"I'm sorry, Miss Susie, if you'll excuse me one second."

Susie turned her gaze in his direction, annoyance narrowing her eyes to slits, but when she recognized Malcolm she flashed him with their full hazel glory. "Mr. McCall! How lovely it is to run into you here! Perhaps you regretted leaving so abruptly yesterday and sought me out?"

Malcolm had been looking forward to visiting Susie, but only because of the spy working in her employ.

"I can't say that's untrue, but I have a bit of business to attend to with Mr. Bitnam here as well."

"Oh, no need to rush for little old me," she said. "I was just buying some fabric for this week's sewing circle. You know I'm always thinking of what I can do to make our boys comfortable."

He almost admired the cheek of her — she'd packed a brazen lie and an invitation into two sweet sentences. He didn't care who or how many men she cavorted with — one thing he'd found in his travels was that women and men weren't as different as the preacher would have you think when it came to appreciation of the opposite sex. However, how easily she lied was something else altogether. He'd known she was a bully, but telling such an inconsequential falsehood on the tail of a self-serving threat rubbed him the wrong way. It was the height of hypocrisy given his profession, but lying came second to instinct in this field and his gut was telling him to tread lightly with Miss Susie Caffrey.

Still, he smiled at her like she was hot Sunday dinner after the sermon had run long. "There is nothing finer than a woman who throws herself behind the Cause, is there, Bitnam?"

Bitnam nodded his strong agreement, although his gaze was wary when he glanced at Susie. "The Caffreys are a fine family. I was just saying this over dinner at the Davis mansion the other night. It was so heartening to see my old family friend, especially now that Jeff has risen to such great heights."

If Bitnam hadn't been waiting for a letter full of bile about President Lincoln and the Union, Malcolm might have ceded the man some respect for that parry.

"Well, I do believe I'll be going," Susie said, withdrawing her threat by stepping away from the counter. "I'm going to watch the boys drill down at the fairground — I promised Ruf. I'm sure he wouldn't mind if you came along, Mr. McCall."

Another flutter of lashes. Another lie. This was one that could prove useful to him, though.

"That sounds like the perfect pastime. If you give me a moment, I'll be right out," he said, then turned to Mr. Bitnam.

The man's eyes held a warning as he accepted the letter, but his words never turned to more than idle chitchat. Malcolm gave his regrets that they couldn't talk longer, and Bitnam wished him an interesting afternoon.

When he stepped outside and saw the fine Caffrey carriage, and Elle standing beside it, he was sure *interesting* was going to be the least of it. Her hair was pulled back into a simple bun and she wore the same dress she had the day before, but she affected him regardless. She shivered in the winter cold, lacking even the cloak she'd worn the night before.

In his imagination, he offered her his jacket, but Susie wouldn't look kindly on such an act, and neither would Elle.

She glanced up at him and then across the street where Susie stood talking with a dark-haired woman.

The women both smiled genially, and Susie was still smiling when she returned to the carriage and said, "I apologize for keeping you waiting, but I've been keeping tabs on that Owens woman for weeks. She claims to be for the South, but yet she gives medicine to the Yanks locked up at Castle Thunder. Her father was born in New York, you know. Blood shows."

Malcolm had heard of what the prisons were like: conditions were terrible, no matter what side of the Mason-Dixon Line you were caught on. Still, he'd heard some tales from Union boys that would make the skin crawl.

"Giving succor to the Yanks? That is suspicious," Malcolm said, taking note. "Perhaps she's taken the Golden Rule quite literally. 'Do unto others.' "

"Well, too bad for the Yanks God is on our side," Susie said brightly. "And we all know that our God is a vengeful one. Don't just stand there, open the door."

Her last words were directed at Elle, who kept her head down as she took a step past Susie to reach the carriage door and pull it open. Malcolm handed Susie inside and almost waited for Elle to step in before reminding himself that it would be a breach of protocol. He squeezed in beside Susie and waited as Elle climbed in and shut the door. She placed the packages on the seat beside her and then stared out of the window, as if she were in the carriage alone.

"I so miss Martha," Susie sighed. "Now there was a darkie who knew how to serve. I never wanted for anything. She was with me until right before we moved, but she fell ill and I had to leave her behind. Now I have no proper servant, and I'm forced to bring this sullen fool about with me."

Malcolm glanced at Elle, who showed no sign of hearing or understanding the conversation. Anger poked at his ribs and made the carriage seem too small for all of them *and* Susie's animosity. He'd had some close calls during his detective work, but such blatant disrespect was one thing he'd never had to tolerate. Even when he'd posed as a lowly dock worker he'd been treated well for the most part. Was this what Elle had endured for weeks upon weeks? Not only the inherent violence of posing as a woman enslaved, but the constant barrage of unprovoked cruelty from Susie?

"Shall we go, miss?" the slave driving the carriage called out.

"Yes, Reibus!"

The carriage pulled off and Malcolm fought the urge to look over at Elle, to catch her gaze with his and let her know that this flirtation with Susie was a farce. But that would serve no purpose but to assuage his own guilt. Providence had landed him alongside Senator Caffrey as they'd waited for the ferry to Richmond, and he could not waste this opportunity. He was playing a role, and a Confederate soldier wooing a senator's daughter wouldn't give her slave a second thought in this situation. He inhaled sharply through his nose and then directed the entirety of his focus on Susie.

"How are you finding Richmond otherwise?" he asked, moving a smidge closer to her. His gaze was all for her. In these moments he usually imagined there was a delicious feast laid out before him, but this time Elle's voice echoed in his mind. It was rough but sweet — like a nettle dipped in molasses. "Oh, it's delightful," Susie said. "There's been such a sense of camaraderie since the war began."

Outside the carriage, they passed by a crowd jeering up at the windows of a tobacco factory that had been converted into a jail for Union soldiers. The next building over was nearly dwarfed by the huge painted letters advertising slave auctions.

"Our refusal to lick the boots of the North has allowed the true ingenuity and kindness of the Southern people to shine. We're not afraid of a little hard work," Susie said, then prattled on about sewing and canning and other matters of little import to Malcolm. She finally paused as the whine of metal against metal filled the air, and when he gazed out he saw that they were passing the Tredegar Iron Works, where the sound of ordnance production was a constant. When they got far enough away to resume the conversation, she looked up at him with bright eyes.

"I wish you could have been here the night Sumter fell! There was such a revel! Men shot their guns in the air and everyone danced with abandon." She leaned closer to him, her chest thrust up and out. "Women were grabbed and kissed in the street, which was quite nice as long as the fellow was handsome."

The way she looked at him left no doubt as to whether she grouped him in that privileged category.

"That sounds like quite the revel, indeed," he replied. He'd heard stories of how people had celebrated in the streets after Fort Sumter had fallen, but he had been in Washington, receiving updates of the terrible siege via telegram. In that moment, the war became a tangible, unstoppable thing.

And Susie had celebrated.

"Is that a battery over yonder?" he asked.

They had moved out of the city's busy downtown area now and were on a less occupied road, heading toward the fairgrounds.

Susie looked at him, surprised by the change in subject, and then turned to follow his line of sight. "Yes, they surround the city and protect us from attack by land or sea." She moved just a bit so that the hoops of her skirt would press into his leg. "There's something quite attractive about a man who has the safety of our nation always foremost in his mind, although I do hope you busy yourself with other pursuits from time to time."

"Oh, I'm a man of many pursuits, Miss Susie, and earthworks are the least interesting by far," he said. He had to fight every instinct to turn away from the woman and toward Elle, who sat silently but whose presence was a persistent physical sensation just outside his peripheral vision. What must she think of him after what had passed between them on the hill? For the first time, he felt foolish as he performed his seduction to gather information. He didn't fear he would fail — failure wasn't in his repertoire — but rather that the woman he truly wanted to trade flirtations with would never take him seriously in the aftermath of his success.

Again, he sensed the pull of Elle's presence and fought the idea that so much as a glance was allowed him. Instead of risking them both, he forced his mind to the task at hand: pulling the wool over Susie's eyes when she expected him to pull it down her thighs. He let his gaze rest on the swell of Susie's breasts as he made a mental note to wake up early and check the earthworks to get precise measurements. It was likely that someone else had sent the information along already, but a glut of information was preferable to a lack of it.

"Although I have to admit," he continued, "there's nothing I enjoy more than exploring new terrain, searching out trenches and discovering what secrets they hold."

He'd imbued each word with an insinuation that couldn't be missed from fifty paces.

Susie's eyes shone with mercenary joy. The expression was the same he'd seen glinting in the eyes of the men whose plots he'd thwarted over the last year: a taste for adventure, for something to elevate what would be a boring life to one filled with glorious exploits. He couldn't fault her for that; he could have been a bursar as well as he could have been a spy — he lived for a good exploit, too.

Her fingers played with the braid of laurel

pinned to her breast, highlighting her décolletage. "Well, Mr. McCall, if you're done ogling the earthworks, I can help with —"

Her words were cut off by a loud bang echoing through the hills. The carriage shook violently from side to side, tipping perilously close to going over. The crack of wood splintered the concussive echoes that followed the initial blast. The calming voice of the carriage driver as he tried to steady the horse was outmatched by Susie's frightened screams.

An instant later, the carriage rocked back onto both wheels and the horse pulled to a reluctant stop. Susie was curled under one of Malcolm's arms, pressed against his chest. Malcolm looked down to find that his other arm was stretched across the carriage, holding Elle down against her seat. Her eyes were wide and wild, but she hadn't broken character by emitting so much as a whimper. He was the one threatening their roles. He released her before Susie saw, even though pulling his hand away and using it to pat the back of the weeping belle felt all kinds of wrong.

The carriage door swung open to reveal the driver, Reibus. His dark brow glistened with sweat and his gaze scanned the cab, taking everyone into account. "I'm sorry. I never seen this horse take a fright before, but whatever that noise was spooked her good. Everyone all right?"

"No, I am not all right!" Susie pushed off of Malcolm and hustled out of the carriage, reluctantly taking Reibus's hand as she stepped down. "I refuse to go another inch with you driving like a maniac!"

"The carriage broke, ma'am," Reibus said, eyes downcast, hands behind his back. "Can't drive it anywhere, nohow."

Before Susie could express her displeasure at that, hoofbeats in the distance drew their attention. "Oh, thank goodness," Susie sighed as she gazed toward an approaching carriage, one nicer than the one that was currently in a state of disrepair. She held up her hands and waved them dramatically. When the carriage pulled to a stop, Rufus and a few other soldiers spilled out.

"What happened here?" he asked, glaring at Malcolm.

"I was coming to see you and nearly lost my life in the process!" Susie said. Tears brimmed in her eyes anew as she approached Rufus, and he took her hand in a gentle way that seemed at odds with his ox-like nature.

"There's room in our carriage," he said.

He shot Malcolm a cool look. "Room for one."

"Is there room up front, maybe?" Susie asked. "My driver needs to go get some help to handle repairs." She then turned to Malcolm, batting her lashes. "You don't mind waiting here a bit, do you? There have been so many new people flooding the city, one never knows what type of unsavory character could happen along and take advantage of my misfortune. That would be disastrous with all the purchases I made in town today! I need someone big and strong to protect the carriage. I know Daddy will be so happy you did."

"I don't mind at all," Malcolm said. Susie had already flounced away and was being tucked into the carriage like a piece of fine china, but he was glad for her foolishness because in her haste she'd forgotten something more valuable than her shopping. As the soldiers' carriage trundled off, he turned back and leaned against the door. A fine mist of snow fluttered down, sticking in his lashes.

"It seems we're marooned," he said. "I don't mean to be forward, but if I sit inside with you, I think you'll find it much warmer."

Elle said nothing, and he wasn't sure if it

was because she was keeping up her role or because she despised him.

"Okay, I admit it. I'm the one seeking warmth."

Her head snapped up and her furious gaze clashed with his.

"Platonic warmth," he corrected. "Would you really leave a fellow detective out in the snow?"

Elle looked all around them, making sure no one watched, and then retreated deeper into the carriage until she was pressed against the opposite door. "You may enter," she said. "But . . ."

Her hands went to her skirts and began to gather the fabric. Malcolm felt a pang of heat as the first patch of silky brown skin was exposed and then a sharp electric zip that nestled in his groin as her calf and knee were revealed — he almost didn't see the shiny silver reflecting the winter sun. She'd slipped a knife from a sheath that was strapped to her leg. When he looked up, a harsh smile graced her lips. She ran a finger over the flat of the knife, then slipped it back into the sheath and lowered her skirt. "Lest you attempt to recommence your activities from last night," she explained.

Malcolm nodded and pushed himself into the carriage. He sat down and closed the door, keeping as much distance between them as possible. She'd meant to warn him off, but that brief, glorious expanse of leg was nothing less than pure temptation.

It was going to be a long wait.

CHAPTER 5

Elle's neck was stiff, and not because she'd been whipped to and fro by the runaway carriage before Malcolm's strong hand had grabbed her and held her steady. His touch had shocked her into calmness, and she still wondered at the fact that in a moment of calamity his instinct had been to protect her. Being this close to McCall after their encounter on the bluff should have filled her with only fury, but there was another sensation in the mix that she refused to acknowledge. One that was becoming too well-acquainted with the contours of his palm and the rough calluses that graced it.

She drew herself up straighter, pressed her legs together more tightly. The jab of her sheathed knife into her thigh was a reminder of the precariousness of her situation, but also of the sensitivity of the skin there, and of how good it might feel to be caressed by a hand other than her own. . . .

She hadn't thought of such things since she'd cut off relations with Daniel. How long had it been — one year? Longer? As soon as her friend had begun to consider their temporary arrangement as a precursor to marriage, she'd ended the sexual aspect of their relationship. She'd encountered many fine men offering their services since then, but the risks were too high for a woman like her and the returns too few. Especially with a man like McCall.

She thought of how he'd been with her on the bluff: so natural and relaxed that she'd temporarily taken leave of her senses. He'd disarmed her, lulled her into a sense of security. And then he'd made her burn for him.

One may smile and smile and be a villain, she reminded herself. Best to recall Shakespeare's tragedies and not his comedies when it came to Malcolm.

She dared to look across the cab of the carriage and found him already watching her. His expression was neutral, but his eyes . . . she'd seen that color and intensity only once, when a savage tempest had struck during her return to America, tossing the ship about on the waves like a bundle of twigs. She'd barely weathered that storm — if she allowed McCall any further

119

liberties, she'd be forsaken like the less fortunate ships that had splintered to pieces in the wide, wild ocean.

She glanced away from him but knew that he still watched her. She usually hated the feeling of being observed, but she didn't get the sense that he was searching for a flaw, or for an explanation of her existence. He seemed content to simply regard her, which was unnerving in an entirely different way.

"You haven't proven yourself to be a good detective, but anyone worth his salt would be thinking about the earthworks or the blast that spooked the horse right now, not gawking like he had a ticket to the side show," she said.

"As the soldiers who were kind enough to get rid of Miss Susie for us weren't in a rush, I doubt the Union has started their invasion of Richmond. It was likely ordnance being tested. Or testing itself," he said. She heard the fabric of his damnable uniform scrape over the stiff seat as he shifted. "As for the earthworks, I couldn't exactly jump out of a moving carriage to examine them, now could I? I plan on taking a long walk early tomorrow morning and gathering information."

"Don't pretend you weren't enjoying yourself with Susie, whether it was playacting or not." She'd meant to talk to him about the earthworks, but the way he brushed aside his behavior slid snugly into the notch of her annoyance, pushing it forward like a moving gear.

"I'm trying to retrieve information, which is to both of our benefits," he said, leaning toward her. "How else should I behave toward her?"

Anger flared in a rush of heat up Elle's neck.

"Funny that, when you wanted information from me back in Baltimore you insinuated I was a whore and threatened me. Should I feel slighted that you're all lashes and flirtation with Susie? But I've forgotten, you're the noble Malcolm McCall, who doesn't see my people as inferior, so I shouldn't make assumptions."

She stared at him and, this time, he could not hold her gaze.

"I won't make excuses for that. I apologize," he said. His expression was somber, as if he actually felt ashamed. Whether he really was, she'd never know. Such was life when dealing with a roguish detective.

"Do you carry a pencil and paper for taking notes?" she asked in a tone that insinuated she doubted he would do anything so sensible. His apology she ignored. She wouldn't give him the pleasure of forgiveness when she was still so piqued, at him and herself.

"I do," he said, reaching into his jacket pocket. "Not all of us are blessed with a memory like yours."

Elle rolled her eyes. "You get to walk the streets unaccosted, flirt as you please with whomever you please, and generally carry yourself with an air of omnipotence even if what you know could fit in a thimble. I, on the other hand, can remember every chamber pot I've scrubbed at the Caffrey household. What a *blessing.*"

She wouldn't have thought it possible, but Malcolm McCall was actually capable of blushing, profusely, and was doing just that as he clutched his pencil and ledger. Elle felt a pang of regret. The man had saved her once before. She could at least be cordial with him.

Oh, you'd like to be more than cordial.

His expression of shocked incredulity bordered on . . . she didn't want to admit the word that was bobbing to the surface of her mind at the sight of his creased brow and exaggerated frown. "A thimble?" he asked. "Truly?"

"I'm sorry," she huffed. "That was mean-spirited. You didn't create this society we live in, even if you reap its benefits. I'm just tired and angry after spending an entire day being told what a disappointing slave I am. As if working myself to the bone for no compensation is something I should aspire to be better at."

She looked out the windows again to be sure no one was approaching, then turned back to him. "Besides, I'm sure you have at least a ladle full of knowledge sloshing around up there if you're a Pinkerton. Now, about the earthworks: There are six of them set in a demi-circle around the city, mostly on hills and other elevated points. They average about thirteen feet wide, ten feet deep, and hold from six to sixteen guns ranging in caliber. Obviously, the approaches from Manassas and Fredericksburg are the most heavily armed." He was still looking at her like he'd been dropped on his head, so Elle reached over and tapped his pencil with the tip of her index finger. "You should be writing this down. And I do hope you're using some form of encryption in that booklet of yours."

Malcolm finally stopped staring and got to writing. The only sound in the cab was the scratch of lead on paper and the icy tinkle of snowflakes hitting the carriage. Elle took a deep breath, surveilled the road again. It was odd to be there alone with him, uncomfortable in a way she hadn't imagined.

In the novels she'd read, carriage rides were where men and women held intimate conversations and got to know one another. It struck her that Malcolm had already played that scene out with Susie; Elle was only useful to him for information.

And warmth.

The sensation of his fingertips slipping over her collarbone on the bluff had warmed her indeed. She shook her head, dismayed with the bent her thoughts kept following like a rut in the road. Malcolm McCall was nothing more than a low seducer, even if they were for the same cause. She refused to fall for his tricks as easily as that feather-brained Susie Caffrey.

"How did you get this information?" he asked as he wrote. "And what was the depth again?"

"Ten feet," she said. "And who do you think built the batteries that will 'keep Richmond safe by land and sea'? Certainly not the men who claim they would sacrifice anything as they fight for freedom from oppression. They will sacrifice much, but not the sweat it takes to dig such large trenches."

Malcolm finished his notes and looked up at her.

"The slaves who dug the batteries passed on the information to you?" Malcolm asked, then shook his head. "Of course. They'd know the measurements in their bones."

"They dug throughout the summer," Elle said, and that anger that had come upon her as she set the dining table returned. "A swampy, humid Virginia summer. They built the means of protecting the city that enslaves them. You said yesterday that you knew my people weren't inferior. Have you tried passing on that information to your fellow man? Or does pretending to be a Rebel allow you to act out all those things you pretend you're above?"

Elle sucked in a breath. That had been an unkind cut, one he didn't deserve. The man just got her back up, though.

Malcolm tucked the ledger and pencil into his pocket and adjusted his cuffs. When he moved from the seat across the carriage to the seat just beside her, it wasn't done quickly. It was slow, deliberate, either to give her a chance to leave the carriage or to intimidate her with his bulk.

She sat firm and looked up at him, unblinking.

"Give me your knife," he said. His voice

125

was deeper than it had been, and heavy as a stone.

She scoffed. "You must have your own, Johnny Reb."

Regretting her words was one thing, taking orders from him quite another.

His hand went to her skirt quickly, and though she pushed him away, that didn't stop him from reaching her sheath and pulling out the knife. He avoided touching her skin with his own, but his pinky grazed her thigh as he pulled his hand away and devil take her, she *felt* it. Everywhere.

As she watched in confusion, Malcolm positioned the sharp tip of the knife at his breast, right where his heart beat beneath the gray fabric if the anatomy book she'd read was correct. His other hand gripped one of her own and closed it around the hilt of her knife. This was all done with the same controlled anger that had carried him beside her.

"If you doubt my commitment to the Cause, or the words I spoke to you on that bluff, you may as well get this over with now."

He exerted the slightest pressure on her hand, pushing the knife's tip through his jacket. She knew it pressed into his skin now, and she glared up at him.

"What trick is this?" she asked.

"This is no trick," he said gravely. "You may scorn me, but if you doubt me — if you cannot trust that I mean what I say to you — I'm already a dead man."

Elle looked up into his eyes. She sensed no malice or ill will, but the intensity of his gaze was an undeniable force that held her in place.

"If your life expectancy rests on my opinion of you, I hate to tell you this, but you haven't very much longer to live," she said.

Malcolm's mouth twitched, and she saw him resist a smile before continuing. His voice was still serious. "If your opinion of me is so low, we will accomplish nothing together. I overstepped my bounds last night —"

Elle made a sound of irritation.

"I was wrong to touch you that way, especially after promising you would be safe in my presence. I cannot say that the desire has left me, because that would be a lie." He exhaled softly. "You're right. I won't say I've had an easy life, but I'm a man who hasn't wanted for much. That doesn't mean I'm not a damned good detective. That doesn't mean I won't put the Union above my own wants."

"Petty wants," Elle sniped, annoyed that

he was making such a scene when there were other matters of import at hand.

Malcolm shook his head. "I know all of the ill that could be read into my desire for you, but there is nothing petty about it."

It was strange. His warm hand was still wrapped around her fingers and the knife hilt, and Elle was still spitting mad, but there was something else filling the carriage besides her confused annoyance. The air throbbed with something dark and fierce and, despite all her stock of knowledge, unknown to her.

Elle pulled her hand and the knife from his grip and slipped it back into its sheath with shaking hands. She'd thought to shock him with its revelation earlier, but he'd turned the tables on her, as he seemed to each time they met.

"You have quite a flair for the dramatic, Mr. McCall." Those were the only words she could manage. She looked out the window again, watching the meager snowflakes drift to the ground and melt. It was the slight rock of the carriage that alerted her to his movement.

"You say that like it's a bad thing, Detective." The velvety richness of his voice joined the throb in the air and Elle tried not to savor it. "I think I'll take some air. The

128

driver should be returning soon and it wouldn't do for the windows to be fogged up when he returns."

"Don't you think they'll find it bizarre that you're out in the cold while I'm inside?" she asked, ignoring his implication.

"If they do, I'll come up with some reason or other for it," he said, his gaze searching the horizon line.

Because that's what he does: Act as the situation demands of him. You'd best keep that in mind.

He rubbed his hands together, then stuffed them into his pockets. "I'm supposed to dine with Caffrey tonight, but I don't think we'll be able to talk more, given your own tendency for the dramatic."

Elle gave a sigh of her own. "Tomorrow morning I'll be doing errands for the Caffreys downtown — alone this time. MacTavish the grocer is the man to see about getting correspondence to the Capital, if you don't already have a means of sending your messages in place. If I see you there, we can share information and see if we'll even be of any use to each other."

She sat up primly in the seat, looking away to show she didn't care about his reaction.

"I'm sure we'll find something of mutual interest to us, Miss Elle."

With that, the door shut between them.

As it should be.

She busied herself with recalling the entirety of *The Art of War* until Reibus returned, if only to remind herself that only a fool would trust the no-good, sweet-talking detective in a Rebel uniform standing right outside her door.

CHAPTER 6

Staying with the carriage, and helping with the repairs upon Reibus's return, had garnered Malcolm even more favor with the senator. Over a meal much too sumptuous for wartime fare, he'd repeatedly brushed off any accolades for his behavior and talk of reimbursement. He'd already received his reward: time spent alone with the vexing Elle.

Dinner at the Caffreys' had gone well: Susie had resumed her flirting, Rufus had continued his glowering, and Malcolm and the senator had talked long into the night over glasses of whiskey. He'd played his jovial role, but all night Elle's words had echoed in his head, probing at his own fears. If he could fit in with the senator and Susie so easily, was he really much different from them? That fear, and thoughts of Elle and her knife sheath, had made for a fitful, restless night.

The next morning found Malcolm back downtown, in the barber's chair. The barber shop was always a good place to find information; the profession was third in line after priest and barmen in the list of those strangers to whom a man would bare his soul. Fourth, really, if you included adventuresses. Men loved to boast and conjecture as they sat in the leather chairs or waited on benches for their trim.

He straightened his hat and smoothed his sideburns as he stepped onto busy Main Street and began walking with the flow of foot traffic. The haircut hadn't been entirely necessary, but it didn't hurt to have Susie think he'd gotten all cleaned up for her. Still, it was Elle's reaction he'd thought of as the barber clipped away. It was her hand he imagined smoothing his hair back before she leaned in to kiss him. . . .

He hadn't gotten any valuable information during his time in the chair, only news of the latest skirmishes and what the odds were that the blockade would be broken before springtime. As usual, the men had spoken of the weakness of the North and the impending victory of the South, but there was a fear in their eyes borne of the scant goods in the marketplace and the thread-bare dresses and darned stockings worn by their women. They'd thought the war would be over and won in a week, but instead it pressed on with no end in sight.

Now he wound his way through the crowd, giving hearty hellos to the acquaintances he had cultivated during his various trips through Richmond. He made friends easily, and always had, despite his generally solitary nature. The talent proved quite useful for infiltrating groups of Rebel plotters, but Elle seemed to be proof against this particular charm of his.

Jesus, man, get ahold of yourself.

A tumbling sensation in his chest seemed to auger danger ahead. He'd been infatuated before, when he was young and foolish, but never had a woman so relentlessly intruded upon his thoughts. Apprehension raised the hairs on his neck as unpleasant memories rose to the fore — hissed threats of violence and fits of sobbing regret, all fueled by a love transformed by jealousy.

No woman will ever drive me to that madness, or be on the receiving end of it.

Still, Elle's bemusement with his theatrics in the carriage came to him then. She was a woman who'd tolerate no such foolishness from the man lucky enough to have her. But he would never be so lucky, even if he were the kind of man who allowed for such a thing as love. Society had already sorted this problem for him, despite the fantasies that tormented him and drove his hand to his cock like he was a sap-filled youth.

But not necessarily . . . he thought of the Bergers, who worked a small farm in the town where he'd been raised. Mr. Berger was a quiet, serious German émigré, his wife a former slave he'd met when she purchased a horse from him. The investment had worked out well for the both of them. Their marriage wasn't recognized by law, or by many of the townspeople, but they'd been together for as long as he could remember. If their love could move against the tide, was it possible for him as well?

As if summoned by the strength of his meditations, Elle's face appeared before him in the crowd, head down but eyes vigilant, searching. Her hair was hidden beneath a dull scarf, drawing even more attention to the lovely shape of her eyes and the fullness of her mouth. To the dark rings beneath her eyes, too. She looked up and her gaze immediately met his. Her eyes narrowed, and for a moment he thought she'd not look away, not until she had won this minor battle of wills. But then she seemed to remember that a slave looking a man full in the face in the streets of Richmond was not done. She dropped her head again, seemingly searching the ground, but her feet carried her toward him none the less.

"Good morning," he said, although his mind was suddenly full to brimming with the things he really wanted to tell her. *You're beautiful. You're brilliant. I want to strip that dress off and make you cry out with pleasure.*

None of those things would be remotely appropriate, even if they didn't have societal constraints against intermingling, but the words welled within him all the same.

"I didn't see you last night," he said. "I hope the morning finds you well."

She gave him a curt nod, unable to speak while others were around. He longed to hear that rough-sweet voice of hers, even if it were castigating him as she had on the bluff and in the carriage. But she was playing her role as a mute, and as he saw a man approaching from his peripheral vision Malcolm realized he would have to play his role, too.

"I'll reply to Master Caffrey's message this afternoon," he said to Elle, patting his pocket as if he'd just placed something there. For her part, she simply nodded as if she knew what he was talking about.

"McCall!"

The portly older gentleman who approached them shook Malcolm's hand enthusiastically, but his eyes flitted to Elle.

"How you doing, son? Hope I'm not interrupting nothing."

"No, Willocks, this gal was just giving me a note from Senator Caffrey. I dined with them yesterday and I'm supposed to call again this evening."

"Ah, so she's only a messenger then," Willocks said, eyeing her rudely. "I could think of a few other uses for her."

Malcolm clenched his teeth and plastered a smile on his face. Hadn't he offered her his protection and now he stood grinning at a man who harassed her? His promise to her couldn't supersede the one he'd made to his country. Willocks was damned lucky Malcolm was such a patriot, or the lecher would have tasted Malcolm's backhand for the next week.

And who will protect her from you?

"This one? She's nature's own fool," Malcolm said blithely. He needed to warn the man off, even if it made him seem like a prig instead of one of the boys. "Can't even talk. No fun in that, is there?"

"As long as the parts down below work, who cares if she's a little soft in the head?" Willocks asked, then laughed at his own lewdness.

Malcolm felt his impotent rage keenly, spurred by the knowledge that he couldn't demand satisfaction for the insult. That he might be the only person on that crowded Richmond street who thought it an insult, besides Elle, added to his frustration.

"You may go," he said to Elle dismissively.

She turned and walked past Willocks, a blank look on her face as if she hadn't just been subjugated before him. Malcolm's gaze followed her over the man's shoulder. He watched her step into a small dry goods store, perhaps belonging to the grocer MacTavish she'd mentioned the night before.

"A bit too dark for my liking," Willocks observed after she had finally disappeared from view. "Still, it's a shame that she's simple. With those hips, she'd make a good breeder."

God must be testing my devotion to the Cause, and testing it sorely, Malcolm thought as he nodded his agreement with the man.

He'd been traveling in Rebel crowds for some time now, and the people were just as varied as in any state in the Union. Some men were funny, some were gentle, some went out of their way to help a stranger. Occasionally, a pang of guilt would assail him after he'd gained some kindhearted Southerner's trust and used it against him. Although he could never forget his duty or the danger it entailed, Malcolm often wished that his enemy wasn't an enemy at all. But the people he'd encountered on this trip to Richmond thus far erased all guilt. They were like walking parables, reminding him of this scourge that must be wiped out from the nation.

"I hear Senator Caffrey is to have a ball in a few days' time," Willocks continued. "Some folks say that he's rubbing it in the face of those who have nothing, throwing a lavish party while people are starving from this here blockade. But I hear tell that he's fixin' to remedy that problem very soon."

Malcolm put his anger aside and clapped a hand cordially on Willocks's shoulder. "You mean we've got something in the works that'll show these Yanks what for?"

"Mayhap," the man said with conspiratorial glee. "Grand plans for the Confederacy are in the works. Will you be here for the ball? I know you were helpful down in Charleston, and we might need the services of a man like you."

Malcolm had received some of the best information of his career during his stay in Charleston. He'd undercut a plan to infiltrate the Navy and ferreted out a nest of vipers living in the Capital and sending information to the Rebels, all while pretending to be a dyed-in-the-wool Confederate. The raid on the secessionists in the Capital and the failure of the infiltration had never been connected, allowing him to trade on other small Confederate "successes" he'd spearheaded in lower Carolina despite the overall Rebel losses. He could only hope the upcoming ball would provide the same windfall of information.

"I wouldn't miss it for the world."

"Excellent. I'll see you there, then."

Willocks hobbled off on his gouty legs, and Malcolm watched him with a friendly grin that faded as the man gained distance. Meeting Caffrey on the ferry to Richmond had been coincidence, but every good detective knew there was no such thing. Something had drawn him to the senator, and it seemed that what he'd thought to be blind angling had landed him a whopper. He needed to get word to Washington that something was brewing.

Telegraph stations were still too unsecure in the Capital, accessible to any literate man who desired to read the correspondence. Pinkerton was having a private presidential telegraph station built, but until then Malcolm would have to do things the old-fashioned way.

He made for the grocer's with haste. He was glad Elle had told him of the place; it was a valuable connection to be made in a city where allegiances were constantly shifting as people flocked to the new capital as quickly as others fled the war.

He walked into the dusty general store, gaze searching the dim, cluttered space for Elle's head scarf. Her hair had smelled of roses when she perched on his lap on the bluff. The tight curls had been soft against his cheek, and he'd wondered how it would be to undo the two braids and run his hands through the dark mass of hair, to feel it pressed against his chest in the aftermath of lovemaking.

His groin tightened at the impossible fantasy, quite inopportunely as she was only a few feet away from him now. The grocer stood before her at the counter, his white hair standing up every which way and clad in a shirt that was more patches than not. When he caught sight of Malcolm, his demeanor changed.

"Can I help you, sir?" he asked. His tone would have seemed cordial to anyone else, but Malcolm was familiar with the mild contempt that underlay the man's brogue.

"I believe you can," he said with a smile. "I need to get letters out with some haste."

"I don't have letter runners here, sir, you must be mistaken. Perhaps you should try another establishment," MacTavish said, a razor's edge still hidden beneath the hospitality in his voice. Malcolm recognized it as the same tone that laced his mother's sweet cadence when conversation turned to the English, like there was a bitter taste in her mouth and they were at fault for it.

Elle cleared her throat and MacTavish looked at her. For a moment she seemed to debate what to do; then she widened her eyes in Malcolm's direction and gave a stiff nod.

"Aye," MacTavish said, scanning the store for any customers who may have wandered in. When he was certain no one lingered behind bushel or shelve, he swung up the wooden counter to allow them to pass through. "Follow me to the back. Quickly now."

Elle followed and Malcolm pulled up the rear, glancing behind him to make sure they moved unwatched.

The grocer led them into the small room. There was hardly space for all three of them along with the desk and chairs, although it apparently served as a meeting place for those involved in abolition and the protection of the Union.

"This lad is a friend of yours then, Ellen?" MacTavish asked.

Ellen.

Ellen and Malcolm. The Lady of the Lake. Even though she detested a particular Scottish poet, she had to know the significance of that name pairing, of the fated lovers in the midst of war. She shot him a displeased glance and he realized he'd spoken her name aloud like a lovesick fool.

"Friend of mine? No, more like a pain in my rear end," Elle said, still avoiding his gaze. "But he's a friend of Abe's, and that's all that matters."

She stood as far away from him as the small room would allow and stared at a horrid example of needlepoint with extreme interest, as if the cure for what ailed the nation was hidden in those crooked stitches.

"I've had the good fortune of becoming friendly with the master of Elle's household," Malcolm explained. "I've just run into an acquaintance from a previous journey, and he gave me information regarding a ball to be held at Elle's place of employ. There are murmurs of breaking the blockade."

"When haven't there been?" Elle asked.

"This man insinuated that something or someone at the ball might be the key to doing more than talking about it."

Elle cut her eyes in his direction. "He gave you this information? Just like that?"

Malcolm shrugged. "What can I say? People like me."

Elle rolled her eyes at that, but he thought the hint of a smile played at the corners of her lips. It was more likely a grimace of annoyance, but he'd take what he could get from her.

"Here's paper, ink, quill that's still usable," MacTavish said. He licked the end of the quill and tested it, then motioned for Malcolm to sit just as a bell chimed.

"A customer," MacTavish whispered, heading back to the front. "Elle can help if you need anything."

He closed the door soundly behind him and then they were alone.

"That man smells as if he's been gargling with whiskey," Malcolm observed in a low voice. "Are you quite sure about his ability to be of service in such a state?"

"Do you doubt my ability to discern a reliable ally from a useless drunk?" Elle asked in a whisper, then sighed in resignation. "Yes, he drinks to excess now and then, but he's never given us reason to doubt him.

MacTavish has helped the Loyal League and other networks on numerous occasions, and before that he helped smuggle untold numbers of escaped slaves up North. Besides, no one suspects an old lush of undermining the Rebellion."

Malcolm had to agree with that.

"I trust your judgment," he said as he settled in to write.

"Oh, thank you. While that is kind of you, I don't have quite the same need for your approval that you have for mine."

Ouch. When he was a boy, his brother had shown him a drawing of a little creature called a hedgehog in an encyclopedia of animals. It was as cute a creature as a boy could hope for, but its back was covered in sharp quills to keep predators away. He reminded himself that he was just the sort of predator Elle was used to, but that didn't lessen the sting of her words. Or his nonsensical reaction to them.

He wanted to go to her, to take her in his arms and soothe the frustration of their earlier encounters away. But Elle stood ramrod straight, her fingers tangled against her skirt. It was clear that she didn't want soothing, or anything, from him. Her quills were out, and had likely been sharpened during each of their previous encounters.

Instead of further trying her, he sat at the desk and jotted down three short dispatches, hoping the information would dovetail with some other correspondence heading for Washington, or perhaps put his fellow detectives on the right trail. He added her information about the earthworks, just in case it hadn't been received before.

He noticed she had some correspondence of her own clutched tightly in her hands. They hadn't yet shared much with each other, he realized. He was fairly certain that was his doing.

"Would you like to read my letters to see if anything proves useful to you?" he asked, pulling his train of thought back onto the correct track.

"Yes, and you can read my correspondence as well. The letters regarding these matters, that is."

She pulled a few papers from her packet of letters and passed them over as he handed her his scant three. His eyes lit on the signature before anything else.

Ellen Burns.

Her former master had been a Scot then. Did she associate his accent and origins with enslavement and cruelty? One day he would ask her, but for now he would read.

As he perused the letters, he came to see

that Elle wasn't exaggerating her talents, and had in fact rather underplayed them. While his letters were cobbled together summaries of his encounters, hers were word for word recountings of conversations, too detailed to be anything but exactly recalled. Beneath each recounted conversation was a brief explanation of how she felt the information could be useful and how it connected to previous conversations she'd overheard, to known information about the movements of the Rebels, and even to relevant historical minutiae that might be useful.

He glanced over the letters in his hand, momentarily silenced by the wonder pressing in at his chest. Elle had taken a seat in a rickety chair in the corner of the room. When he looked over at her, his letters sat on her lap and she stared off into the distance, eyes unfocused as if she were in deep in thought.

"You're incredible," he said.

"I know," she replied in a tone that indicated she was only half listening.

He grinned and continued reading her letters, coming to the account of the day they had met. Had it really been just a few days? She didn't mention the dreadful misunderstanding that had passed between them when he'd intruded upon her in the dining room, he noticed. But she'd recounted knocking over Susie, and the entire conversation at the table after she'd been kicked out — her earnest polishing of the banister had been a ruse as she eavesdropped at the door. He even learned what had passed when he'd left the room — Rufus had gone on about troop movements his drill master had shared with him, the possibility of dangerous soldier movement in South Carolina. That caught his interest, but the next few lines made him cringe. His blood pounded in his temples as he read the words that had been spoken about her, laid down in black ink. The situation was described without anger or condemnation. Just the facts.

He wondered if she would write about Willocks's crude assessment of her that morning and realized that encounters of that sort probably occurred often enough to not merit reporting.

Again he thought of the bizarre promise he'd made her, one that smacked of the chivalry he'd read about in books as a boy. Perhaps Elle had been correct about the Sir Walter disease. He'd wanted to hurt Willocks for his rudeness, but doing such a thing would ruin his cover as a good ol' boy, and worse, mark him as someone who cared for Negroes more than his own. When he'd carried a bleeding Elle through the streets of Baltimore, he'd had to hide her beneath his coat lest someone try to kill them both.

It was the height of egotism to pursue anything further with her. Even if she weren't annoyed by the very sight of him, he wouldn't hide her away forever just to have her for his own. And yet . . .

He folded the final letter back into its envelope, walked over to Elle, and kneeled down before her chair.

"I'm thinking," she said brusquely, not even looking at him.

"I wanted to apologize about this morning —" he began, but she cut him off with an annoyed wave, as if he were a pesky horsefly.

"I don't want another apology," she said. "Words of regret or sympathy serve no purpose in my life at the moment, unless they're spoken before a master frees a slave or a politician repeals slavery and the laws that undergird it." Her words were quiet, but that didn't undercut their strength. "Perhaps that man did me a favor and knocked this idea of you and me being together out of your fool head. In the eyes of society, I'm nothing more than a wench for you to bed. That's just the way things are, and even if we win the war it won't change anytime soon."

She spoke the words calmly, as if the fact that people assumed the worst of her and thought her beneath them because of her skin color was normal.

Because it is normal.

Malcolm thought of everything he'd just read, of the way her intelligence and obvious skill at strategizing shone through in her words, and frustration welled up in him on her behalf. He'd worked with many fine agents, but none had impressed him in the way Elle had. He thought of Elle on her knees in front of Susie.

"How can you stand it, Elle? How can you not be bursting with anger?"

"Where would that get me? This righteous anger you speak of?" She now looked him full in the face, challenge inscribed in the set of her mouth and the lift of her brow.

He hated her calmness and restraint when he was feeling her injustice so keenly. But he knew the anger that pulsed through him wasn't caused by her prim expression, or even the situation that caused it. Malcolm was upset with himself; it galled to think that although he fought against slavery he'd never so keenly understood it's unfairness until he met the brilliant woman before him. She'd been right to get angry in the carriage. His job was far from easy, but the difference in their reception at almost every level, despite her clear superiority, was frustrating.

He'd always prided himself as a friend and ally to every man who sought equality, but was that true? Or had he imagined himself a savior instead?

He shook his head, disgusted with himself. With everything. When he spoke again, his voice was a raw whisper in the silence. "You deserve to be outraged. All of your people do. Why you didn't set this country ablaze a hundred years ago is beyond me."

Elle jumped to her feet, not very much taller than him even though he knelt and she stood. When she spoke, her fury was constrained in a voice that fairly dripped with annoyance at having to explain something very obvious to him. "Because, unlike you, we don't have the *luxury* of being outraged. If we rebelled and set half the country on fire, where would that leave us? You think that would make folks see us as *more* human?"

"Given the way they treat their slaves, maybe it would," he muttered darkly. "Maybe the only way for this country to be cleansed of its sins is to burn them away."

"What, an eye for an eye?" she scoffed. " 'If I cannot inspire love, I will cause fear'? What rubbish." She fixed him with a look that made him regret that the words had even crossed his mind, let alone left his mouth. "The blood of my people permeates the very foundation of this country. Even if everything from the Eastern seaboard to the furthest territory out West was razed to the ground, it couldn't make up for the injustice. And if you think that's what I'm fighting for, what every Negro putting their life on the line to stop the Confederacy is fighting for, then you've misunderstood everything. You've misunderstood *me*." Her hands clenched the letter she held, and she dropped it before she could damage it further.

Her words eviscerated him. He held her gaze, glossy with emotion and tight with impatience.

"Help me to understand," he said. He was still asking of her when he should be giving, but he didn't know how else to proceed.

"We don't want revenge, Malcolm." She looked at him like he was the densest bastard to ever walk the earth. "We want life, liberty, and the pursuit of happiness, just like any damned fool in these United

151

States is entitled to so long as he isn't Black or Red. So you can keep your outrage. All I can do is try to make a difference."

Despite all her talk of not being angry, Elle was fairly shaking with it. She stood barely a step away from him, hands balled into fists. Her eyes were glossy with tears he knew she wouldn't shed out of pride, and she bit her lower lip as if to keep it from trembling. Despite her fury, there was something soft and pleading in her look, something that shook Malcolm to his core. So far he'd seen Elle annoyed, or flustered, or defiant. She was strong, without a doubt. But this despair made her seem vulnerable and quite easy to break should anyone choose to do so.

"Don't you see?" she asked. "This is our homeland, too. We shouldn't have to wreak havoc on the land to be seen as citizens! We shouldn't have to."

Her voice broke on that last whispered word, and something in him cracked along with it. Malcolm rose to his feet, his gaze locked on hers as the tension between them morphed from anger and frustration to something that burned with a much different accelerant. Elle's chest rose and fell as if she'd been running instead of quietly eviscerating him with her truth. Warmth flamed up the back of his neck, the hairs there rising with awareness.

Malcolm didn't know what to say. He wasn't used to being tongue-tied, or to the all-consuming desire to give comfort.

Her eyes darted back and forth, searching his; what she looked for, he didn't know, but in that moment he wanted to give her everything. The feeling streaked through him like hot lead — a desperate desire to please her, to tear down the world and build it anew if he had to. He'd never experienced the sensation. He'd spent a lifetime steeling himself against just such an occurrence, but that meant nothing in the face of his desire to feel her mouth against his, to taste her against his tongue, to kiss the sadness and despair right out of her.

He slid his hands up her arms and tightened them against the rough homespun of her dress, just a little. Just enough to let her know what he wanted of her. Even a simple embrace was fraught with danger and placed the burden of an entire country's horrific origins on their shoulders — he wouldn't force his comfort on her any more than he would his desire. It was something she had to choose for herself, by stepping forward or pulling away. What he wanted wasn't the best choice for her, and was far from the

153

safest for either of them, but he willed her to come to him all the same.

Trust me, he thought as he stared into her eyes. She resisted, and he relaxed the gentle pressure on her arms. Then the tension against his fingertips slackened — Elle had stepped into his embrace, releasing a shuddering sigh as she did. Malcolm gathered her in his arms, simply holding her in the dim, dusty storeroom. In the silence he heard the noise of customers entering the store and MacTavish, who could disrupt them at any moment.

They were on stolen time.

He pressed her close against him and emitted a noise of relief at how right it felt to hold her. She tilted her head up toward him in surprise. Her lips were a dusky rose, slightly parted as if blooming for him, and the sight sent a jolt through him. His mind ceased functioning, and for a moment all that existed for him was her.

What in the hell is wrong with you?

Malcolm had heard men wax poetic about meeting the woman for them and just *knowing,* but he'd always thought of it as people making myths of their own mundane lives. Looking down into Elle's wide brown eyes, he wondered if he'd been mistaken.

There was only one way to find out.

He kissed her.

The kiss was chaste, merely the soft press of his mouth against hers, but Malcolm was nearly undone by it. Her lips were so soft, warm, and lush, and her kiss was sweet, tasting of cinnamon. Warmth settled heavy in his stomach as she responded, her mouth meeting the pressure of his.

He didn't know when their tongues joined the fray, or even who initiated it. Everything was blocked out by how *good* it was, their shared desire filling him with a terrible ache that swelled through him from his toes straight up his spine. Dear God, had he ever felt anything like this? A simple kiss that hit him like a horse hoof square in the chest?

Elle was responsive, meeting each stroke of his with one of her own. Their tongues sparred now, as if continuing the argument they'd been having but on more sensual terms. Malcolm's hands moved between them, up her waist to skim the outline of her breasts. He caressed the undersides tenderly, gently kneading as he explored their heft and circumference.

Her hands flew to his lapels, clutching at them as he grabbed her waist and whirled her around, seating her on the edge of the desk. In an instant, he had her skirts up around her knees. His fingers encircled her ankle, feeling the birdlike bones flex beneath the cracked leather of her old boots. The texture beneath his palm changed as his hand worked its way up; smooth, warm skin greeted his questing hand. She gasped as he caressed the length of her calf to her knee with one heavy stroke, and the look of heated surprise that brush of skin elicited spurred him on.

"MacTavish could walk in at any moment," she breathed. She didn't push him away. Her lips were moist and plump, abraded by his kisses. Her eyes were bright; it seemed he had finally provoked something other than consternation in her.

"Well, then, we'd better be quick," he whispered. His hand continued its course, straight up her thigh, and just as he cupped her mound, the dampness of her drawers pressing into his palm, she shook her head and slammed her legs shut. It was like a steam engine running out of coal, the way she went from hot to cold on him.

He pulled his hand away. "Elle?"

When she looked at him, he expected fury, as she'd displayed the night before on the hill, but instead there was only confusion and sadness. As he watched, her expression went blank. She hopped down off of the desk and straightened her dress, then took a deep, shuddering breath.

"I should be getting back now, or Mary will be sending out a search party for her bags of meal," she said calmly, as if he hadn't just kissed and caressed her. As if his cock weren't so hard and his mind so jumbled that he didn't know what to do with himself. She turned and gathered up the scattered letters.

"I hope I can see you again soon," he said.

Her back was to him, so he couldn't see her face when she replied. Couldn't read truth or falsehood in her eyes. "You'll be over to see Susie and Senator Caffrey, so I expect we'll meet by and by," she said. "But do not hope to see me again. Do not hope for anything more from me, other than Union business. I've already told you this cannot be, and yet you persist."

Malcolm was learning many lessons in MacTavish's back room, including what true rejection felt like. He couldn't say he liked it, the sick, sinking feeling caused by Elle's words.

"You returned my kiss, Elle, and with fervor," he challenged. "What am I supposed to make of that?"

"That even a woman who knows better can appreciate a moment's distraction." She turned and raised her brows at him. Now even the sadness was gone, and all that remained was a coldness that could freeze the James over in an instant. "It was just a kiss, Malcolm. Now your curiosity has been sated and we can do what we're meant to be doing. I hope you didn't expect that one demonstration of your prowess would be enough to change my mind."

She laughed. Laughed! If Malcolm hadn't felt her trembling under his hands mere moments before, he would have believed her.

"Get this fool idea out of your head, Mc-Call. I will not have you."

Malcolm felt a strange desperation twist up his insides. He didn't believe she really felt nothing for him, but that was of no importance. If she was determined to push him away, she would. Her stubbornness was one of the things that made her so attractive, but it was not his ally.

"I know you don't take me seriously, but I . . . I feel something when I'm with you." He saw her face screw up, and kept talking before she could stop him. "I know I'm not entitled to anything. Everything in the world conspires against anything being possible between us, but the world can go screw."

He'd never spoken such words to a woman before. He expected them to work like a skeleton key, unlocking the warm, vivacious woman who had just kissed him as if her life depended on it. Elle remained firmly shuttered.

"The world?" she asked, incredulous. "The world can go screw, indeed! It is I, Ellen Burns, who says we shouldn't be together. You claim to respect me, yet you cannot accept that perhaps there's one woman in the world who doesn't want you? I'm sure Susie Caffrey will kindly fulfill any services you need rendered in my stead, and that would be much more helpful to the Cause."

"I don't want Susie Caffrey," he said, and he knew that she understood the unspoken words that followed. *I want you.*

"All that we seek in this world is not always provided, Mr. McCall," Elle said. "Maybe it's time you learned that. You obviously haven't if you think that there is anything more to say on the topic of you and me."

Her gaze was hard. Malcolm could see why she made an excellent detective. Still, he was one of Pinkerton's best for a reason. Even if she wanted to believe her words were true, she was bluffing him. He thought better of calling her on it.

"You're clear to come out, unless ye want to continue this staring match." MacTavish poked his head through the door, his boozy scent permeating the room again.

"Here are the letters, Tav," Elle said, tearing her gaze away from Malcolm to hand the grocer the packet. "These are very important, be sure they get there as quick as can be."

"At your service, love," he said, giving her shoulder a squeeze as she passed.

They walked out into the main area, Elle pretending she didn't know Malcolm as she picked up her purchases and left in silence. Malcolm watched her go, surprised at how much it stung when she didn't look back.

He turned to find MacTavish looking at him suspiciously. He lifted his hat to the man. "Good day."

"Humph," was all he got in reply. The old man turned and began tallying receipts, and Malcolm walked out into the bustling street, drawing back just in time to avoid being barreled into by a huge red-haired man. Rufus.

"Pardon," Malcolm said by way of greeting, and moved to continue on his way, but Rufus stepped in front of him, his chest nearly pushing Malcolm back into the store.

There was no greeting or other segue into conversation, simply a brusque declaration. "Susie is mine."

Malcolm grimaced. Is this how he'd appeared to Elle, a possessive fool who wouldn't take no for an answer? Had he been this ridiculous in the thrall of his desire?

"I'm very happy for you," Malcolm said, clapping the younger man on the back a bit harder than necessary. "Perhaps you should relay that information to her, though. Much like the lands out West, she doesn't seem to be aware that she's conquered territory."

Rufus's eyes narrowed. "You can keep up your fancy talk, McCall, but watch that you stay away from that which don't belong to you."

Elle's incredulous laugh rang in Malcolm's ears and a burst of anger flared in him, heating the back of his neck.

"I'm not a man who gives up easily, young Rufus," he said. "Not in battle, and not in matters of the heart. Now, if you'll excuse me."

He pushed past Rufus, whose beefy body barely registered the insult. Let Rufus think he was speaking of his dainty Southern belle. Malcolm had the kiss of a real woman thrumming in his veins, and he couldn't settle for anyone less after that. In fact, he was worried that he couldn't settle for anyone else at all.

CHAPTER 7

Elle knew that, outwardly, she was composed. She was practiced at withdrawing her true self behind an impenetrable barrier; such a skill was necessary when one was trotted about and forced to perform humiliating acts for strangers. Being asked to recite poetry or recall tracts of literature wasn't degrading in and of itself; it was people's reactions that had made it feel like something tainted. For a brief period, when she was very young, she'd thought that people were impressed with *her*. The first time an angry, indignant man had asked how a darkie could possibly possess her memory and intellect had remedied her of that belief. The question had reduced her to tears, but by the end of her tenure with the abolitionists, she'd mastered the art of the cool glare.

Thus, no one in the Caffrey household could tell that her thoughts were in tumult as she quietly sorted through the cornmeal, searching out the grubs that were vying with hungry Virginians for the meager stores of food. But the grain wasn't the only thing that had been infiltrated; thoughts of Malcolm had gotten past her defenses and ate away at her attention.

What had happened the previous day in MacTavish's back room had been unacceptable. She'd been on the verge of making an important connection between their information when he'd interrupted her with his pathetic apologia; the usually well-oiled machine that was her mind had run off the tracks when he'd knelt before her. His mere proximity had shaken her, and when he touched her — oh, she couldn't think of it. It was wrong for someone who looked like her to react in such a way to someone who looked like him, and while he wore a Rebel uniform no less. She felt like the worst kind of traitor.

That she, who had been appointed a freedom fighter for her people, would now cavort with the enemy could not be tolerated. And yes, he was the enemy, despite his allegiance to the Union. It could not be otherwise with such an imbalance between them; one wrong word from him and she would lose her life, whereas his sex and skin color inoculated him from harm at her hand.

Yet, he'd saved her in Baltimore. That had been no small feat in the midst of a crowd of crazed men looking for the slightest sign of affection for the North. And something had compelled him to offer her his protection here, although he hadn't recognized her. Or had he? Perhaps this was all some trick, like the one he'd pulled in the carriage.

"You still sorting that meal?" Mary asked benignly enough as she walked up to Elle, although what she meant was, "This is taking you entirely too long."

Elle nodded apologetically and hurried her pace, and Mary smiled in approval. Elle was glad she didn't have to speak. Who knows what she would have blurted out. *A white man kissed me and I enjoyed it. I can still feel his touch on my skin, and last night when I went to bed, my hands retraced his path. . . .*

Dammit, this was ridiculous. Elle repressed a shudder as one of the worms curled in her palm before she threw it into a bucket with the others. She took both the bucket and the worm-free meal and headed toward the kitchen, dropping the meal off with one of the grateful cooks. She grabbed

164

a woven basket as she headed out the back door, toward the henhouse.

"Hey there, Elle," Timothy said. She hadn't seen him since he made his request for her to pick up a package. "How did it go the other night?"

Curiosity glinted in his hazel eyes as he regarded her. Timothy wasn't much taller than her, and he was skinny as a billy goat to boot. His size and demeanor led people to underestimate him, but the man was intelligent and wily, and he did nothing without careful deliberation.

Elle scanned the backyard; there was no one about to see as Timothy followed her into the small structure. Perhaps it would be better if there was. A dalliance with a fellow slave could serve as useful cover if they ever had to slip away on Loyal League business. People were more forgiving if they thought you were snatching a moment of joy during the bleak drudgery of working without respite.

"Why didn't you tell me that the package was a man?" she whispered, masking her voice beneath the cooing and clucking of the hens. Feathers floated in the air around them as chickens hopped out of their path or scratched at the ground in anticipation of feed. She let her tone say what her words

165

did not: *a white man.* "Was this some kind of test? Something LaValle put you up to?"

"Since when is it a problem for you to meet a man to discuss the Cause? I know you've been in more compromising situations than that." Timothy scrunched up his face in confusion. "McCall is one of Pinkerton's top detectives, a legend in the field and the war ain't even half-started yet. You're one of the best operatives the Loyal League has, so it made sense for you two to meet, even if I wasn't off doing the devil's work."

"You're right," she said. She held the bucket away from her and overturned it, stepping out of the way as the chickens rushed to feast on the grubs. "It just took me off guard, is all. And I can't say I like him overmuch."

"Aw, I thought that you two would make a mighty fine team," he said. "That, or hate each other. I guess I was right."

He chuckled, but Elle found nothing funny about her situation. If Malcolm hated her, it would make their situation much more tenable. She shrugged. "I sent some correspondence about the movements of the troops that dunderhead Rufus Sewell spilled when he tried to impress Susie two days back. I suggested that the Capital try to

166

intercept the regiment if they can, since there's intelligence that they're providing reinforcements to Fort Sumter." The loss of the fort still smarted, and anything that could be done to prevent further entrenchment would help.

Timothy nodded, rubbing the grizzled scruff on his chin. "I've been busy tracking troop movements that are either part of some greater strategy or proof these Rebel boys got no idea what they're doing. Seems like regiments could be massing to make a move, but I don't know if I'm seeing a pattern or pure foolishness."

They agreed to keep each other updated. Elle hesitated as Timothy turned away from her, but then took a deep breath and asked one of the many questions that had plagued her since her night on the hill.

"Do you think McCall is truly trustworthy? I must say, the lack of plain old common sense he's displayed during our meetings has not inspired the greatest confidence in him."

It inspired quite another array of emotions, ones that she wasn't willing to sort through, now or ever. Her back was to Timothy, and when she turned she found that he was studying her. He worked his lips a bit, as if chewing over some idea, and then shook his head. "I can't say for certain, Elle, but the man seems all right to me. You got the best instincts I know. Trust your gut, gal."

He gave her a faint smile and then tramped out of the chicken coop, leaving a trail of disgruntled fowl in his wake.

Elle looked after him, part of her wishing that he hadn't spoken so kindly. Her gut was telling her that Malcolm could be more than merely an ally, and *that* was more dangerous than anything she'd encountered in Richmond thus far.

Elle returned to the kitchens, losing herself in the monotonous act of cleaning, prepping, and making order. For a moment, she thought back to how doing her daily chores had been a source of comfort to her in her regular life, how it allowed her to shut out the information her brain was constantly processing whether she wanted it to or not. It wasn't quite the same being forced to do the work for someone else, and without thanks or recompense. A pang of homesickness hit her then. Would she ever walk into the neat little parlor where her parents sat by the fire again, or would this infernal war would rob her of that bit of happiness, too?

The little bell in the kitchen jingled, and Elle felt her jaw clench with a preemptive surge of anger and annoyance.

Susie wanted something, and Elle would have to go provide it. She hadn't expected this to be the thing she most dreaded every day when she agreed to pose as a slave, but Susie's constant jibes made Elle choking mad. If she'd been allowed just one cutting remark, or even a glare that wasn't accidental, she'd be able to tolerate it. But she had to take the abuse and act like such behavior was what she deserved.

Elle walked toward the parlor and took a deep breath. Missus Caffrey's cloying voice filtered through the air like powdered sugar, choking with its sweetness. Susie was unbearable, but she'd been created that way in a Frankenstein fashion, cobbled together bits of the Southern belle her mother expected her to be.

"And really, I know that makeup is wanting right now, but you simply must do something about how sallow your skin is." Missus Caffrey was pinching at Susie's cheeks when Elle walked in, and not playfully. Elle saw tears spring up in the woman's eyes, but she didn't pull away. "Lucinda is floating about town looking like a ripe peach. You can't go about like one that's fallen off the tree and been trampled underfoot, darling."

Elle walked up to them and paused, head bowed.

"Perhaps if you paid more attention to this kind of thing, John wouldn't have gone off to war without offering for your hand. With the way this war is going, claiming our brave young boys, you'll have to compete to win a man's attentions."

Elle glanced at Susie, who sat with a stiff back and a blank expression. She was many things, most of them unsavory, but being an annoying wench hadn't made her any less beautiful.

"I try, Mother. I've been trying. You can't blame me for the shortcomings of the men around me." Susie said the words haughtily, as if she didn't care, but she tugged at one of her curls without thought, ruining its set.

"What do you think this life holds for you without a husband?" Missus Caffrey asked. "Don't think your . . . exploits are unknown to me. You may have your fun, but without a husband you are powerless. I worked hard to ensure your father chose me out of all the women fawning over him, and I got exactly what I wanted."

She motioned to the fine furnishings and paintings that adorned the room.

Susie's lip curled. "What power do you have, Mama? Picking out patterns, then

170

changing your mind the next month and having them done again? Making a fancy menu that you don't even know how to cook yourself?"

The crack of skin meeting skin, hard, echoed through the room, shocking Elle.

"There. Now you have some color in your face," Missus Caffrey said in the same pleasant tone she would have used to ask Susie to pass the salt. With that she turned and walked out of the room.

Susie's hard gaze turned to Elle. "What are you doing standing about?"

Elle inclined her head toward the rope Susie had tugged to indicate she wanted to be waited on. Was it such force of habit that she'd forgotten she'd called for a slave?

"Never mind. Get out of my sight, you ugly thing." She picked up one of her gossip sheets and turned away.

Elle nodded and headed back to the kitchen, the angry heat in her blood making her feel like she might leave singed footsteps on the carpet behind her.

Susie was lashing out and Elle just happened to be there to take the hit, but the words still stung. She knew that, just as she knew that looks didn't matter a bit, that it was intelligence and fortitude that carried one through the twists and turns of life.

Still, the words had hit her at a soft spot. She could catalogue in her mind all the things people considered beautiful, straight from hundreds of source works. Skin pale like cream, light eyes in shades of blue and violet. Lips that seduced with their pink sweetness. Hair that flowed like silk. Elle remembered when she was on the road with the abolitionists, how they tutted and pulled at her hair as if it was something designed to spite them.

All the supporting text of years of devoted reading and remembering pushed up behind Susie's careless insults, giving it power, but one memory began to crowd the other words out.

"I think you're beautiful. Maybe the loveliest woman I've ever clapped eyes on."

She shouldn't care what Malcolm said or thought — he wasn't a man whose words should carry weight with her. But as she recalled the many ways he had annoyed her with his looks and flattery and caresses, her anger slowed from a boil to a simmer. It seemed an annoying rake of a detective could prove useful after all.

"Elle!" Timothy whispered, but his voice was urgent. She didn't see him at first, then realized he was in the pantry.

She walked in with a smile, determined

not to let Susie's cruelty affect her. When she saw the look on Timothy's face, her smile faltered.

"Read this." He handed her a note and pushed her into the pantry, away from prying eyes. "I'm sorry, Elle."

As Elle scanned the scathing letter from LaValle, she sank down onto a sack of peas, unable to stand the weight of her disappointment. The words swam in front of her eyes and she searched her brain for how they could be true.

Malcolm McCall came to mind again, but any goodwill she felt toward him had been crushed by the letter she held in her hands.

McCall was a dead man.

CHAPTER 8

Malcolm awoke in the comfortable bed of his fine hotel room, but he may as well have slept on a rock. He'd spent his day quashing thoughts of a woman who didn't want him and in whose presence he lost all sense of reality. She was just a woman — three fifths of a woman if the Constitution was to be believed — and yet he couldn't shake the taste of her lips or stop reliving that moment when her mouth had opened to allow his tongue entry.

He'd never been a man for severe infatuations; he'd cringed in vicarious shame whenever one of his comrades had confessed to such weakness. He'd never been one for love in any form; not after seeing the havoc it wreaked upon his father. The once-proud man had loved Malcolm's mother with every fiber of his being, and after the Clearances and their wretched trip to the Americas, he'd been undone by the very thing that had once sustained him.

A memory came to Malcolm then, from their first small Kentucky cabin that was more hovel than home. It was before Father had pulled himself together, before that brief period when the McCalls had prospered. When it had seemed they would shake the ghosts of Scotland that hadn't been scoured away by the Atlantic's relentless waves as they were pushed toward the Americas.

His mother had been cooking at the wood-fired stove, humming the little tune that always made Malcolm think of warm milk and stolen hugs before bed. He'd felt a surge of love for the resilient woman with hair like copper wire. But when he'd turned to his father, a sick feeling had crept up in his throat. His pa stared across the room with sunken eyes that glittered with a wild possessiveness. The look in his eyes had been love, but love that had been corrupted, like a tree whose root rot has finally begun to wither the branches.

"Did you like it, Catherine?" his father had asked, then paused to slug his whiskey straight from the bottle. He spoke through gritted teeth. "Did you truly fight them off, or did you moan as you took them into you, one by one?"

His mother hadn't answered, or even turned around; she'd simply stopped stirring the boiling potatoes and walked briskly out of the kitchen. His father's face had immediately crumpled with regret.

"Cath, I'm sorry. Jesus, I didn't mean that. I love you, *a chuisle mo chroí!*" He hadn't gone after her, though. He'd placed his head in his hands and wept, mindless of the starchy water boiling over and hitting the stove with a hiss. Malcolm had run and taken over his mother's duty. He looked to his younger brother, Ewan, who had his face stuck in a Latin book he'd borrowed from a neighbor. Reading was his favorite form of escape. Don, his sister, was still a burbling babe, unaware that she was a daily reminder of all that had gone awry for them.

That was when Malcolm had learned the *true* power of love: It could take a good man, hollow him out, and fill him with something caustic. He'd steered well clear of it as he grew into a man, and his nomadic lifestyle had aided him well in his avoidance. But now there was Elle. Elle with the sharp tongue. Elle with the brilliant mind. Elle who was a million times too good for a man like him, but who would always be seen as less than.

Malcolm thought of her bleeding in the

streets of Baltimore. The men whose group he had infiltrated had laughed as she fell, or ignored her, as if a bleeding woman shouldn't be a shock to Southern Gentlemanhood. Malcolm could already feel that anger he'd seen in his father creeping into his blood; maybe it was a curse, placed on the McCalls that fateful day when the English lapdogs had swarmed into their village. Or maybe it was the only recourse of a man who couldn't protect the woman he cared about.

She's not your woman. Oh, that was true, but not for lack of wanting it to be so.

Malcolm sighed. Pinkerton had joked that thirty-two was a bit old for a detective, and perhaps he'd been right. He was going soft or his brain was addled. There was no other explanation for his preoccupation with the woman. None that he wanted to admit, that is.

Malcolm performed his morning ablutions, dressed in the thick woolen uniform that was comfortable in this January cold but had given men heatstroke during the marches in the warmer months. He stared at himself in the reviled gray and for a moment he was weary. The constant pretending, the fear of discovery, the rootless nature of his life. What he'd for so long thought of as a boon was now beginning to feel like a burden.

When he'd strapped on his gun, pulled on his hat, and stepped outside into the quiet side street where his hotel was located, he began to feel more like himself. He set his mouth at the perfect angle to signal he was thinking of something amusing, but private. He kept his gaze before him, a bit unfocused to show he was deep in thought. He'd long since discovered that presenting an air of contented solitude was the quickest way to have loquacious people approach.

It took about two minutes, and that was on the long side.

"Oh, Mr. McCall! Say, Mr. McCall!" A youngish man was quickly approaching, maneuvering his way between carriages pulled by emaciated horses and drivers that were only marginally better nourished. The blockade's effects were showing more and more every day.

The man arrived, eyes bright and out of breath from his exertions.

"Just the man I want to see," the man said excitedly. "Just the one." He stared at Malcolm in adoration, unblinking.

Malcolm gave an inward groan as he realized what the man was about. The sweaty, panting men were always after the same

178

thing. Glory.

"Well, sir, tales of your exploits as told to Senator Caffrey made today's paper. I just want to shake the hand of a man who came so close to ridding our nation of the scourge of that traitor Lincoln."

"Well, I failed at my task, so I'm not worthy of any special attention," Malcolm said. He'd succeeded, of course, spectacularly so since President Lincoln had escaped the Rebel plot unscathed. He wished he could rub that knowledge in this man's face. He was so tired of the spineless hangers-on who thirsted for blood as long as someone else's hand was on the hilt of the sword or pulling the trigger. He wasn't pleased to hear that he had made the papers either. Even if the rags bolstered him as a son of the South, making headlines was the sort of attention a man like him didn't court.

"Well, that's not true. It's just heartening to know that fellows like you and Stevens are working in support of Davis's government. We beat the tar out of the Northmen at Manassas, and it's only a matter of time before we've defeated them completely."

Malcolm looked away in a show of modesty, but the truth was he couldn't look the man in the eye. This misplaced nationalism was another kind of corrupted love, and it was just as unpalatable.

He gave the man a friendly clap on the shoulder. "I'm sure you're right, friend. I'm sure you're right. Good day to you."

There was nothing further to say. Although he was positive the stranger could spend days pontificating on the righteousness of the Confederacy, he had no tolerance for such tomfoolery at the moment.

Malcolm wound his way through the city, seeing what drew his eye. He meandered down side streets and stopped to chat with an old acquaintance. He hooted and cheered at an intersection as a regiment of young soldiers marched by.

He told himself that he was simply surveying the city, seeing if there was any intelligence that could be conveyed to the Capital, but when his boots carried him to MacTavish's store he admitted the truth: Although he'd do anything for the Union, he was in search of something other than secessionist plots.

He stooped through the door into the dusty store. Many shelves were empty, and they would remain so if smugglers didn't get through with goods. If he'd wanted bread or oats, he would have been sorely disappointed, but he wanted Elle and it seemed luck was on his side.

She stood at the counter, her back to him. She only turned because MacTavish glared over her shoulder at him. When she moved toward him, he was so taken with the heat in her eyes and the scowl pulling at her pretty lips that he didn't notice the gun until it was pressed into his belly.

"Have you changed your mind since our carriage ride? If so, I prefer the knife." He kept his voice light. He didn't want to die, but if she was to be his executioner, then he might consider it.

"I'm going to take him to the back, Tav," she said. Her voice was low and lovely and altogether dangerous. There was a thread of something in her words, the way they caught in her throat, that warned him of just how angry she was. Had he been mistaken about her? Could she possibly have reason to turn on him? Perhaps he'd underestimated how seriously his kiss had offended her.

"Elle, what madness is this?"

"I'm wondering the same thing myself, McCall," she said through gritted teeth. "Why don't we go discuss it further? Alone."

She pressed the gun into him and the most ill-timed thread of desire began to unspool in his belly.

"As you may have noticed, I'm more than amenable to spending time with you," he said quietly, using the lazy tone he knew annoyed her. "No need for drawn weapons."

"When dealing with possible traitors, a gun is a valuable accessory. Now, are you going to move or am I going to shoot you?"

Malcolm didn't know what she was about, but the anger in Elle's eyes grabbed his attention. She wasn't one for histrionics that he could tell of. Something had to have occurred for her to resort to such brusque behavior. He decided not to resist. The room was small and he would have the size advantage, despite her weapon.

"I'll come along. This is the most eager I've ever seen you to be in my presence, after all. Well, I guess that's not entirely true." He paused, waited for the spark of acknowledgment to light her eyes. She glared at him. "Ah. Now I'm worried that you'll shoot me before the interrogation even starts."

"As you should be," she gritted out. Her eyes held his as he marched past her, past MacTavish, and into the dim back room. He sat on a chair that felt as if it would give way beneath him at any moment and wondered if she'd planned it to make him feel unsteady. His brother, Ewan, had told him of such tactics, but Elle was in the detective game, not counterintelligence.

"Bar the door," Elle said over her shoulder to MacTavish. "And leave us be. If I need help disposing of the body, I'll call for you."

Despite his precarious situation, Malcolm smiled. Damn, she was impressive. If she didn't kill him, he'd tell her so.

CHAPTER 9

"When last we met here, we shared information that was sent on to the Capital. Information about the movement of Rebel troops," she said, leaning back on the desk. Her hand clasped the gun against her skirts, and she pushed away thoughts of the path that Malcolm's hand had traveled the last time they were in the same space. It had been wrong then, but now that he was possibly a double agent, it was galling. "When the Capital sent troops to waylay that movement, they were ambushed."

She stopped talking and stared at him. She wished to intimidate him, and she wasn't sure she could do that around the lump of emotion in her throat.

Malcolm raised his eyebrows. "I understand that this is upsetting, but I don't see why it calls for drawn weapons and back-room interrogations. If you have something to ask me, then ask it."

A tract of text popped up in her mind's eye, a common occurrence since she had so many of the dad-blamed things committed to memory. " 'No man, for any considerable period, can wear one face to himself and another to the multitude, without finally getting bewildered as to which may be the true,' " she said.

"I don't know what you're quoting at me, but I do know what it implies," he said. There was an undercurrent to his voice that she hadn't heard before, one that reminded her that despite his easy demeanor with her, Malcolm was a dangerous man. Possibly a treasonous one.

Elle hated the assuredness of his voice, as if he were the one in charge. She was tempted to raise her weapon, but instead she laid it on the table beside her, showing that she wasn't someone who would hide behind her revolver. She kept her hand next to it, though; she wouldn't let ego be her undoing, either.

"You are the only other person besides me who was aware the Union possessed that information. Now good men lay dead or taken off to Confederate prisons," she said, trying to hide the shake in her voice. "I will know if I was betrayed."

When she'd heard about the ambushing

of the regiment, her heart had dropped. She didn't want to believe it was Malcolm, but the words of Sun Tzu had sprung to her mind, unbidden: *"It is essential to seek out enemy agents who have come to conduct espionage against you and to bribe them to serve you. . . . Thus double agents are recruited and used."* Malcolm had sought her out . . . and the bribe he'd given her? The kiss she'd fallen into instead of running from.

Malcolm straightened in his seat, making his massive size, compared to hers, even more apparent. His brow creased and his eyes narrowed.

"I will tolerate only so much of these shenanigans, Miss Burns," he said. His voice was rough with suppressed anger. "I will not have my loyalty questioned after all I've done to serve my country."

"I have the blood of twenty men on my hands, Mr. McCall," she said. She stood, no longer wanting the support of the desk. "I cannot worry about bruising your feelings. If they're so tender that they cannot withstand a simple line of questioning, perhaps you've chosen the wrong profession."

She stared at him and he held it, but she saw the anger drain out of his expression. It was replaced by sadness. No, that wasn't right — it was pity. "Twenty men? Lord above. I'm sorry, Elle. Was it the information about the troops massing to move to South Carolina?"

She nodded, hating the sympathy in his voice.

He sighed. "Is this the first time you've had a bad batch?"

"Batch?" she asked.

"Of information." He placed his hands on his thighs and she remembered how strong they had been beneath her as they hid on the bluff. How, beneath the fear of discovery, it had been nice to let someone else carry her weight for just a moment. She was weary, and this war had only just begun. Maybe she'd been wrong to spurn Daniel. Even if she didn't love him how a woman should love her husband, having someone to sink into after such a blow would be wonderful.

Malcolm ran a hand through his hair. "I know how you feel. On one of my first missions during this conflict, I passed on bum information. I'd been told that Confederate troops were setting up camp in a certain section of wood and passed that information along to my superiors. When the Union forces showed up, there was a camp, but it was empty. It was an ambush, and there were no survivors. Those men had gone there on my word, and they died because of it."

She bit her lip against the anguish that rose in her throat.

"Why should I believe you?" she asked after a moment. "I've already seen that you lie as easily as you breathe. It's not as if you would confess your treason."

The words were harsh, but they came out heatless; her fiery surety had burned down to ashes. She had relayed information that resulted in tragedy, but she still trusted her gut. Despite the fact that killing him would make her life a damn sight easier, she didn't think he had betrayed her. Worse, she was relieved.

"I already offered to let you kill me," he said with a shrug. "You missed your opportunity and now you're just going to have to trust that, although I lie for my country, I wouldn't lie to you."

"And why is that?" she asked.

"I'd tell you, but I don't think you'd believe me." His eyes were dark with an emotion that didn't match his grin.

"I could still shoot you," she said. He raised his brows, and she looked away from him. "I need you to be straight with me,

McCall: Did you share what you read in my letter with anyone?"

"No one," he said. "I didn't even write it in my ledger. You can't know what happened. The likeliest thing, with the way this war operates, is that it was simple bad luck that fell upon those men. Or, since the information was thirdhand at best, who knows how many others heard it and passed it along?"

Elle nodded. He was right, but that didn't make her sadness disappear. Of all the hundreds of books she'd memorized, none had provided her with a good answer to the dread that sat heavy in her chest. The burden seemed too great.

"How did you move past it?" she asked. She didn't want to be told to soldier on. She'd thought to exercise her fury on Malcolm, but he'd played no part in this. Now all her pent-up emotion had no vent. She stood, walked a few steps, and then realizing she'd nowhere to go, sat on the rickety wooden stool with a thump.

Malcolm rose and walked toward her, and she knew already that he wasn't going to offer her a clap on the back and a swig of bourbon, as she'd seen other operatives coddled in their lowest moments.

He pulled up a stool beside her. The wood

creaked under his weight; then he was sitting so close that her shoulder pressed into his biceps. The way he leaned into her was friendly, but his nearness made her senses stand at attention. She thought of moving away from him, but it was nice to have something solid to prop her up. He smelled of leather and wool, and his warmth seemed to draw some of the fear and anger from her.

"It's a hard thing, Elle, but you cannot let this shake your confidence. It could have been a devious trap, or it could have been simple conjecture like half the things you hear in this city. Either way, it's not your fault."

"That doesn't bring those men back," she said. She leaned into his warmth, promising herself it was just for a moment.

"Neither does flagellating yourself," Malcolm said quietly. "What would you say if a fellow operative came to you feeling sorry after passing on bad intelligence? Would you tell them to go jump off a cliff? And remember now, you're not giving the advice to me, so be kind."

A low laugh rose in her throat, despite her despair. "I would tell them . . . that the best thing they could do to honor those fallen soldiers would be to work hard and discover

190

information that helped the Union win."

Malcolm nodded, but he didn't lean away from her. In fact, he settled in closer so now their knees touched, too. Part of her itched to shove him away. She couldn't understand why being close to him felt so good, even as her logic railed against it. She hated how her body had gone warm and her stomach fluttered with anticipation every time he moved an inch.

"Are you still planning on killing me?" he asked. "If so, you should call for reinforcements. I think you might need more help than that wee scrap of a Scotsman to carry my body out."

His voice was calm as he spoke to her, but his pulse raced — perhaps even faster than her own. She could feel it. Heat wound sinuously through her body, flaring as his hand began to move up and down her arm. The touch was meant to be soothing, but the pull of his fingertips against the fabric of her dress was erotic, despite his intentions. Despite her common sense.

"Not if I chopped you into pieces first," she said. "I can dress a deer lickety-split; I imagine an annoying detective wouldn't be much different." She looked up at him, feeling his laugh roll through her. The sound resonated in every part of her body, like

191

when she stood too close to the church bell tower. There was nothing holy or sanctified about the sensation Malcolm's laugh caused in her, though.

"I still feel like I failed," she said, trying to distract from the increasing heat along the seams where their bodies touched.

She pulled away from him then, remaining seated but leaving some distance between them. It wasn't right allowing him that kind of liberty. An even deeper shame pressed at her, piling on to the self-doubt that was already shredding her sense of purpose.

You're a disappointment. To your country. To your cause. To your people.

Elle stiffened, the blows of her own thoughts more painful than Malcolm's lack of response. What was she doing? What had she gotten herself into? And how would she ever make things right?

Malcolm sighed and finally spoke. "And what if you did fail?" he asked finally. There was no censure in his words. "That tends to happen to human beings every now and again. No one expects you to be perfect, Elle."

Her breath drew sharp into her lungs at his words. He was wrong, of course. All of those years on the abolitionist circuit, her

192

years as a teacher, her trip to Liberia. People had always expected perfection from her, as if her flawless memory superseded her right to be a human being. She didn't know when she'd started believing it, too, but she had.

She let out a startled laugh. "I'm allowed to make mistakes," she said. "I'm allowed to fail and not feel like I've disgraced my entire race? Imagine that." Her voice was tight with emotion, a pent-up ache that sought release somehow.

"You're allowed that. That and more," Malcolm said. She couldn't see his hand, but she felt the warmth of it beside her arm. He'd reached for her, but hesitated, and although her logic was firmly against the idea, some villainous part of her willed him to move his hand that inch closer that would bring contact.

It seemed that insurrection was catching.

His fingers grazed her sleeve, tentatively, and then his grip tightened. His large hand was a circle of heat as it encircled her arm. His hand slid up, the fabric of her dress dragging against his rough palm as it squeezed the curve of her biceps and caressed the round of her shoulder, moving up the slope there until the back of her neck was cupped in his hand. His touch against her sensitive skin sent little blips of pleasure through Elle, like messages down a telegraph line. *More. Stop. Please. Stop.*

"You're allowed whatever you want, as far as I'm concerned. What do you want, Ellen?"

"I want . . . comfort." The words came out deep, rough. Elle was ashamed to discover that she was trembling, her duplicitous body plainly broadcasting the desire she wished she could hide from him, and especially from herself.

"Can you be more specific, love?"

She couldn't. All the fancy words she had accumulated over the years were stuck in that logical portion of her brain, the part that knew what she was about to do next was madness.

She kissed him.

She could feel his surprise in the stiffening of his body as her mouth pressed against his. That was all it took to knock some sense into her. She started to pull away, but then his mouth opened wide against hers and his tongue pushed past her lips and there was no escaping. One arm crushed her close to his side, pulling her halfway onto his lap, and the other cupped her chin, tilting her head back for him.

"Mmmmmmm." The sound he made was familiar, but somehow obscene and inviting at the same time. It was the groan of a man who had tasted something delicious, and that something was her. Chills of delight traveled over her body, all heading toward the bundle of throbbing sensation between her thighs. His hand left her chin and followed, curving over her breasts and down the plane of her abdomen as if her desire bade him come quickly, the desire that she'd flatly deny if her mouth wasn't pressed against his.

His hand slipped under her dress, atop the loose folds of her drawers and cupped her mound. "Malcolm." His name slipped from between her lips as if to stay his progress. She knew she was damp there and the weakness embarrassed her. Her chagrin didn't stop her from lifting up, pressing her sensitive nub into the heel of his hand as he rubbed it in rough circles.

"Is this comfort enough, Elle?" he asked. His palm massaged her through the rough fabric, each controlled twist of his wrist sending a burst of pleasure through her. Elle could feel his touch in her breasts and in her toes and in the impossibly delicious feeling that had her inner walls clenching in anticipation of being filled. She thought of what it would be like to have Malcolm hard inside her and she let out a ragged pant. If his palm could do this to her, unassisted by those digits that supposedly made man the most superior of animals, she was afraid of what else he could wring from her.

"Yes, it's enough," she said, although she hoped he wouldn't stop. The way he looked down at her was dangerous. It was the look of a man who would not be deterred, not in war and not in making love. His fingers replaced his palm and she swallowed a cry, her head lolling against his shoulder as the increased pressure sent even stronger bolts of all-encompassing pleasure through her.

His other hand slid up to her neck, and she felt a gentle tug as he wrapped her plaits around his hand — once, twice — and gently tugged her head back to place a trail of kisses along the exposed path that led from her jaw to her collarbone. His lips lingered in the notch of her neck, and she could feel the fluttering of both of their pulses combined where their skin met.

"You think I want you for a taste of something taboo," he whispered. "But you're any man's dream: intelligent, brave, and so damn lovely I can't tear my eyes from you. That's why I want you."

She shook her head. Malcolm used his grip on her hair to angle her head back and kiss her, his tongue tracing her bottom lip before slashing over her entire mouth.

"Yes, Elle," he said. His fingers circled faster, urging her toward completion even as her back arched and her hips bucked wantonly. "Take your release, lass."

She looked into his eyes. "No," she whispered, then bit her lip against the moan that fought to follow the word out into the silence of the back room. That's when the sensation burst in her, pure and bright and sweeter than anything she'd ever felt before. There was no sadness or recrimination in the heat that raced through her body, just pleasure. Just Malcolm.

He eased his hand away as her shuddering subsided, and she leapt from his lap and onto wobbly legs. She could feel his gaze seeking hers out, but she refused to meet it.

"We shouldn't have done that," she said after a long moment. "We shouldn't have done that," she repeated, as if saying it twice was a charm that could undo what had passed between them. "But it made me feel good. *You* made me feel good. What does that make me?"

The enormity of what she'd allowed to pass was too much to process. Perhaps it had been another Elle who parted her thighs for the rogue across the room? The one who looked ready to sink to his knees

— to sink into her — if only she gave him the go-ahead. Her quivering knees were a testament to her physical reaction, but the ridiculous thoughts that now swarmed her mind were much worse. She wanted to run her hands over his body. She imagined what his face would look like as his climax took him, and just the thought made her shiver with want.

He shook his head and shrugged. "I can't answer that, but I can tell you it makes me happier than a fish in the James."

She glared at him. Of course the fool would say something like that. He wasn't the one who had betrayed everything he believed in, so it was fine for him to make silly jokes about the river . . . the river that passed right through Richmond . . . where they had seen men planning to move something. And what was that she'd read in one of Malcolm's letters?

All shame and dismay were lost as the realization that had been on the edge of her consciousness the last time they'd been in MacTavish's back room finally coalesced. The text of the letters she had intercepted at the Caffrey's and the information from Malcolm's reports flashed in her mind's eye, the relevant parts jumping out at her.

"Ironclad!" she whispered excitedly. Elle

felt a rush nearly as good as the climax she'd just experienced as the random information formed into unified theory.

"Pardon?" Malcolm asked. He adjusted the tented groin of his pants. "I'm not familiar with that particular euphemism, but I'm not opposed to it."

Elle rolled her eyes. "I'd been trying to piece your information together with my information when you . . . interrupted me the other day. You said in one of your letters that one of the men coming into the city on your boat said he had been recruited for a big project at Tredegar. The ironworks," she said excitedly. "Meanwhile, both Senator Caffrey yesterday and your friend the other day —"

"Willocks is not my friend," Malcolm interrupted.

"— your friend mentioned breaking the blockade. I'm sure you've heard about the scuttled Union ironclad that the Rebs scavenged to shore up their paltry navy. Ironclads are the only boats with enough armor to go head-to-head with the boats being used in the blockade. The men on the bluff seemed to want to bring something large along the river. Perhaps parts —"

"— that are needed to finish repairs to the salvaged ironclad," Malcolm finished for her. "Given that Tredegar is the only place in the south that could produce the materials needed for such an undertaking, you just might be right."

Elle and Malcolm stared at each other in silent communion; both knew what it would mean if her theory was correct. The possession of an ironclad would turn the tide of the war, allowing the South to rip through the blockade and regain control of their coasts and rivers. Once the trade routes were reopened, ships laden with cotton could make sail for England to barter for money and ammunition. The Confederate army could move soldiers freely along the coasts, and the influx of goods and manpower would mean that the rebellion could continue indefinitely. It would mean that the Union could be lost.

"This cannot be allowed," Elle said.

Malcolm gave a brusque nod. "We need to send word immediately. They're building another Union ironclad, but if it's not done in time . . ."

Elle paced the room, unable to still the excitement her deduction had roused in her. She may have recently sent misinformation, but she'd just discovered something huge enough to make up for that error a thousand-fold. If she was right, the course of the war could soon be irretrievably changed, for good or ill.

"It would be a death blow to us. We have to let the Capital know of our suspicions and that we plan to get them hard proof as soon as we can," she said, grabbing a sheet of paper and jotting down the information in a code that only her Loyal League brothers would be able to decode. "I'm guessing our best chance to get that proof will be at the ball. All those Rebs drinking and trying to outdo each other with how much classified information they know."

"We?" Malcolm asked, his tone just a smidge too pleased for her liking. "A moment ago you nearly killed me, and I don't mean those little noises you kept making while you were perched in my lap."

Elle narrowed her eyes at him. The cheek of him to talk of their momentary distraction when there was work to be done.

"I shall let you live for now, McCall. But only because I need someone with unfettered access to Caffrey's heart and mind. Your flirtation with Susie, and the senator for that matter, should make you privy to information I can't access, and we need as many sources as possible."

Even she heard the edge to her words at the mention of Susie's name. If one were a silly man with ridiculous ideas about what was possible in their world, one might think she was jealous. She knew better than that, though.

"Yes, I'll be by soon, and while I'm there I'll have to flirt with Susie. She's got connections to the local Vigilance Committee, and even though those groups are usually hokum, she might have information that's helpful. But don't dare think I'll enjoy it knowing that, in a perfect world, I could be spending my time with you instead."

"In a perfect world you wouldn't know me," she said bluntly. She finished writing the letter and folded it into a neat square. "You don't have to explain yourself to me."

Malcolm stepped close to her, nearly as close as he'd been as they sat on the chairs.

Comfort. That was all it had been.

Apparently, Mr. McCall wasn't of the same opinion. His hand rested atop of hers. "If you feel even a little bit the way I'm feeling, I'd damn well better explain myself before going and flirting with that pile of crinoline known as Miss Susie Caffrey."

Elle didn't know how to react to his words. One part of her felt victorious, while the other hated him for continuing this charade. She pulled her hand away.

"The quote you scoffed at earlier was from

a book called *The Scarlet Letter.* Do you know what the story entails?"

Malcolm shook his head.

"A woman gives in to her desire, partakes in a forbidden romance, and ends up reviled. And her lover, how do you think he fares? If you guess that they're meted out the same punishment, you are wrong."

"What does some work of fiction have to do with the desire we feel for each other?" Malcolm asked.

"Everything. Why should I believe that were I to proceed with this affair, which I shall not, that you wouldn't desert me as soon as things get rough? That night on the bluff, you wouldn't even pretend to introduce me to your parents, and now you want to lay claim to me?" she whispered. "And they say women are fickle."

"My father is dead, Elle, so you can't meet him," he said. She whipped her head in his direction. "I told you about the Clearances. When the men came to our town, they brutalized the women, some of them in front of their own families. My father was at his shop when the men came. I tried to stop them, but I was too small, too weak. My mother begged them to put me out of the house before they hurt her. . . ."

The pain in his eyes was so stark as to

make Elle believe she was talking to a different man. There was no flirtation, no sly jokes.

Elle's breath froze in her lung. The story was so familiar, whispered among the women in the slave quarters and, after she was a freedwoman, at the quilting circles and church dinners. They warned of what could happen if a man, especially a white man, wanted to have his way with you. She didn't need Malcolm to elaborate; she'd heard of all the ways a man could violate an unwilling woman. Those stories had laid the foundation for why she shouldn't care about a man who looked like Malcolm, but her heart hurt for him and his mother all the same.

He continued, not waiting for her to speak. "Mum was bad for a while after, but she recovered eventually. She had to, or what would my siblings and I have done? My father was never the same, though. It was like, in addition to taking all he'd worked for, they had taken my mother from him as well. He'd failed to protect her, and even though she didn't blame him, he blamed himself. Despite being the one who had been victimized, she poured her energy into bringing him back around once we got to Kentucky. For a while it seemed to work.

But he eventually took his own life."

Malcolm closed his eyes, as if proofing himself against some memory. For the briefest of moments, he looked very young and very frightened. Elle thought that perhaps that's who he really was under all the layers of the subterfuge that made him a prized Pinkerton.

She grasped his hand. "That's horrible, Malcolm. Unspeakable. I couldn't have known, but I'm sorry I said something hurtful all the same."

Strangely, Malcolm smiled at her. "There's no need for apology. Besides, I know he would have liked you. When he was well, he loved nothing more than a woman with a smart mouth."

Elle's gaze jerked up to his face. The ridiculous man. He could claim his father would like him gallivanting around with a black woman only because he'd never have to prove it.

"That's a compliment," he said, just as the door to the back room opened. "I'm sure the rest of my family will like you fine, too."

He plucked the note out of her hand and handed it to MacTavish. "Apologies, but she decided to let me live. Pass this note along, will you?"

With that, he swept out of the room, as if he'd been the one in control the entire time.

"I should have killed him," Elle said. MacTavish gave her a grim nod in agreement.

CHAPTER 10

Elle knew what it was to have a secret, but never one that left her feeling as if her entire being was a vessel designed to keep it safe. She fairly vibrated with excitement at the conclusion she'd come to with Malcolm, but two days had gone by with no word from her superiors. The impatient part of her wanted to scream from the rafters that the ironclad must be stopped. She was finally glad of her subterfuge of muteness; she didn't trust herself otherwise. After sharing her suspicions with Timothy, she'd kept her mouth shut. Still, every moment spent without taking action seemed like time wasted.

Her tasks at the Caffrey mansion now chafed even more: unjust, unpaid, and unlikely to let up as the ball approached. While the senator was busy with wartime affairs, his wife had little to do but obsess over the presentation of their home. She took what little power she had quite seriously, and every slave felt her anxieties.

Mrs. Caffrey had Elle scrub the parlor floor on her hands and knees twice in one afternoon, and when Senator Caffrey lingered too long in appreciation of Elle's work, the damned woman spilled a glass of port on one of the sofas and demanded Elle make sure the pale blue satin was spotless. "And this time without shoving your behind in the air like a baboon in heat," she'd said in a sickly sweet voice. Elle wanted to tell the woman to get on all fours and clean herself if she wanted the senator's attentions so badly — maybe he'd mistake her for a slave and try to mount her — but that wouldn't have been acceptable. So she'd scrubbed in frustrated silence.

And then there was Malcolm. He made his regular appearances at the house, glad-handing the men who might have valuable information and spinning yarns about his adventures in thwarting the Union. If she hadn't known him to be a Pinkerton, she would have believed every word he said without a second thought. She who had been trained in all the tells that showed a man was lying.

Something about that didn't sit well. She no longer thought Malcolm a traitor, but

208

the fact he could deceive people so easily was disconcerting. Ms. Mary Shelly's words appeared in her mind's eye: *"When falsehood can look so like the truth, who can assure themselves of certain happiness?"*

Malcolm wanted her to trust him, but reality made that nearly impossible. She'd heard enough of the exploits of her fellow Loyal League members, and the things the senator's guests spoke of when the ladies retired to the parlor. Men saw women as playthings more often than not, and she'd been foolish enough to let Malcolm get under her skirts — and her skin.

His persistence was bothersome, but it also nourished a small, withered place within her that dared to hope someone could want her just as she was. She hated comparing Malcolm to Daniel, but her lost friend had also been her only experience with love. She'd thought herself satisfied with their arrangement, camaraderie, and carnal pleasure, but she'd never felt more than the deep fondness of friendship with Daniel. And it was for the best, in the end. He'd thought her memorizing skill a neat trick, but as they grew older he'd seemed more and more ashamed of it, of the fact that she'd always know more than him no matter how hard he tried to catch up. And he hadn't thought a woman could handle the rigors of working for the Union, or that one should even try, despite his support for the North and desire for freedom for their people.

And here I am proving him right, falling for the first man who gives me a tingle, Elle thought as she dabbed at the couch, soaking up the last remnant of dark alcohol. She shook her head and gathered her cleaning supplies. She refused to flagellate herself any further. She'd called herself every despicable insult that could be hurled her way — adventuress, bed wench, traitor to the race — and none of that stopped the ungodly fascination that Malcolm held for her. Even as she watched him lie and told herself not to trust him, she was further ensnared. Charm wasn't required to be a Pinkerton, so she was told, but in McCall's case it surely didn't hurt.

As the Caffrey house bustled with guests who had arrived for an impromptu gathering, Elle realized she'd been kept so busy with all the small details her position entailed that she hadn't had time to check the senator's office that day. With the guests leaving soon, he would retire to his desk to write correspondence that had to be sent off first thing in the morning.

Elle left the kitchen and moved stealthily toward the servant's staircase. She grabbed a candle to enter the dark, unlit space and nearly walked right into two warm bodies engaged in less than savory behavior. The two forms quickly jumped away from each other.

"Please don't tell anyone," a familiar voice said. Elle raised the candle, illuminating Althea, one of the kitchen girls. There was a nervous snicker. Ezekiel, one of the cooks in training. His voice, still teetering between boyishness and manhood, cracked as he spoke. "It's just Elle. She ain't gonna tell nobody. She *can't* tell nobody."

The words were harsh, but she knew he meant no harm by them. Elle had noticed growing warmth from the other slaves since she'd had her literal run-in with Susie. It had been much to her benefit, for now they spoke more freely in front of her, spreading the gossip they garnered from others.

Althea hit at his arm with a rag she had in her hand. "Hush, Zeke!" She turned to Elle and rolled her eyes. "My cousin Ben is coming up from down Carolina with his master. Ben is mighty cute, and I know he'll want to meet you."

Zeke dropped his head back to show his impatience. "Do you gotta talk about this

211

now?"

Elle stifled a laugh. She remembered her first kiss, how they'd fumbled and groped until they both burst out laughing at the ridiculousness of it. The memory was bittersweet because, of course, she had to think of where Daniel must be now, and the life he was consigned to. She sighed and raised a hand, pretending to cover her eyes as she passed by the teenage lovers. She moved the hand to the side and winked at Althea, drawing surprised laughter from the girl. The sound soothed Elle's sadness; who knew what the future held for Althea and Zeke as the war marched on without an end in sight. If they could snatch a few moments of euphoria in a stairwell, she wished them well. Best that they enjoy such amusements while they could.

Elle left thoughts of the teenaged sweethearts behind as she crept into the senator's office. Luckily for her, his confidence in the sanctity of his home meant he wasn't overly cautious with his affairs. There was a pile of correspondence, but it had yet to be opened and she didn't have enough time to reproduce a seal. She was about to give the situation up for lost when she noticed a folded-up billet. She snatched it up, hoping it was a something that could be of use, but it was a list of names and, next to those names, prices. The list of slaves for sale in Richmond that week. She thought about the boy Timothy had gone to pick up and the plentiful household staff and wondered if Caffrey intended to keep buying humans just because he could, like Susie with her baubles. Her stomach lurched at the thought.

She was turning to leave, the list she had scanned already imprinted in her memory, when an entry three lines down from the bottom became more than an innocuous jumble of words. What she'd read without thinking now stopped her in her tracks.

Daniel — $800 — 28-year-old male, healthy stock, uppity but will be a great asset once broken. Broad, strong, good teeth. No abnormalities save for a missing left earlobe.

It had to be a coincidence. It had to. But she remembered the day the neighbor's savage dog had gotten loose and tackled the gangly young man to the ground. She'd jumped on the dog's back and nearly gotten her hand mauled, but Daniel had escaped intact — minus one earlobe.

The room seemed to tilt as she resumed

her stride toward the door. Her body was heavy as she forced herself out of the office and toward the stairwell — it wouldn't do to be found insensate in the senator's office when she had no reason to be there. It was some survival instinct that guided her, because grief had seized every other part of her mind and held it tight.

Once broken. Broken.

Daniel could be in Richmond. Daniel, who had been in her life for almost as long as she could remember living, and who she had hurt so badly during their last encounter. Elle was halfway down the now-deserted stairwell when she realized she had forgotten her candle. For a moment, she thought to leave it; she didn't know if she could go back in knowing that foul document lay on his desk, innocuous in its pure evil. But if she didn't, she risked more than herself. If Caffrey found a burning candle in his office he would demand to know who had been lazy enough to forget such a thing, and it would reflect on all the other slaves.

She whirled and retraced her steps, hurrying now. She'd already pressed her luck in entering unnoticed once. She slipped in, retrieved the candle, and slipped out. She realized she'd been holding her breath, as if to protect herself from the corruption of the sales billet. She was almost through the door of the servants' staircase again when a hand closed on her shoulder. To her great surprise, she didn't drop the candle. And to her great chagrin, relief coursed through her at the familiar touch.

"Susie started caterwauling about you not bringing her a tisane," Malcolm said. "I thought . . . I had a feeling you might be up here. You should get downstairs before she gets out of hand."

Elle had been holding herself together, but Malcolm's words slammed into the most sensitive part of her, shattering her self-control. She had put up with so much, with so little complaint, but she wasn't allowed even a moment for her own grief. For the first time since arriving at the Caffreys', Elle forgot why she was there and what she was doing. Not so much forgot as couldn't be bothered to temper herself.

"I should get downstairs, should I? So I can wait hand and foot on a spoiled chit who's never done a day's work, unless you count batting your lashes as hard labor?" The words came out low and harsh, and the hot tears that spilled out enraged her even more. "Let her get out of hand. Let her lay one hand on me and I'll . . . I'll . . ." She gasped back a sob. There was nothing she could do. Nothing.

Malcolm pulled her into the stairwell and closed the door behind him, pulling her close to his warmth. Fool that she was, she let him.

"Elle, what's wrong?"

Everything.

She shook her head against his chest. "You're right. If Susie is sniffing after me, I should go."

Malcolm rubbed his palm over the small of her back. "Rufus had cornered her before I left, so you have a moment or two. Tell me what pains you like this?"

It was the concern in his voice that did her in. He couldn't fake that worry, that strain that said he was already preparing to shoulder whatever burden she would lay on him. Elle took a shaky breath.

"Before I left for Liberia, my closest friend, my former beau, asked me to marry him." She felt Malcolm stiffen, but he kept stroking his hand down her back in comfort without missing a beat.

"Did you accept his offer?" Malcolm asked. She'd been twisting herself in knots over how slick Malcolm was, but he couldn't keep the hesitation and fear out of his voice when he asked her that question. She thought to lie, to keep the comfortable distance of a man between her and Malcolm's intentions, but to use Daniel in such a way seemed wrong.

"No. I loved him very much, but not in that way." She pressed her forehead into Malcolm's chest at the thought that followed. *He didn't make me feel how you do.* Enough. She pulled away from him and wiped the tears from her face with her sleeve. "While I was gone, he sank into a despair. One night after he'd imbibed too much, he was coerced by slavers and kidnapped down South. Daniel was a free man, born free. And I just saw a list of slaves for sale with his name on it."

"Are you sure it's him?" Malcolm asked. There was no doubt or hesitation in the question, just determination.

"No, just a name and a matching descriptor that could be chance." She shook her head, every muscle in her body tensed against the knowledge that her hands were tied. "Even if it is him, what am I to do? I can't break into a slave market and free everyone. That would start a manhunt for abolitionists and Northern spies in Richmond, and I'd be risking everything we'd worked for. Timothy, MacTavish and his group, the various Loyal League agents in the area. With the information we have, I could be risking the Union."

Malcolm nodded. "If anything alerts them to a strong Union presence, and a break-in at the slave market would do just that, they could change their plans for the ironclad and we'd have no way of knowing if we were right until too late."

Elle tried to think of another way to free Daniel, but her mind kept imagining him beaten and starved, dragged out before men who would grab his haunches and check his teeth like he were so much livestock. Living in the North, Elle had known of the slave markets. She'd read as much as she could about them, heard tales from the people escaping enslavement who passed through her parents' home. But it was there in Richmond where she saw the monstrous made mundane. The slave market was located sickeningly close to the grocer's, just another establishment to purchase goods. She heard the cries of mothers torn from children, of men separated from their wives. . . .

Elle felt something inside her being crushed slowly: hope.

"Just because we can't free him ourselves doesn't mean I can't see if something, anything, can be done through my contacts." He placed a hand on her elbow, lightly and with no hint of possession. "Elle, you know how I feel about you, but this is something else entirely. The other day you described us as 'we,' and I took that to mean you and I are partners now. I'll do whatever I can to help in this matter."

Elle thought she would tumble down the stairs, so struck was she by his words. *He knows what to say to gain a person's trust,* she reminded herself. But still, a warm, happy feeling was spreading from her chest, pushing out against the crushing despair that had threatened to extinguish that which drove her on. New words sprang into her mind, not those of a Chinese general, but a British author whose works had captivated her in an entirely different way. *"And so she shuddered away from the threat of his enduring love. . . . Had she not the power to daunt him?"* She'd recalled the same quote from Gaskell's *North and South* when Daniel had proposed they marry, but somehow the words had lost their effect. With Daniel, she hadn't immediately remembered the lines that followed later in the novel. *"Why did she tremble and hide her face in the pillow? What strong feeling had overtaken her at last?"*

She didn't know what to say, only that she should proffer some response to such a

219

declaration. Before she could gather her thoughts, which had been blown willy-nilly first by thoughts of Daniel and then Malcolm's presence, the door to the stairwell opened. Malcolm's reflexes were quick, but Mary still turned a hard eye on him and Elle as she entered. This wasn't the adolescent shenanigans of Althea and Zeke, and she doubted Mary would pretend she'd seen nothing as Elle had.

"I seem to have taken a wrong turn while looking for the privy," Malcolm said, and sidestepped Mary to exit into the hallway. Elle schooled her features into a study of nonchalant confusion.

Mary pulled herself up to her full height and looked down at Elle. Her expression was stern, erasing the years of age and experience that Elle held over her. "I told Susie I sent you to clean up here, and that you wasn't lazing around somewhere. Was I lying?" She held her candle up to Elle's face and neck, seeming to examine them for signs of molestation, and then her mask of annoyance faltered and she took Elle's hand. "Has that man tried anything? To force himself on you? You'd tell me, wouldn't you?"

There was a panic in Mary's voice, a vulnerability that Elle hadn't thought possible in the young woman. Her nostrils flared and her eyes were wide. This reaction could only be one borne of experience with such terrible matters. Elle clutched the woman's hand and shook her head, desperately trying to signal that she was fine.

Mary nodded, pulled her back up straight. "Okay," she said, obviously still disturbed. "Okay. But the way that man lookin' at you . . . be careful, girl. I've seen that look before and it don't lead nowhere good."

Mary's unconscious echoing of Elle's own words that first night on the bluff shook her. What could possibly lie ahead for her and Malcolm? Could she really stake anything on the fact that he seemed to care about her? Daniel had cared about her, too, up until the point where she wouldn't do as he bade, and they hadn't had the obstacle of race between them.

"Robert says change is coming for us," Mary said. "But I know one thing that'll stay the same — these men think they are entitled to not only the sweat off our back but every other part of our bodies to boot. Be careful, no matter how that one sweet-talks you. Just because he don't hold you down, don't mean he's not forcing you."

Elle nodded again and looked away. She couldn't meet Mary's eye with the truth of her words hanging between them.

Her friend sighed and briefly squeezed her shoulder. "If you think he gonna try something and you ain't safe here, well, Robert and me could help if it came to that," Mary said cryptically, then brushed past her down the stairs, leaving Elle feeling more alone than ever.

She regretted so many things in that moment — not being able to respond to Mary, not being able to help the slave who could be Daniel, and perhaps most of all, not being able to fight her growing affection for a man she should have been running from in the opposite direction. She had no news to back up her claims about the ironclad, and nothing new to report to her colleagues. The souls of those men who had died from her false information seemed to crowd into the small space of the stairwell, smothering her in her own incompetency.

She dragged herself quietly down the stairs, feeling like an unmitigated failure. Hopefully her colleagues were faring better than she, or else the country was in dire straits indeed.

CHAPTER 11

Anything to preserve the Union, Malcolm reminded himself as Susie preened in front of him the following night at another impromptu gathering at the Caffrey mansion. Senator Caffrey had suddenly excused himself nearly an hour before, leaving Malcolm to Susie's tender mercies. He fought hard against the fatigue-induced irritation with the woman. There wasn't a thing he liked about her, and he was sure there was only one thing she liked about him, but that didn't mean she should bear the brunt of his frustrations.

"I am so sad that you'll be leaving us shortly," she said. "While it's every Southern man's duty to fight, it does leave a girl lonely."

"I'm sure you'll get along fine," he said, then raised his glass to her. "When I'm freezing out in the trenches, it will warm me just a bit to know that there's a woman thinking kindly of me."

Susie giggled, and Malcolm thought he'd much prefer Elle's unvarnished conversation to this flowery small talk. The note he'd written to her, in case they did not get to speak, was a weight in his pocket that would only be lessened when he knew she had it in hand. He told himself it was simply because he'd helped undercut the Confederacy in a small way, but he knew the information contained therein would please her, and that had become of paramount importance at some point over the last week. His brief glimpse of her hours earlier hadn't done anything to sustain him. Seeing her on her knees scrubbing the floor had angered him but also unlocked an odd memory: his mother cleaning the house and his father coming up behind her, pulling her to her feet and sweeping her into a dance as he sang a Scottish ballad. That was when things were good between his parents, when the drink and the anger hadn't muddled his father's mind.

Malcolm wondered what it would be like to partake in such domestic drudgery with Elle. To wake up beside her in their own warm home, to help with the wash and play with their children as she cooked them a meal. The fantasy was more than agreeable to him, even as Susie's words reminded him of how unrealistic it was.

An enslaved woman passed in front of them, her expression dour as she cleared glasses from a nearby table.

"My word, you'd think we'd sentenced these darkies to death the way they've been sulking about," she said, fanning herself in the closed air of the room. She wore some cloying scent that made Malcolm's throat itch and his eyes burn, and each flick of her fan wafted more of the smell in his direction. "I know things are scarce in town with the blockade and all, but you don't see us complaining," she said as a slave gave her a cool glass of water to sip. She didn't even look at the man.

Malcolm mused that perhaps he'd been premature in shielding her from his annoyance.

"Hopefully, the blockade will be broken soon," Malcolm said, giving a nod of thanks as he took a glass of brandy. He swirled the drink in his glass and then pinned Susie with a smile that had proven to be quite effective with the opposite sex. She wasn't the only one who knew how to flirt. "I've heard some talk these past days that we're working on something to that effect. I'm assuming it's on account of ladies needing their silk stockings."

He glanced suggestively at her skirts, as if imagining what was beneath. In reality, he thought of the silky skin of Elle's thighs as he'd caressed them, how she had thrown her head back with abandon when he touched her. Something in his thoughts must have translated into his eyes, for Susie blushed and leaned toward him.

"I don't know much about this tiresome blockade," she drawled, "but I know a great deal about silk stockings should you ever desire any hands-on instruction." She raised a delicate brow at him.

Malcolm looked her in the eye. "I just may take you up on that offer one of these days if you aren't careful, Miss Susie."

Just then the senator walked over with a slight, pale man dressed in stained trousers and a threadbare jacket. He held a fine, though battered, hat in one hand and swept the other hand over his thinning hair as if checking that at least some of his coif remained.

"May I present Mr. Alton Dix," Senator Caffrey said. "McCall, this man is a true son of the Confederacy. He's been working on a special project for weeks, and tonight he's taking a well-deserved break."

Malcolm stood and grabbed the man's

hand, shaking firmly. Dix was the cause of the senator's abrupt departure earlier in the evening, and so he was the man whom Malcolm needed to speak with the most.

"Mighty fine to meet you, Mr. Dix," he said in a reverent tone. "You must be a smart fella if they've got you working on a special project."

The man looked down shyly before answering.

"Oh, I wouldn't say I'm over-smart," Dix said. "But what I do know, I know well."

"And what is that?" Susie asked, standing and placing her arm through Malcolm's. "Do tell, Mr. Dix."

Malcolm should have been happy that she asked the question instead of him, likely so she could report it to the gossip rags, but the dismissiveness of her tone irked him. She spoke to Dix as if he were a child presenting the grownups with something he'd found in the garden.

Dix shot Senator Caffrey a nervous glance, as if asking for permission. The senator nodded, but his eyes held warning all the same.

"I'm an engineer," he said. "Before the war, I was in the business of building ships."

Were you now? Malcolm thought. The familiar sense of elation that occurred when he was on the right path in an investigation

227

surged up in him. He imagined it was akin to the sensation of a wolf on the hunt spotting an oblivious deer.

"A shipbuilder? I've always found that profession fascinating. It requires such precision and eye for detail," Malcolm said, leaning slightly away from Susie. She tugged him closer to her and then looked up at him with wide eyes.

"Mr. McCall, I'm terribly parched. Could you escort me to fetch some punch?"

He'd just seen the chit drink an entire glass of water, but he supposed she meant parched for attention.

"Would you like to join us, Mr. Dix?" he asked, hoping to continue the conversation. But the man eyed Susie, who ignored him instead of also requesting his presence.

"That's all right. I'm very tired, as I've been working and traveling all day. I'll have to take my leave early, and I haven't had a chance to make my rounds," he said. He gave Malcolm a wary smile. "Perhaps we'll continue this conversation upon my return. Will you be at the ball?"

"I will, and I look forward to talking to you. I greatly admire a man who can conjure something as grand as a ship from numbers and measurements," he said, shaking the man's hand warmly. The man seemed surprised, but then returned the gesture with a kind smile, unencumbered by nervousness.

Gotcha, Malcolm thought.

Susie pulled him toward the punch bowl before Senator Caffrey and Mr. Dix had even turned away.

"God, that man was tedious, standing there and sweating like a donkey," she sniped. "And those clothes! How did he get in the front door with those? Why, even this fool is more put together than him."

They had reached the punch bowl, where Elle stood with a ladle serving out drinks. She wore a green-and-white-checked poplin dress that, despite its obvious age, fit her perfectly. Her ample bosoms were accentuated by a double row of white buttons along the front of the dress, and the waist was cinched tight with a length of frayed green ribbon. Her hair was different today, loosed from the plaits but pulled back into a bun covered by a piece of cloth that functioned as a snood. Wisps of her hair escaped at her temples, framing the face that haunted his dreams more often than not now. Malcolm remembered how her hair had felt in his hand as he pulled her head back and kissed her.

And then he insulted her.

"I don't recall the man doing anything to

warrant being compared to this simple thing," he said, remembering how Susie had interrogated him about his behavior toward Elle before. He couldn't show her any kindness, but he hoped she saw the irony in the insult he had chosen. "Besides, I'd hardly think that a naval engineer would be expected to be the height of fashion. He's a shipbuilder, not a fashion plate. I look forward to learning more when he returns for the ball."

He glanced at Elle. Her expression was blank as she filled a cup for Susie, but he knew she was listening, recording all of the information in his words for later processing. She handed the cup to him, and when her fingers grazed his, a jolt of raw awareness passed through him. Usually the thrill of a mission blocked out all other emotions, but since he'd met Elle he felt like nothing more than a love-struck schoolboy who couldn't concentrate on his lessons.

"Well, just because he's important doesn't mean he can dress like a poverty-stricken farmer. This society has rules for a reason," Susie said, still stuck on Dix's outfit. Malcolm pitied the flaying the man would get in the gossip columns the next day, then reminded himself that Dix was a Rebel.

"And what reason is that?" he asked,

masking the challenge in his question with a smile.

"To separate people like us from them," she said, pointing at Elle. "Animals." She leaned closer and gave a throaty laugh, one that was well practiced and designed to seduce. "Although I do sometimes enjoy giving in to my baser instincts, Mr. McCall."

Malcolm simply stared at her. Hopefully she thought him enchanted by her wit.

"But enough about that," she said, back to being a coquette. "Papa told me that you like poetry. I have been practicing something to perform for my Ladies of the Rebellion meeting. Last time, Lucinda Smith performed and I have just the thing to top her."

She cleared her throat dramatically. "Oh, that these two solid breasts would melt, thaw, and resolve themselves forsooth," she said, her mangled performance uttered with the conviction of the veriest actor who strutted the stage of the Globe.

A violent fit of coughs erupted from Elle, some of them sounding suspiciously like laughter. She turned her back to them, shoulders shaking. It took all of Malcolm's skill to mask his own laughter, which bubbled in his chest, drawn from him by Elle's mirth.

"That was . . . splendid," he said, the feeling in his words enhanced by the laughter beneath them.

"I knew you would like it! Recite something for me now," she said, looking up at him with unadorned desire.

He thought for a moment, trying to recall a line that would do for the moment. He glanced quickly at Elle — for her such a task would be quite simple, given the endless knowledge in that fine brain of hers. Then a line came to him, from a verse he'd had to repeat in front of the family hearth on many a chilly winter's night. Elle seemed to have an aversion to quality Scottish literature, but he was quite sure she knew *The Lady in the Lake.*

" 'And seldom was a snood amid such wild luxuriant ringlets hid, whose glossy black to shame might bring the plumage of the raven's wing.' " His eyes were on Susie, but every other part of him stretched out toward Elle.

Susie stood blushing before him, then batted him with her fan.

"My hair is brown, silly," she said, then slid her arm through his again.

"Are you planning on monopolizing Susie's time the entire evening?" Rufus stood at her other side now. His cheeks, and his courage apparently, had been warmed by whiskey's sweet embrace. His gaze was fixed on where Susie and Malcolm's arms were joined, and Malcolm was glad that a glare couldn't cause bodily harm. If that were the case, his arm, and perhaps other appendages, would have been scattered across the parlor floor.

"I wasn't aware that Susie had arranged to spend her time with you," Malcolm said, withdrawing his arm from hers. "Far be it from me to cause strife between two old friends."

"Where are you going?" Susie asked. "It's just Ruf, I can see him anytime."

"Not if I get killed fighting for President Davis. You'll miss me then." Rufus spoke these words with a wishful vengeance, as if he hoped for his own demise just to teach Susie a lesson.

"Too true, Rufus," Malcolm said as he handed Susie off. "I'm sure she'd love to hear more about life on the battlefield. Indulge her in your tales of derring-do."

"Don't I get to choose whom I talk to?" Susie asked, indignant. Malcolm regretted his action instantly. Yes, she was a pawn in his quest for information, but he needn't treat her as one.

"Do you really not wish to speak to me?

I'll go —" Rufus began, but Susie stopped him with a sigh and a pat of the hand.

"Ruf, you know I always want to talk to you. But I'm sure even you are a mite curious about our Mr. McCall." Her eyes ran over Malcolm's body suggestively; then she looked up at him, all pouty seduction. "But I guess I'll have to get him alone one of these evenings and then I'll see what he's all about."

Malcolm was shocked at her boldness, but Rufus was gazing at her as if she were the most angelic creature to have graced the earth.

"I think you're overestimating how interesting I am, Miss Caffrey," Malcolm countered.

"Not hardly," she replied with a wink as Rufus pulled her away.

Malcolm began making his way toward the senator, who now stood with his wife and a few other of the Richmond elite. He heard the ringing noise of ceramic on ceramic and turned to see Elle rearranging the punch cups with her back to him. She glanced over her shoulder, her eyes briefly landing on his before she turned back around. To anyone else observing, she had been scanning the room to see if anyone else required a drink. But when she reached up and pointedly adjusted her snood, Malcolm couldn't help his victorious smile.

Perhaps the night hadn't been a waste after all.

CHAPTER 12

Elle had tried to steel herself against Malcolm. She'd decided that she would feel nothing as she watched him play Susie's escort, but then he'd managed to say just the thing to inspire that unbidden intimacy with him once more. She'd once seen a traveling show where a supposed Indian swami controlled a snake with just the motion of his hand, making it sway this way and that. Malcolm seemed to have the same power over the darkest, most volatile parts of her, calling forth forbidden feelings with the slightest touch. Unlike the snake-charming show, she couldn't see the strings that bound her to him and didn't know how to cut them — or if she even wanted to.

Elle cleaned up her area and carried the dirty glasses to the kitchen, where she was immediately pulled into a group of slaves chatting during a lull in their service. Althea's round, girlish face beamed at her as she introduced her cousin Benjamin.

"This is her, Ben! The one who pushed Susie right onto that griddle cake behind of hers and didn't even get a lash for it!"

A handsome man of average height with skin the color of oak stepped forward and took her hand. His smile was warm and open, and when he clasped her hand between his two work-worn ones, Elle felt her cheeks warm. For an instant, a glimmer of hope arose in her; perhaps this man could inspire the same desires Malcolm did. But as she looked up at him, all she felt was the pleasure of making his acquaintance and irritation that she couldn't ask him any direct questions lest she ruin her disguise.

"Well, I guess they must have looked on that sweet face and decided it would be a shame to make her cry," he said, and there was a chorus of agreement and a few sounds of encouragement at his flirting.

"Susie didn't always used to be such a heifer," Althea said. "We used to play together every day. But once she had her debut she became too much of a *lady* to talk to the likes of me."

The girl tried to say the words breezily, but Elle could see the hurt in her eyes. Althea had lost a friend and gained a callous mistress. It was a story Elle had heard often enough to know that it was a pain that would never be healed. It didn't always turn out that way, though: Her mother's friendship with the master's son had opened the boy's heart, and eventually led to freedom for her family and the other slaves he'd inherited. But her family's story was all too rare.

"You should be glad of that," Ben interjected, his strong accent evidence of a Deep South plantation at some point in his history. "Massa Dix ain't got no true friends of his own and he tell me everything. How he's wishing for a family, but can't find a woman to take him. How Davis is riding him like the devil to get finished with this ship he building. If I got to hear about that ship one more time!"

He shook his head, unaware that Elle's attention had become totally focused on him. Ben worked for Dix, the man Malcolm had mentioned. What did he know?

She tapped his arm, and when he looked at her she raised her eyebrows to show she had a question. She first drew in her body small and mimicked rowing a boat. Then she raised her eyebrows again, hoping he understood that it meant there was a second part to the question. She threw her eyes wide to show she meant something large and pretended she was turning a large steering wheel, shading her eyes with one hand as if she were looking far out to sea.

The small group erupted into laughter.

"You silly, Elle," Althea said, and Benjamin regarded her with a wide smile.

"You want to know if the boat is big or small?" he asked. "I ain't seen it, but I think it's big. Taking them forever to work on it, and it still ain't ready yet."

Elle's heart kicked up for sure now, not because of the man smiling at her, but at what his words meant. His master was building a big boat, and if the conclusion she'd reached at MacTavish's was correct, that meant the South was on the path to having a blockade-busting ironclad.

She jumped excitedly, the frustration of not having words forcing all her energy into her miming. She strutted back and forth, pretending to sip a drink and chat with a person next to her. Then she was suddenly in full battle mode, loading an imaginary canon and sticking her fingers in her ears as she waited for it to go off. She looked over at Ben and the others, who were still laughing as if she were a simple girl putting on a show.

"Oh, it's a warship," he said. "I don't know much more than that since I shut my ears and start dreaming of the Promised Land when he gets to yapping."

Elle's heart sank.

"All I know is he's mighty secretive with the plans for the ship. He don't let no one into his office, not even me."

Ben sounded offended at that. The connection between master and slave was a strange thing, indeed.

She inclined her head to him, sank into a mock curtsy of thanks.

"I best be goin'," Ben said. "We have to head out tomorrow morning for some business he got to attend to and then we got to come back the next day for this silly party. I hope he don't make me wear that fancy coat and tie. He always tell me I got to dress up so he don't have to."

"What time you heading out?" Althea asked, and Elle could have kissed her.

"Before sunup, so I got to go back to town with him to get him ready for bed," Ben said, smothering a yawn. "G'night, y'all."

There was a chorus of farewells, and Elle tried to be inconspicuous as she walked out with him to the coach he had to prepare. She had one more question for him, and hoped he would understand. It took her a fair few attempts, but finally comprehension illuminated his features.

"Where we headed?" he confirmed. "I don't rightly know, Elle. Wait, you stay at town, right? Where's your room? I can give you a ride if it's close to us. We're at the Lancelot Inn."

Excellent, Elle thought. Finding out information was thrill enough, but now she couldn't wait to tell Malcolm that they were on the right path.

Ben placed his hand on her shoulder in a friendly way, trying to pull her wandering attention back to him. Just then, a shadow fell over both of them, and she knew without looking that it would be Malcolm.

Ben turned and gave him a friendly smile.

"Need help saddling your horse?" he asked, his ebullient nature not alerting him to Malcolm's dissatisfaction with the scene.

"No, it appears you've got your hands full," he said.

Anger pulsed through Elle at the suggestion in his tone. He'd just spent half the night flirting with Susie. The woman had had her hands all over him, and Lord only knew what had happened when they left Elle at the punch bowl. Now he was standing before her all tensed and tightlipped, looking like he'd sucked on a crab apple, because she was talking to another man? The nerve of him.

"I'm just getting Massa Dix's coach ready," he said, letting go of Elle's shoulder. "Seeing if this lady needed a ride into town. Won't take but a minute to help you out."

Ben's relentless friendliness seemed to break through Malcolm's anger.

"That's very kind of you, but no, thank you," he said. "Good night."

And then he turned and headed for the stalls without giving Elle so much as a second look. Spiking anger made her feel hot and shaky despite the cool winter night. He'd chosen the worst possible moment to reveal he had a jealous streak.

The nerve!

Elle clenched her fists and bit back the words she wanted to shout after him. If she couldn't speak to him of Dix's departure, then she would just go by herself. In fact, maybe it was better that way. She'd done just fine gathering intelligence before she knew Malcolm McCall existed, and that didn't have to change because of some unwise choices in a back room.

The disheveled man Susie had been insulting earlier in the night stepped up to the carriage and Ben helped him in.

"I'm giving this lady a ride to town, sir," Ben said. "If that's okay with you."

"Of course it's okay," Mr. Dix said. "It's

242

not safe after dark for a woman in times like these. She can sit up front with you."

Elle found it disconcerting that the man possibly responsible for the South's resurgence was seemingly kind. Many slave owners would have told a strange Negro to walk on home, darkness be damned, but he hadn't. Humans were a most confusing and incomprehensible species, that was one thing she knew for certain.

She was glad for the ride after the exhausting day. She spent the time listening to Ben do enough talking for the both of them, occasionally lapsing into snippets of song. By the time he dropped her off at the boardinghouse, she was about ready to pass out. She walked up the rickety steps and let herself into her small, dark room.

Elle didn't know if she'd ever been as tired. Mostly from the work, but also from her disappointment in Malcolm. She didn't want to be disappointed in him, because that would mean the emotion that had been nudging at her since she had met him wasn't just a brief infatuation.

"Who wishes to fight must first count the cost." She wasn't exactly at war with Malcolm, but Sun Tzu was still right. What had happened between them before could be discounted as a passing whimsy, but if she

acknowledged the way her eyes had burned with tears when Malcolm turned away, what then? What did she expect from him, and even if he weren't playing her for a fool, would the uphill battle be worth it? It seemed that every aspect of herself was in conflict with another: free versus slave, loyalty versus duty, womanhood versus work.

Elle sighed, a deep and world-weary exhalation that was forced out of her by the worry and confusion that occupied the space in her lungs. All she wanted to do was crawl into bed and drop into the mindlessness of sleep: She'd have a dangerous day ahead of her thanks to Ben's information and she'd have to be alert. Losing sleep worrying over any man that wasn't Jefferson Davis would be ridiculous. She started unbuttoning her dress and then stopped, struck a match, and lit a candle so she wouldn't have to fumble about in the dark.

"Holy Mary, Mother of God," she exclaimed, nearly dropping the candle. There, sitting quite comfortably at the edge of her bed, was Malcolm McCall.

CHAPTER 13

Malcolm didn't give Elle time to kick him out.

"I'm sorry."

He was sorry for getting angry in the stables and sorry for riding off without saying a word. He should have been for surprising Elle with her dress half-unbuttoned and her thin shift clinging to her bosom.

When he'd come upon the scene in the stable — her smiling up at a handsome man, a handsome black man at that — all reason had left him. He knew that men found her attractive. He himself could barely think if he looked upon her for too long. He knew that she inspired lascivious thoughts in white men who wished to use her for her body. But seeing her smiling up at Dix's slave had driven home a harsh reality: that she might prefer another man over him, a man who might be able to understand her better than he ever could. One whom the world expected her to be with, like her Daniel.

The thought had been nearly unbearable. And even though he immediately recognized his mistake, that hadn't eased the tightness in his chest. He'd felt too close to the man he never wanted to become — his father, who would spear his wife with his words because his love for her had been tainted by jealousy. Malcolm hadn't been able to look at her, to let her see the raw emotion that had driven his foolish anger. But he let her see it now.

He stood and met her gaze, trying to peel back the layers of defenses that were necessary for his work — and the many that had been erected before he ever knew what a Pinkerton was.

"I was jealous and I was wrong," he said, then repeated what he thought to be the most important thing. "I'm sorry."

"How did you know where I'm staying?" she asked, setting the candle on the bedside table and crossing her arms over her chest. The flickering flame bathed her in warm tones, highlighting her high cheekbones and her sweet lips, which were drawn tight in anger.

Malcolm shrugged.

"I'm a detective," he said. "You don't

know where I'm staying?"

"He's staying at the Spotswood Hotel, Mother," she drawled in a passable imitation of Susie. "It's where the Davises stayed! I do believe that he's a man of means. What do you know of the McCalls? There's a family that's made a sum of money in the railroads, do you think he could be one of them? I don't care if he's poor, though, I just want him to be mine!"

Malcolm shifted uncomfortably as she fixed her gaze on him. He knew what was coming, and knew that he deserved it.

"I had to watch you making cow eyes at her all evening, to hear you talk about me like I was an idiot right to my face, but me merely speaking to a man is reason enough for you to treat me like a harlot and storm off," she said. She was pacing back and forth now, her agitation growing more visible with each circuit she made. She stopped and faced him, eyes shining in the candlelight. "I needed you tonight, and you left me standing there like a fool!"

Her words didn't surprise him, but the hurt behind her anger did. This wasn't like the other times she'd chastised him, and he couldn't tell if that was a good thing or if all was lost.

"Elle." He didn't know how to explain

how the thought of losing her had knocked the sense out of him. It was madness, and if it frightened him this much, it would send Elle running for the hills.

"I'm here now," he finally said, knowing it wasn't the right answer but unsure of what to say in the face of his glaringly unkind behavior.

She stopped with her back to him, so he couldn't see her face.

"You say we're partners, and you've sure spent a lot of time telling me I'm wrong about you. You expect me to trust that you'll stand by me no matter what, but the first little thing that sets you off, you're on your horse and thundering down the lane."

The betrayal in her voice stung, and the dread of losing her surged strong. He'd failed her, once again causing her pain instead of protecting her from it. It seemed the more he cared for her, the more easily he hurt her. Is that what love was? A finely honed blade that would cut at the slightest pressure?

"That's the second time you've made me feel like a fallen woman with no provocation. I should take my knife to you for the hypocrisy alone." He was surprised she didn't brandish her weapon, but he could see how fatigue weighed down her every motion.

"I'm good at pretending, but when it comes to the real thing I'm compass-less," he said, taking a step closer to her. "The way I feel for you, the quickness and intensity of it, that scares me more than anything else I've faced in this war. When I saw that man talking to you in what looked like an intimate way, it made my heart drop into my shoes, and I acted treated you unfairly because of it." He twisted a hank of hair between his fingers. "I feel like I keep doing things that hurt you when all I want is to make you happy."

"Maybe you can't make me happy," she tossed over her shoulder. "Ever think of that?"

"No," he said, his answer as much a surprise to himself as it seemed to be to her. He reached out and turned her so that she faced him, and moved his hands to her chest. She stiffened, ready to retreat, until she realized what he was doing. He carefully slid each button back into its hole, re-situating her dress. "No, I haven't thought that, and I'm not inclined to start now."

He buttoned on in silence, his eyes trained on his task instead of her face. As he moved to slip the last button through, her small hands rested lightly on top of his.

He looked into her wide eyes. "It seems gauche to give this to you now, after acting like such a fool. I'm not trying to buy my forgiveness. I meant to give it to you before I treated you so poorly."

"What are you on about?" she asked.

He reached into his pocket and passed her the note. He didn't have her memory, but he knew most of the short message as she read it aloud, her voice growing progressively more strained.

"M —

The slave named Daniel has been purchased from bondage, after much haggling, by a local woman, a true Unionist who specializes in this type of rescue. I do not yet know if he is the man you search for, but he shall be free, whatever the case. Will have more info shortly.

— A."

Elle's hard expression crumpled in on itself as she fought to control her emotions.

Malcolm frowned. "I wish we could be certain it was him —"

Elle touched his forearm to stay him. "I dearly hope it's Daniel. If it's not, a man who was enslaved is now free, and that is no small matter. Thank you."

"Don't," he warned. He knew he should've been happy with the way she was looking at him, but he wasn't. "When you were angry with me just now, I knew it was how you truly felt. Don't be kind to me out of gratitude. I didn't do anything but pass the information along to someone who takes an interest in these matters."

"Okay, Fitzwilliam. You'd rather I focus on your behavior before you presented me with this miraculous letter? Fine. It was blue-bellied, undignified behavior and I expect better from you. Don't you ever even think of treating me like that again," she said in a tone that had him standing up straighter and swallowing hard. She fingered the note and then placed it gently on her rickety dresser. "I shouldn't admit this, but I never felt so alone as when you walked away from me."

Malcolm felt hope flood through him like the Mississippi topping her banks. She wasn't only speaking of their work — it wasn't just him caught up in this storm of emotion. He wasn't alone in sensing the connection between them that defied society and common sense.

"I won't," he said, and he meant it. "I

won't ever leave you again, I promise."

His lips pressed to her forehead, a chaste kiss that shook him as much as their more heated moments because she returned it after a beat, dropping a soft kiss on his chin in return. He wasn't sure that she believed his words, but he believed them and that would have to do for the both of them.

She shook her head and emitted a mirthless chuckle, although her eyes still flashed with emotion. " 'The expert in battle moves the enemy, and is not moved by him,' " she said as she walked away from him and went over to a small table that had a ceramic bowl of water and a bar of white soap beside it.

"Shakespeare?" he guessed, and she rolled her eyes.

"Not all that sounds profound is from the Western canon, McCall. Sun Tzu was an ancient Chinese strategist. I had to memorize his words before I became a detective."

"So you apply military strategy to our interactions now? I think I preferred the Hawthorne," Malcolm said. "I thought we already established that I'm not your enemy." He was disquieted by her words, by all that lingered beneath the surface of their every interaction.

"No, we established that you are for the Union," she said. "Honestly? Your behavior confounds me, but then, so does my re-action to it. To you." She dipped a cloth into the water and rubbed it against a thin scrap of soap, and the familiar smell of roses filled the room. Malcolm's nostrils flared, wanting more than just her smell. He wanted her taste and her touch, too.

"Elle —"

She raised a hand to stay him. "Now I shall tell you what I would have if you hadn't ignored me in the stable. The man I was talking to, Ben, is Dix's slave," she said as she brought the cloth to her neck and wiped it slowly across. "He says that Dix is heading out somewhere tomorrow for an important meeting. They leave before dawn. I intend to follow them and see what this is about."

She spoke the words calmly as she lathered the cloth again and ran it over her face and up her arms. He knew she was performing an act of daily hygiene, but the sight of her made him want to fall to his knees in sup-plication. Instead, Malcolm walked over to her and took the rag from her hands. She'd done enough scrubbing that day.

"And how do you intend to do that?" he asked, rubbing the cloth along her neck, massaging her through the rough material.

"I'm a detective," she said, throwing his

words back at him. She leaned her head forward to give him more access as he caressed her neck with the soapy rag.

"I'll go with you," he said, moving the cool cloth down to the juncture of her shoulder and neck, and massaging the taut muscles there.

"I wouldn't be opposed to that," she said. "As long as you don't act a fool again."

Malcolm knew better than to promise her that.

"What would you have done when you got home tonight if I wasn't here?" he asked, pressing harder against a knot of muscles. She hissed, but then relaxed as the tightness eased. She placed her hands behind her, against his thighs, to steady herself, and his manhood thickened as if stretching toward her splayed fingers.

"After cursing you to hell and back? I would have done what I'm doing now. What you're doing now," she said, her voice breathy. "I would have undressed and washed. I feel like a pig that's been rolling in the mud all day."

"You are far from that, lass," he said. "But if it's a bath you want, I can give you that."

He wanted to see all of her, to run his hands over each curve and indentation of her body until he had them memorized. As his mind was far less refined than hers, it would take him a very long time.

She turned in his arms and took the cloth from him.

"I don't want you to bathe me," she said, looking up at him with trepidation. "I want something that is the very last thing I should be seeking from you, but which you provide so very well."

A sensation of pins and needles ran up and down his spine at the shy words spoken in that smoky voice of hers.

"Comfort?" he asked. She gave him a prim nod, as if hiding her desire would make her feelings for him more acceptable. Malcolm was tired of talking, of pretending, of not saying the right thing. He grabbed her by the chin, tilted her head up, and kissed her. Her hands went to his shoulders, the pressure of her pulling herself into their kiss an unexpected addition to his excitement. His mouth moved over hers slowly, but not softly. He intended to show her exactly how he felt since his words kept failing him.

His hands encircled her slim waist and she gasped into his mouth, seemingly responsive to his every touch. He could feel the heat of her through her dress, just as he had the first night he touched her, and he wondered what it would feel like to be skin to skin with her, finally freed of the encumbrance of their clothing. It was his turn to groan then, and she licked up into his mouth.

Their tongues played a cat and mouse game, tangling and then retreating. She responded to his kisses, but there was still hesitation in her touch. Her thin fingers slid over his chest, brushing over his pectorals as if petting some unfamiliar and possibly dangerous animal. Pleasure radiated out from each point her fingertips pressed into him, and he pulled her closer, heedless of the full erection that tented his pants and pressed into her belly.

"Dear Lord," she murmured against his lips, and Malcolm felt as if he could take on the entire Confederacy himself in that moment. He pulled her into a more secure embrace, their lips still locked, and then spun and deposited her onto the bed. She drew her legs up beneath her skirts and knelt, looking up at him with shining eyes and glossy lips.

"I could have saved some time by leaving these undone," he said as he crouched and retraced his path as he unbuttoned her dress. He undid them slowly, running fingers beneath the stiff fabric panel to caress the soft weight of her breasts beneath. He had her raise her arms and then drew the dress up over her head. She wore a thin beige chemise that clung to her every curve.

Malcolm had been to many dubious establishments on his various missions, but no show girl decked out in sequins and lace had ever been sexier. A surge of desire stirred low in his groin, the desire to drive into her and claim her as his own. He resisted the impulse to move quickly — Elle was far too important to ever be something he possessed by brute strength. Instead, he reached his hands out and caressed her, dragging his hands over the thin fabric and then pulling that up over her head, too.

Her smooth skin was warm to the touch, soft as silk. Her breasts overflowed in his hands, but her nipples were small and nearly flat, barely pressing into his hands even though they were tight with need. He smoothed his hands down her waist, over the flare of her hips, cupping her ass to hold her steady. And then he leaned forward and drew the tip of a breast into his mouth, his tongue playing over the textured areola again and again just to hear the sighs and moans the action pulled from Elle.

"Malcolm," she whispered, and her voice made his whole body shake with need.

Her fingers slid into his hair as he lavished attention onto her other breast, and the reaction it stirred within him was so strong that he nipped at her. She arched her back, pressing her breast forward, closer to his tongue and teeth.

"I want to see you, too," she said, pushing him away. "I want to see you out of that uniform that signifies everything wrong with this world."

He stood and quickly unbuttoned and pulled off his jacket, followed by the homespun shirt beneath it. He reached for his trousers, but Elle leaned forward then.

"Let me," she said. Her voice was confident, but she fumbled as she undid his belt, unbuttoned the fly of his pants, and sent his pants and drawers southward. It did something to him, to see her nervousness; her hands hadn't shaken like this when she'd pulled her gun on him. Trickles of pleasure skimmed through his body as she worked, but when his cock sprang free and into her waiting hand he bit back a hoarse cry.

She wrapped both of her small hands around his shaft and stroked him, from his root to his head, and back down again, as if savoring the heft of him. He rocked his hips forward, increasing the friction on his member. It felt wonderful, but he knew if she continued the motion he would spend himself much too quickly.

He gently pushed her back on the bed as he extricated himself from the warmth of her hands. When she was flat on her back, his mouth moved to her cheek, grazed her lips, skimmed her neck, and made its lackadaisical way back toward her breasts. His hand slid down between them, fingers finding the slick cleft between her thighs and pressing gently, rubbing softly at first but with increasing pressure as she began to writhe beneath him. Her hands gripped his arms and clasped frantically as he rubbed in time with the rasps of his tongue against her breasts.

She moaned, her fingers moving to his chest to scrape up over his nipples as she pulled at him. "I need more, Malcolm."

His eyes flew to hers in question, the brown depths fathomless in the candlelight. She hesitated and then nodded. Malcolm felt a sweet relief at her signal; not because he would claim her, but because she'd asked him to.

He slid up the bed, leaving his cock perfectly positioned at her entrance and, as he kissed her like she was his dearest treasure, he nudged his manhood between her folds and into the heated core of her.

She was tight, and the entry was slow going, but when he filled her completely she fit him like a silken glove.

"Oh, my Ellen," he breathed into her mouth. She wrapped her legs around his waist, thrusting her hips up and squeezing his cock even more tightly within her, and he was lost to sensation. He pumped into her with abandon, circling his hips and driving up to hit that perfect spot that made her buck and cry out and bite into his shoulder to mask the noise.

He rested his weight on his elbows, cupping her face with his hands as he fused his lips to hers. But as he continued to move over her and in her, Malcolm felt a waning in Elle's passion, a mental withdrawal from their lovemaking that stopped him mid-thrust.

"What's wrong?" he asked. He didn't understand how a woman who had been so vibrant in his arms could suddenly feel miles away from him despite the fact that his cock still pulsed within her. And then he felt the scalding tears begin to pool where his hand met her cheek. Her eyes were plaintive as she tried to turn her head away from him.

"Elle?" His heart thudded heavily in his chest. "Have I hurt you?"

Malcolm was totally unmoored. He'd been with a fair few women, but a roll in the hay usually required little emotional commitment from him. It was uncharted territory to have the woman he wanted so badly weeping in his arms; he had no idea how to make things right.

"No," she said. She sounded miserable, and almost angry. "Everything felt so good. You didn't do anything. . . . It's just —"

She made a sound that was somewhere on the spectrum between an annoyed laugh and a sob, and Malcolm rolled over onto his back, holding her slight frame against his chest as she fought against her tears. She crossed her arms across his pectorals and rested her chin on them, head turned away from him.

He thought of Daniel, the man he helped free. Maybe Elle had changed her mind about his proposal. She wasn't a virgin — perhaps she'd been struck by a memory of a man whose company she preferred in the bedroom. His blood ran cold at that possibility. He withdrew from inside of her, but still cradled her. He'd promised to keep her safe, and he would, even if it was from himself. He spoke the next words and forced them to be true. "What is it, Elle? You can tell me. I will do anything I can to make things right."

"You can't help with this. I can't stop thinking, you see," she said, turning her tear-stained eyes up to his. "All my life, I've been taught that this is wrong. I've been told that men like you only want women like me for one thing, and I should never give them that thing. And now here I am, wanting you so bad that I can barely stand it, but I can't stop thinking what if —"

What if they're right? He finished her unspoken words. *What if he is just using her?*

Frustration flooded him; not at Elle, but at a world that had forced her into that mind-set. He hated that she didn't feel safe with him, but it was a necessary defense. He didn't know how to make her see how much he cared for her, or even if he should try. He rubbed his hand over her back soothingly.

She was entitled to feel the way she did, given everything he'd seen in his trips through the South. The leers that had been directed at her in the past few days alone were bad enough, and they were benign as those threats came. No matter what angle their relationship was viewed from, he ultimately held the power, even if he chose not to wield it.

"Perhaps we should desist before it's too

late," she whispered, although she still clung to him.

"It's already too late for me," he said with a sigh. "But I cannot imagine how hard this is for you. I understand your hesitance, even if certain parts of me don't currently reflect that." She gifted him with a choked laugh, barely more than a cough, but it was something. He rolled so that they lay on their sides, facing one another. He could see the fear in her eyes and hated that he was contributing to it. "I know you have plenty of reasons to shut your heart and lock it up tight, but you've infiltrated mine as surely as you have Caffrey's household. I'd always reckoned that such a thing would be a hard task, but you seem to have accomplished the feat without even trying."

"It's my heart that concerns you, is it?" she asked. She gave him an appraising look, as if searching for a falsehood in his words. He ran his hands over her hair, down her back, and over her buttocks, repeating the soothing motion as he spoke to her.

"If I was the type of man who sought a tumble with the taboo, there are much simpler ways to go about it," he said. "Ways that don't involve my brain being so muddled by your presence that I can barely think straight. Elle, I spent a whole afternoon wondering what your voice would be like! And once I had heard it, I wondered what my name would sound like on your lips. And once I'd heard that, I wanted even more."

"You wanted my body," Elle stated flatly.

"I want all of you," he said. "But you're not mine for the taking. I'll make do with whatever meager scraps you're willing to give me."

He could see the tumult of emotions reflected in her eyes. Her hands moved to his biceps, as if she would either push him away from her or pull him close but hadn't decided upon her course of action. Malcolm didn't move, but spoke the words that came to his mind freely and without hesitation.

"I want to be skewered by that sharp tongue of yours, always. I want to hear every mundane childhood story, and then some. I wanted to know everything about you, from your favorite color to your first spoken words."

"I love the color blue," she whispered, her gaze locked on his. Her leg slipped over his hip, positioning his cock at the notch of her warmth. "And my first word was actually four: *son of a bitch.* My parents learned quickly that I would repeat everything the adults around me said and, later, that I never forgot those things."

Malcolm laughed.

"What season makes you happiest?" He withheld the groan that sought escape as the heels of her feet pressed into the bed on either side him, anchoring herself as she sank onto him.

"Autumn," she said on a gasp as her core clenched around him. She pushed him so that he lay flat on his back and she could control the pace of their lovemaking. "Up North where I live, the forest looks like a sea of flames when the leaves change."

"Your favorite song," he said, circling his hips as he pushed into her, savoring how perfectly they fit.

She closed her eyes briefly in her pleasure and then gave a little laugh. " 'Hallelujah,' " she breathed as she rolled her hips, taking him in even more deeply. "That is, Handel's *Messiah.*"

"Book," he gritted out as he lifted his hips. Her hands were splayed on his chest now, providing her with support as she rode him. They were working at a steady rhythm now — him gliding into her hot, slick core and her bearing down to meet him thrust for thrust.

"Too many to name," she snapped, annoyance clear in her tone, and Malcolm laughed and moaned at the same time. She swiveled her hips during her downward motion, adding a new and wonderfully delicious friction to their joining.

"I'll know them all one day," he gritted out. "I'll learn everything there is to know about you and it still won't —"

"Shut up and kiss me," she commanded, and Malcolm leaned up and did just that. This was the real Elle now, beautiful and unafraid as she pressed her lips to his and rode him with abandon. This was who she was when she was allowed to be free from fear.

He rolled her beneath him, his knees chafing against the mattress as he thrust into her. Their kisses were wild and erratic, matching the henceforth unknown pleasure that held his body in thrall. Malcolm felt a new sort of rapture as they held each other, fused by their passion. He knew that she was giving him something even more dear than her body; the trust in him that allowed her to let go and enjoy their lovemaking.

Their intimate sounds filled the air, and her hushed cries egged him on toward climax. Her core spasmed around his member, and he slid his hands down to cup her by the ass, holding her in place as he drove into her with a last furious barrage.

He was so close, was amazed that he hadn't spent himself yet, when she clamped around his cock, squeezing him with rapid muscular undulations as her back arched beneath him with enough force to lift his hips clean off the bed with her.

Her passionate wail echoed in his mouth, entering his body like a spirit that possessed him. He cried out then, too, as his body stiffened and sensation spread from the soles of his feet to his belly. He quickly withdrew, giving himself a last stroke with his own hand as his seed surged forth, spurting onto her stomach as she trembled beneath him.

There was silence in the aftermath, nothing but their ragged breath and the pounding of Malcolm's heart in his ears. She looked up at him with eyes that were drowsy with pleasure, but hesitant as well, as if unsure what to say.

When he was sure he had his bearings, he rolled away from her and retrieved the soapy cloth. He lay beside her, cleaning his expenditure from her stomach, sliding the cloth between her legs and over her thighs. He couldn't speak just yet, so he simply kissed her as he worked, following a trail from the shell of her ear to her lips. Then he put the cloth aside and held her close to him in the cool Southern night.

"We're in trouble now, aren't we?" she asked, running her fingers over his chest in a motion that brought him ever closer to slumber.

Before that night, his definition of trouble had included the possibility of capture, torture, and death. But now he knew there was something much more terrifying a man could face: love.

"That we are, my sweet Elle." He ran his knuckles over her jawline.

"Sweet? I should have killed you when I had the chance," she said. She snuggled closer to him.

Trouble, indeed.

CHAPTER 14

Elle stood in front of her trunk naked, searching for the items she would need for the day's journey. It was dark, but she remembered exactly where she had packed each piece of clothing. She focused all of her thoughts on the act of retrieval, trying to ignore Malcolm's soft snoring behind her. He was curled up in the center of the bed, having grabbed her balled-up sheet when she slipped out from his arms.

Glad to see I'm so easily replaceable, she thought tartly, although she knew it wasn't the truth. She'd never felt so cherished in her life as when he'd held her close. But part of her missed the reassuring doubt that had marked their previous relationship.

What had occurred between them opened up an entire world of possibility that should have been unthinkable. She'd been relying on his lack of seriousness to save her from her own desire. But she'd been mistaken to think that Malcolm was the type of man who would act on a whim when it came to matters of the heart. Now they were both plummeting without a safety net, and Lord knew where they would land.

She sighed and tried to focus on the task in front of her. It frightened her, this deviation from her mission, but her instinct told her that chancing this trip to follow Dix would be worth the risk. LaValle wouldn't mind if she had something to show for it, and if she turned up nothing, he wouldn't need to know about the trip at all. She was in the business of gathering information, and that info didn't always arrive on one's doorstep. She was glad that the fever going around gave her an excuse for not showing at the Caffreys', but she would still pay dearly for it, even if she pleaded she was too sick to move. She'd take whatever punishment they doled out, although the possibilities frightened her. *Anything for the Cause.*

She lit a candle — they would have to set out soon, and Malcolm needed to wake up and prepare — then slid on her drawers and trousers, and the soft leather boots one of her students back home had outgrown. Staring into her cloudy shard of mirror, she stuffed her hair into her rough wool cap and pulled it down over her ears, securing it with pins so it wouldn't fly off at an inopportune moment. She pulled out a length of fabric and was about to begin the awkward task of binding her chest when Malcolm's eyes blinked open and his hand patted the bed beside him, searching. Then his gaze focused on her from across the room and a slow smile spread across his face.

"Good morning, young fellow, have you seen a pretty little thing about yea high?" he said in a voice still cloaked with sleep. He hovered his hand just over the mattress.

"I'm not that short," she said, lashing the fabric at him. He caught the edge of it and pulled her down onto the bed with him, sliding an arm around her so her breasts were pushed up against the coarse hairs of his chest.

"Now you are," he whispered in a gravelly voice before pressing his mouth over hers. He kissed her long and slow and deep, making her go soft with need. Elle despised the rock-hard excuse for a mattress, but having Malcolm there made her consider the possibility of never leaving it. There, in her shabby little room, there was no one to look down on her for the way Malcolm made her heart beat quickly and her knees go weak.

Feels like home, she thought as she caressed his stubbled chin, then chastised

271

herself for allowing such an absurdity to cross her mind.

"It's nice to hold you like this, to let all the madness of the world swirl around us as we sit comfortably in the eye of the storm," he said. "It makes me think of one of those Scott poems I had to memorize, one that I thought quite innocuous until this very moment. I know you're not an ardent admirer of his work, but it seems fitting. 'One hour with thee! When sun is set, oh, what can teach me to forget, the thankless labors of the day.' "

He recited the lines in a voice that had dropped an octave with desire and ached with need. His Gaelic burr accentuated each syllable, giving sensuous twists that loaned the words new and erotic undertones. Perhaps she would have had more affection for Scott if she always heard his poetry in this way.

He paused and smiled at her expectantly. A new desire bloomed within Elle, in addition to the fluttering in her belly. She wanted to join in his recitation. Not to one-up him or to prove anything, but for a reason that was new to her: for the enjoyment of it.

" 'The hopes, the wishes, flung away,' " she continued where he left off, the knowledge shared between them deepening their connection as much as the warmth of his arms banded about her. " 'The increasing wants and lessening gains, the master's pride, who scorns my pains?' "

" 'One hour with thee,' " Malcolm finished the verse on a rasp, his eyes dark with feeling.

The words hung between them, leaving Elle feeling exposed. They were as intimate as any declaration of ardor, and maybe more so. She'd performed poetry for audiences before, but she'd always done so without feeling. She'd shared her body and her heart with another before, but never her mind. She'd thought those things must be kept separate.

Until now.

"We have work to do," she said. It was a statement of fact and a reminder of purpose, both. "Get dressed."

"I'll add this to my list of reasons to destroy the Confederacy," he muttered. He snuck in a kiss and then rolled away from her to pull on his clothing. When he'd buttoned and buckled and arranged everything just so, Elle handed him the binding fabric and raised her hands above her head.

"For this particular mission, it won't do to be jiggling about as we ride. Can you bind my chest?" she asked. She wished his hands could be on her for another reason, but their task superseded any physical desires.

"Anything for the Union," he said with exaggerated sadness as he cinched the stretchy fabric tightly around her chest. His fingers skimmed her bare skin, sending little jolts through her that distracted her from the unpleasant sensation of being bound. It'd been weeks since she'd worn a proper corset, and although she'd felt uncomfortably underdressed at first, her breasts had apparently adjusted to their freedom.

"There you go," he said as he pinned the last of the fabric in place. "The most attractive mummy to walk the streets of Richmond."

She smiled as she slipped on her homespun shirt and oversized jacket and handed him his hat.

"Time to go," she said, heading for the door. She had the feeling she was forgetting something, then ran back and rummaged under the mattress to pull out her gun and ammunition, placing it in the satchel she'd slung over her shoulder.

"That was under the bed the whole time?" Malcolm asked, shaking his head. "I knew I nearly died last night, but I thought from pleasure."

Elle laughed and stepped up to him, grabbing his collar and pulling him down to her height for one last kiss. The movement surprised both of them; perhaps because it had happened so naturally, as if it was out of habit. Disappointment descended upon her then, because she knew that once they stepped through that door, the fantasy they'd woven the previous night would be destroyed. She could show no outward attachment to this man beyond those allowed by the strictures of society.

"From this point out, I'm Earl," she said. "If anyone asks, I'm your boy. But don't —"

She swallowed against the sudden lump in her throat. She knew that at some point in their charade he might have to do something that would upset her. She could deal with it, and as a black woman in a country that saw her as nothing more than chattel, she'd had to be strong enough to deal with a heavy load. But everything had changed between her and Malcolm. She couldn't bear to have him treat her badly if they could avoid it.

"I know," he said, squeezing her hand. "But we need to acknowledge now that if a situation arises where I have to treat you like a slave, then I'll have to do it. I'll go out of my way to avoid it, but you know that if there's the slightest suspicion that I'm for the North, we could be killed. I've had some very close calls for far less innocuous things. In Tennessee, I was chased by a mob because they thought I *walked* like a Yank. I've talked my way out of a fair few bad turns, but I can't risk having something happen to you because I didn't want to hurt your feelings."

He was right. Elle knew he was right, and still the prospect of him treating her harshly made her stomach churn. She nodded and made to move away from him, but he gently tugged at her sleeve, holding on until she looked back at him.

"I'm aware that I have the upper hand in every way save one, but don't think mistreating you would be easy for me," he said, his voice rough. "Don't think it doesn't chip away at my soul every time I have to say and do terrible things to gain the enemy's trust. I've done a lot of acting, and I'm good at it, but no amount of patriotism will make having to disrespect you easy for me. Understand?"

She saw the trepidation in his eyes; he was an expert at schooling his emotions, but he didn't hide anything from her in that moment.

"What is the one way you don't have the upper hand, pray tell?" she asked. The skepticism in her tone was purposeful, a sharp and thorny prod that would push him away from her, even if just for a moment. The danger of what she'd gotten herself into made itself more apparent each time she glanced at him and longed for something that could never be.

He didn't answer her, simply looked at her in a way that made her feel as if the flames of Charleston themselves could not have burned more strongly than he did for her.

She shouldn't have asked.

"Let us go," she whispered. "We need to get to the stables to rent horses," she said. "It's getting closer to dawn and we need to be ready to make chase. And I need to send a message to Timothy telling him to spread the word I've got that fever that's going around. That should make them glad of my absence."

"Whatever you think is best, Earl," Malcolm said archly as they stepped out into the still darkness.

A cool breeze made Elle shiver. On mornings like this it was hard to believe that

Richmond would be hot as a tar pit in a few months. The thought of summer warmth made Elle feel cold inside. Where would she be then? Where would Malcolm? More importantly, would the country be united by then or would it still be embroiled in this macabre battle?

At the stables, they took out two older but seemingly sturdy horses. All the fastest and freshest horses were being used in the war effort, so they didn't exactly have the pick of the litter, but they were lucky they hadn't ended up with a couple of old nags.

Elle's message was slipped to the stable boy with explicit delivery instructions. They gave him a few coins for his trouble and then they were off.

"The Lancelot Inn is located just off of the main road," Elle said in a low tone as they rode along, her horse staggered just a bit behind his for appearance sake. "There are some horse trails that lead out the back and toward the back roads, but they have a coach, so they have to leave the stables via the main exit. You stay around this corner here with the horses and I'll hide in this empty trough. That way I can see which way they're going."

Malcolm grinned at her, apparently impressed with her summary.

"Good thinking, Earl," he said, reaching over as she handed him the reins. She dismounted, looked around just in case anyone else was up extra early heading toward a day of labor, and then hopped into the trough. She had only been half-right about it being empty, unfortunately. Icy water sloshed about her shoes and soaked the hem of her pants. The trough smelled of horse spittle, but the view was perfect.

She crouched there for a long time. Long enough that her knees began to ache and she could no longer feel her toes, and she began to wonder if they had missed Dix heading out after all. She was just about to risk stretching her aching back when the coach rolled out with Ben seated in the driver's seat. Two Rebel soldiers bought up the rear as outriders, indicating that the meeting was, indeed, important.

She clambered out and jogged over to Malcolm. When she was seated on her mount, she told him what she had seen.

"We can follow somewhat closely now," she said. "When the sun starts to rise, then we'll have to fall back."

Malcolm nodded, and they were off. It was a quiet ride, with one of them occasionally trotting up ahead to be sure they hadn't lost their quarry. Elle took in the beauty of the morning, the fading pinpricks of the stars above and the morning call of birds as sunrise drew near.

Their horses picked quietly among the twigs and leaves in the road. She patted her animal's flank as it rode onward, feeling a heightened sense of kinship with the beast, and with the man beside her. She knew that they weren't out for a morning jaunt — it was dangerous business they were about. But there was a peace within her right alongside the nervous excitement. She and Malcolm had agreed to undertake this mission together, and even though their relationship had changed since that decision had been made, he sought no dominion over her and, in fact, followed her willingly.

They chatted as they traveled, ever alert but using the time to learn more about each other. Malcolm regaled her with stories of his family: his ginger-topped brother, Ewan, who had always been quiet and serious to the point of causing worry, and their younger sister, Donella, who thought herself just one of the boys and smarted that she wasn't afforded their freedoms. Elle wondered what it would have been like to have had siblings to share her life with. Her mother had not wanted to risk having another child, fearing the master would see

Elle as expendable and sell her off. After they made it North, she hadn't been able to.

As sunlight started to filter through the trees, Elle began to get a better idea of where they were heading. She pictured the map of Virginia she'd memorized, figured in their approximate direction and speed and Dix's possible intent.

"I believe that we're heading toward the York River, or perhaps the bay," she observed quietly.

"That would make sense given what we suspect," he said. "I wonder if the ship will be there."

A bolt of fear passed through her even imagining what the behemoth of a ship would look like. She'd seen war boats in Boston Harbor, but the ironclads were different. Powered by gluttonous steam engines and lined with protective sheets of metal, the boats were nigh on invincible against an average naval fleet. For the South to have one while the North hurried to replace theirs . . . the Rebels could sail right up to the Capital and no one would be able to stop them.

"If it is, we should try to sink it," she said.

From the corner of her eye she saw him stiffen in his seat. When he spoke, it was in an even tone that masked some much harsher emotion.

"If we find it, you should ride straight on to Washington to alert them of the danger. I'll stay behind to do what I can."

"You think I'd get in your way?" she asked. She knew she was getting her back up over a hypothetical, but it galled her that his first thought was to send her away. She thought they were a team now, but maybe she'd been mistaken.

"I know you wouldn't," he said, his voice conciliatory. "But one of us would have to stay alive and get word to the Capital." He sighed. "And I couldn't ride off knowing what would happen to you if you were caught."

"I don't know if I could ride away, either," she admitted.

He sighed again, looking over at her. She could see his ocean eyes shining in the morning light.

"We'll take things as they come then," he said.

They rode on in silence once more. Elle focused her vigilance on the coach that pounded on ahead of them. The roads eventually became more crowded and they could follow the coach more closely. Regiments of troops nodded at Malcolm in passing, and their slaves did the same to Elle. They were approaching Yorktown, and the bay, when the coach made a sharp turn. Elle knew that a mile or so ahead were the banks of the York River.

One of the outriders turned back and locked his eyes on them in the thinning traffic and then turned back again. He motioned that he was heading back to his companion and turned his horse, his path heading directly toward them.

They'd been spotted.

Elle's heart nearly beat out of her chest. They would have to bluff. She looked at Malcolm and he smiled at her. A lazy smile that broadcast such a lack of concern that Elle felt her pulse slow and the tightness in her neck ease up. She was excellent at what she did, and so was he. She thought back to their first meeting on the bluff.

They'll be too busy focusing on charming old Malcolm McCall, he'd said, and Elle had seen firsthand that he had not been exaggerating.

"Is that one of your friends, sah?" she asked when the outrider was within hearing range. She could bluff, too.

"I think so, Earl," he said, and added

under his breath, "and if he isn't, he will be soon."

Elle could only hope he was right.

CHAPTER 15

The soldier's eyes were narrowed in suspicion as he approached. He was young, too young to be facing death on a battlefield by Malcolm's thinking.

"Where y'all two heading?" the soldier asked. Sandy hair poked out from beneath his gray hat, which was a size too big for his head. "I seent y'all a few miles back, and now here you are again."

Malcolm studied the boy, who would surely back up his bravado with the gun at his hip but looked uncertain as to whether he was in the right.

"Well, you caught us," Malcolm said, working some of the earnest good ol' boy into his accent. "We was following y'all."

The soldier's hand went for his gun. Elle was stock-still beside him, although her horse pawed at the ground, probably sensing her unease.

Malcolm held up his hands in mock surrender.

"I'm not from these parts, and neither is my boy. We got turned around looking for a meeting, and when I saw that coach and you two riding with it, I thought maybe I'd follow and see if you was heading where I'm heading."

"Why didn't you ride up and ask?" the soldier asked gruffly, still suspicious.

"What man you know of who cares to admit he can't make hide nor hair of where he's at?" Malcolm asked with an incredulous laugh. "I'd rather be hogtied than ask for directions."

The soldier cracked a grin.

Gotcha, Malcolm thought, then focused on looking repentant.

"I apologize if we gave you cause to worry," he said. "I know these Northern men are everywhere trying to stir up trouble."

"You don't know the half of it," the soldier said. "Running the blockade, ripping up the rail lines, and now you don't even know who you can trust."

"Bastards, the lot of them," Malcolm said. His voice was limned with anger, just enough to get the soldier's attention. "They killed my cousin up at Manassas, and that was the day I vowed to destroy every North-man I could. I've done my fair share to give 'em Jesse at every turn."

The soldier nodded somberly.

"My uncle died there, too. Took a bayonet in the gut and bled out." The soldier sucked in a breath and glanced off into the distance. Malcolm wondered how these grudges would be resolved when and if the Union prevailed. Would this war never end?

"You heading toward Mallory's private meeting then?" the soldier asked finally. "That's where we're heading with this Dix fella."

The soldier looked pleased to convey that he was involved in a mission of import. Mallory . . . the name sounded familiar, but the specifics eluded him. Malcolm glanced at Elle, saw her raise an eyebrow at him and give a surreptitious shake of the head.

"No, that's actually not where we're heading," Malcolm said easily. "I guess I should've asked before, shouldn't I?"

"Well, you can ask me now. I got kin from round here, so I know these parts a bit," the soldier said easily. Malcolm searched his brain for any information at all about the area and came up blank. One mistake in direction could be overlooked, but not knowing the exact address of where you were going could get you killed at times like these. He would regret having to hurt this boy or starting a ruckus on the road because he couldn't think quickly enough.

Elle made a sound beside him and then spoke, her voice lowered a few octaves and accent dropped by a few states, too.

"Marse, I believe that place we got to meet is at . . . at the corner of Maslow and West Street. Yeah, that's it." Her voice broke believably enough to be a teenaged boy's. It appeared he wasn't the only good actor.

The soldier glanced at Earl, then his face brightened.

"Oh, near the molasses factory! You must've took a wrong turn off of Main."

The soldier gave them directions to their fictitious meeting and wished them an amiable farewell as he galloped off in the direction of the coach, which had ridden ahead without him.

Malcolm let out a deep breath.

"Have you visited this part of the state before?" he asked, hoping the adrenaline in his veins would evaporate soon. The rush of a near miss was a temporary high, but the jittery residue left behind from such encounters was taxing.

"The molasses we used to get back home when I was a girl, it came in a jar with a little map that showed its location on the label. We ate a lot of that molasses," she said, as if that was why she'd been able to recall the street names that had just saved them from an interrogation, at the most optimistic outcome.

He was impressed, but he'd noticed her sensitivity about her skill. He imagined a lifetime of being treated like an anomaly had made her a bit wary of people expressing interest in it.

"Well, thank goodness for your parents' fine taste in molasses or we would have been in a whole heap of trouble," he said. "Why didn't you think we should go? Who is this Mallory?"

"There would have been too high a chance of someone realizing we weren't supposed to be there," she said, patting her horse as it stamped impatiently. "The senator has recently received correspondence from a Stephen Russell Mallory, Secretary of the Confederate Navy. At a meeting with big bugs like that, we might have gotten ourselves into a situation that we couldn't get out of."

"Well, we know that whatever it is, Dix is coming to Caffrey's for the ball and we'll have the opportunity to find out more then."

"Will we?" Elle said, staring down the

road after the soldier, her expression calculating. "Maybe we should ambush them."

Malcolm nearly laughed. Not because he doubted her, but because it was probably the most arousing thing he'd heard in his life. The thought of her jumping into action filled him with fear, but he admired her strength of will.

"I think an ambush on high-ranking Confederate officials is something we need approval for, Detective," he said. "We know that he's coming to the ball tomorrow. We should head back. We have a ways to go, and we don't want to be out on these roads too late."

It wasn't only the Rebel patrols he feared. These were desperate times, and there was many a man who had no loyalty to either the blue or the gray. They would rob you for whatever they could and leave you bleeding out in a ditch.

"Can we eat? I'm half-starved after all this riding," she said, clutching her hands to her stomach.

They let the horses graze in a clearing far from the road while they ate day-old bread and a bit of butter from Elle's sack, along with a few sips of whiskey from Malcolm's flask. As he watched Elle gnaw at a hard corner of bread, Malcolm realized that this was their first meal together, or rather the first which she hadn't been serving in some capacity. He wished it were under more pleasant circumstances than a brief respite while trying to quell the rebellion, but maybe one day things would be different. Was it insanity to hope that was true?

"What's your favorite food? One day I'm going to make you a feast of everything you like best and then feed it all to you until you're fit to bust."

She let out a shocked laugh.

"You're peculiar, you know that?" she said, but she looked up at him with appreciation. "Only my mama knows how to cook my favorite meals, but I like cornpone with cheese, and her special clam chowder."

"Clams?" Malcolm scrunched up his face and a thought to match his grimace occurred to him. "What will your parents think of you being with me?"

Malcolm had already gleaned that Elle was close to her family. Would she be willing to face ostracization just to be with him? Would he let her? He'd fallen for Elle fast and hard, but hadn't given much thought to the long-term logistics of their relationship. He'd never had to think of such things before, because he'd never imagined settling down. Her words from that first encounter on the bluff echoed in his mind. *"I'm certainly not someone you would bring home to Ma and Pa, am I?"* He realized that it was pure egotism that he hadn't considered asking the same of her. A spike of fear much stronger than anything he'd felt while on assignment chilled his blood. And Elle still hadn't answered.

And what did he imagine she would say? Since that first night on the bluff he could feel how she resisted her attraction to him, and with good reason. Yet there he was, already planning their future despite the fact that she might still think him a dalliance. When it came to people, Malcolm always knew when he had someone hooked. It was something he just felt, like hunger or thirst. He was more certain about Elle than he had been about anything in his life, yet he couldn't feel anything tying her to him other than his will that she have him.

Elle chewed her food thoughtfully, for much longer than even the stale bread required.

"I can't say they would be happy *if* I were to do such a thing," she finally said. He chose not to comment on what her emphasis implied. "Think about it from their point of view: People who looked like you owned us. Like we were animals. And now they should just accept me giving myself up to you for free? I'm still not quite sure what I'm doing myself."

She looked away from him, out into the clearing where the horses grazed. Malcolm choked down his food, his throat suddenly dry as he swallowed. He'd asked her to own up to some realities this morning, and it was only fair that he did, too. Could the hard facts she'd just stated ever be overcome? When they'd been entangled together the night before, he'd thought so, but now he wondered at how fair it was to even ask such a thing of her.

She took a swig of whiskey and wiped her mouth daintily. "I know you already think rather highly of yourself, but there's something about you, McCall. Something that makes me want to know you despite what people like you have done. That doesn't change the fact that my daddy might be inclined to shoot you if I brought you home for dinner."

Her smile warmed him, just a bit, though it didn't melt the icy fear that had settled in the pit of his stomach. Thinking of a future without Elle was a physical pain to him, an itching under his skin he was sure would drive him mad. He wondered again if it were a McCall curse to love a woman too much. Ewan appeared to be immune to the charms of women, more interested in his ancient philosophers, and Don was more focused on freedom than fellows, leaving Malcolm to test that particular theory alone. He prayed he was wrong.

"Remember the last time we were alone in the woods?" Elle asked suddenly, her tone playful. She was changing the subject, and not very subtly.

"It wasn't very long ago, Elle," he said. He remembered the accidental press of their two bodies, and how in that moment he'd felt that something more than chance had pulled them together in such a way. His cock stirred, summoned back to duty by the remembrance of the feel and scent of her. "I may not have your memory, but give me some credit."

She smiled at him and even her shabby clothes and ridiculous hat couldn't hide her beauty.

"Time for us to get a move on," he said, squinting up at the sun. The sooner he was back on his horse, the sooner his arousal would be dampened by the uncomfortable saddle.

"We can linger a few minutes," she said, her teeth pressing into her bottom lip as she regarded the tented bulge in his pants. She reached a hand out and stroked him through the heavy fabric.

"I don't want to chance us getting back too late," he said. He should have been ashamed at the tremor that shimmied through his words, but he wasn't. "Someone might notice that one of us is gone from the city. Or that both of us are."

Her hand on his cock was too distracting for him to continue speaking. He was already completely rigid beneath her palm, with trickles of pleasure coursing down his spine. Her hand moved to undo his pants, and his hips rocked up without his permission, urging her on. His member emerged into the cool winter air and was quickly ensconced in the heat of her hands, a delicious contrast.

"The ball is tomorrow," she said, leaning forward. Her warm mouth slanted over his as her hand squeezed his penis, fingers clenching more and less tightly as they glided up and down. "Anything could happen between now and then. If this is the last moment we spend alone together, I'd like to remember something better than stale bread and cheap whisky. You've given me pleasure at your hand, and I won't be denied the same satisfaction."

Her words were sharp, but he was well

versed in her expressions of annoyance, and it was something else that shone in her eyes now. He understood that when he'd pleasured her in the back room of the grocery, and even when he'd showed up in her quarters, he had taken a bit of her control from her, however much she enjoyed their lovemaking. She was asking for it back now, and far be it from him to deny it to her. To deny her anything.

"What if someone walks through here right now?" he asked. One hand was stretched behind him, propping him up, and he moved the other to her loose waistband, skimming his fingers beneath it and against her firm belly.

She trembled, but continued to stroke him. "We enjoy taking risks, don't we? If not, we're both in dire need of a more suitable profession." She worked him more quickly, running her thumb over the head of his cock and gathering the fluid that pearled there.

Her technique had Malcolm ready to blow quicker than if he had been brought pleasure by his own hand. She seemed to know just what to do to bring him to the heights of pleasure, or perhaps it was simply the fact that it was Elle, caressing him with a fierce tenderness that sent bliss careening wildly through his body. She alternated strong, tight tugs with short, quick, jerking motions. Her other hand scraped at the nape of his neck with blunted nails. Malcolm heaved a breath as her touch pulled him away from the harsh realities of war and into a warm cocoon of felicity.

He loved the way she looked at him as she stroked, with a confidence that was guileless. She wasn't afraid to be open with him in that moment. More than that, she enjoyed pleasing him, as he had her. He was sure that if he slipped a hand into her trousers she would be wet and ready for him. She bent and licked along the sensitive rim of his ear and sensation boiled through him.

"Malcolm, I want to see you climax," she said in a voice that reminded him she had been a teacher once. "I don't often get to choose what memories I retain, but I want this one. Give it to me."

Elle leaned back to gaze at him as she worked.

"Please, Malcolm." She ran her tongue over her lips as she stroked him, and her breathy gasp as he thickened in her hand was too much to bear. He bit back a growl as he stiffened and then pumped up, his seed fountaining down over her knuckles as climax pulled him under. Brilliant sensation swirled through his body as he twisted and shuddered beneath her hand. The bright sunlight created a kaleidoscope of colors as it filtered through his lashes, a visual accompaniment to his pleasure that surrounded Elle in motes of light as he squinted up at her.

"Now we can go," she said deviously as he caught his breath. "I do wonder what the Rebs would say if they knew our greatest detective makes sounds like a little kitty cat when he climaxes? It's adorable, really."

"Elle," he warned, attempting to tackle her, but she evaded his grasp.

"It's Earl, sah," she called to him as she jogged off to gather their horses. Malcolm was giddy — he couldn't recall feeling that way since his childhood. Before his father had gone and his mother had been left to care for three children on her own. He'd always thought working solo was a necessity in his detective work, but being with Elle made what could have been a dire situation rather fun.

"Whoever told you to play mute passed up on an excellent scheme," he said as he packed up their paltry picnic and handed her the sack. "A few naughty words from you to some of these old secessionists and they would keel straight over from a stroke."

"Malcolm!" She playfully smacked his shoulder as he helped her mount her horse.

"Or at least a case of the vapors," he finished, avoiding her kick.

They rode back home at a good clip, not having to worry about being noticed by Dix's coach. The farmers and soldiers they passed in the road didn't pay them much mind beyond the necessary salutations.

Despite their pace, they had to pause to water the horses; then Malcolm's horse got a stone caught in its shoe and panicked, requiring a time-consuming stop that involved calming the horse enough to be able to safely remove the rock. By the time they were approaching Richmond, wintry night had fallen and the stars were the only thing that guided them along the road in the crisp winter air.

"Shouldn't be long now," Elle whispered. He didn't find it odd that she whispered because he felt it, too — the sensation that something wasn't right. It was much too quiet in the dark forest along either side of the road. He was moving his hand toward his gun just as the first shadow stepped into the road in front of them, grabbing at Elle's reins.

Fury and confusion zipped through Malcolm's mind as his reflexes kicked in and he reached for his gun. Elle was dressed as a boy, so it seemed discordant that the bandit was looking at her with such a covetous gaze.

What do they want? he thought, and the answer hit him just as Elle bit the word out.

"Slavers."

"That's right, boy," the bandit said as more shadows surrounded them. "You're coming with me."

CHAPTER 16

When she'd heard what had happened to Daniel, Elle had tried a thousand times to imagine what she might have done in his shoes. Fought? Gone peaceably and hoped for a later escape? Panicked? Now she knew for certain: She wished for her daddy. Daddy wasn't coming, though, and her mind raced to find the next best solution.

Elle glanced up at the night sky, searched for the position of the North Star to get her bearings. They were so close to the edge of town, where there was a chance of Rebel soldiers patrolling the perimeters to drive these bastards away. That she wished for the sight of Davis's boys spoke to how truly dire their situation was.

But there was no one else in sight except for two more men who had stepped out of the forest and surrounded them in the moonlight, guns drawn. Three versus two would have been possible for fisticuffs, but when guns were involved, an extra man and an extra bullet were a more dangerous math.

Her horse whinnied and tried to pull away from the ringleader, but he tightened his grip on the reins, jerking abruptly.

"What is the meaning of this?" Malcolm asked in a low, deadly voice. "You see my uniform and dare try to take what's mine? Let the boy go and leave us be, or you'll meet your death this night and wake up with the taste of Hell in your mouth come morning."

The intensity of his words raised goose bumps on Elle's skin, but words couldn't save them. She didn't want to be taken — every part of her rejected the idea, violently — but there was a good chance she and Malcolm would die fighting these men. From their grizzled beards and patched-up clothing, she could tell they were desperate folk who would have no compunction about killing to get what they wanted. A healthy black woman could fetch them a tidy sum at the slave market; most buyers didn't care if the slave they purchased belonged to someone else, or even if they were actually free.

"You talk pretty, but that ain't gonna save your boy," the man holding her reins said. "That uniform is the only reason I ain't kilt you already. You got two choices: Cut your losses and mosey on along, or keep yapping and find yourself with a mouthful of lead."

She remembered Malcolm's promises to her: that he would keep her safe no matter what, that he wouldn't leave her. Part of her had discounted them as flowery tripe he'd thrown at her before their lives had become entwined by more than service to their nation, but now she knew his history, knew how his father had failed his mother. More importantly, now she knew him; he wouldn't let her go without a fight.

I cannot lose him. Not yet.

It made her heart throb that only on the cusp of death did she realize what might have been despite the rules of a sick society that was destroying itself from the inside out. Death, because she would never allow herself to truly be enslaved again. Death, because waiting for the slavers to ravish her once they discovered she was a woman was not something she'd let pass either.

Death, because one of them had to survive to send word of Mallory and Dix's meeting, and the only way to ensure that was for Malcolm to walk away from this fight. They were the only agents who knew that something was brewing in the port city of Yorktown: that an ironclad was being produced and could soon wreak havoc on the block-ade. Someone had to pass word along that was more than mere rumor, and find out exactly what plan the Rebels were hatching.

"I think its best you get on home, sah," she said, her voice breaking. It made her sound more truly like a teenage boy, but it was from excess emotion, not excess hor-mones. "You've got important work to do, things that are more important than me."

Understanding dawned in Malcolm's eyes like a tempest blowing in from the sea.

"You expect me to leave you?" His face paled, and the tendons in his neck stood out like knotted rope. "I will not."

Elle tried her best to fix him with a glare. "If you die and I'm taken, we're gonna let down a whole lot of people. You know what you have to do."

Tears filled her eyes as heartache exploded in her chest. She would never see him again. She'd worried so much about what society would think and how impossible it would be for them to be together that she'd given not a thought to the idea that their parting ways wouldn't be her choice, or even his. To acknowledge the pained look on his face, to know that it was the last image of him that would be imprinted on her mind, was agony.

And she couldn't even touch him. What

she wouldn't give for one last touch! To feel his smooth lips pressing against hers or to smell the tangy scent of his skin as she nuzzled into his neck.

Her eyes were locked onto his, his despair making her even more resolute. He knew what awaited her. But if one of them didn't get word to the government, then the Deep South could become the reality for everyone like her in the United States, and its new territories as well.

"Best listen to your boy," she heard one of the slavers say. Then she was hauled abruptly off of her horse, landing on her back with a *thud* that knocked the wind clean out of her. Elle gasped and rolled on the ground, struggling for breath as pain radiated through her body. She was still gasping like a catfish when someone pulled her to her feet and began tying rope around her wrists.

"Get along now," one of the men said, poking Malcolm's horse in the flank with the butt of his gun. "Go boil your shirt."

"Go," Elle managed to gasp up at him. "I know what you promised, but go. I'll be fine."

"You hear this codswallop?" the ringleader asked, grabbing the rope that led from Elle's hands and tugging her along behind him as he walked on. "I seen men shit themselves on the battlefield with more dignity. Skedaddle, Johnny Reb."

Malcolm stared down at the man, his brows drawn and an unfathomable fury etched into his face.

The man stopped and stared at him. "I shoulda kilt you already, but I'll give you a sporting chance. I'll give you to the count of three. One —"

"Go," Elle urged, wishing with all her might that this was a bad dream she would soon startle awake from, sweat-soaked but safe in her dingy room at the boardinghouse.

The third man, who had been standing silently with his gun turned toward Malcolm stepped up to her and pulled at her sack, bringing it around front. He struggled with the knot for a second before giving up and snatching her hat from her head instead, not even waiting for her supposed master to leave before beginning his looting. The pins ripped at her hair but were unable to withstand the forceful tug. Now the man stood with her cap in his hand as the pins rained over her shoulders and her hair billowed out in an unruly cloud.

"Two —"

"The boy's a girl! A woman!" the hat thief announced, ripping aside the lapels of Elle's jacket and running a hand over her bound chest as Elle stood in shock. She'd hoped she would be able to attempt an escape before they discovered her disguise.

Three faces turned to her in shock, but one remained fixed on the men with deadly calm. Elle had seen that hawk-like look before.

As the man holding the rope turned, its hold slackened and her arms dropped. Her hands made contact with her rucksack and she groped through the fabric for the heavy weight that had sunk to the bottom corner. There was no time to get it out, and she knew that she needed to act now. Her fingers shook, nearly numb from the tight binding of her wrists, but she found the hammer through the fabric of the bag, cocked the gun, and pulled the trigger. It all happened in a few seconds — her disguise being discovered, a moment of shock — and then the man holding her rope had a bloody hole in his chest, ragged where the bullet had torn through.

He looked at her, the cruelty that had marred his face replaced by a shock that made him look younger, innocent. He spluttered and a mist of blood escaped his lips and bubbled from his chest at the same time.

Elle flushed hot and felt her gorge rise, wondered if she was going to pass out, and then realized there wasn't time for that. There was another explosion of noise and gunpowder, and the man holding her hat went down, too. Her horse reared back with a terrified whinny, knocking the third man to the ground before tearing off down the road.

Malcolm spurred his horse forward, toward her.

"Lift your hands," he commanded.

Elle obeyed immediately, raising her tightly bound wrists just as Malcolm thundered past, grabbing her by the binding at her wrist as if it were the handle of a picnic basket.

Elle gave a short yell as she was hoisted aloft, legs scrambling for purchase against the horse's flanks as Malcolm held her and rode like the devil was at their heels. Never had Elle been more grateful that the name Li'l Bit applied to her, although it still must have taken an amazing amount of strength to hold all of her weight with one arm while controlling the horse. His arm began to tremble from the strain.

"Hold for a moment and I'll climb on," she gasped. The fact that she was still alive and still with Malcolm didn't seem possible.

She felt very peculiar, as if she wanted to sprint a mile and curl up into a ball both at the same time. She'd just killed a man, and even though she knew he'd intended her serious harm, she wished she hadn't seen his last bloody gasp, which would now be engraved indelibly in her mind.

"We aren't far enough yet," Malcolm said, although the veins stood out on his neck from the strain of carrying her.

She was going to contradict him when she looked back and saw the third man running after them, his long, thin rifle trained on them.

"Malcolm, he's coming," she screamed just as she heard the explosion of gunpowder. She felt the flex of Malcolm's thigh as he positioned the horse to turn. He meant to come between her and the bullet, but it was too late.

Elle felt a searing pain in her skull. Malcolm's grip was gone, suddenly, and she flew through the darkness alone.

CHAPTER 17

"Goddammit!" Malcolm roared as Elle was torn from his grasp and landed in a heap a few feet away. There was no time to attend to her while they were under fire. He rounded his horse and chased down the man who had just hurt her, who was running down the road like the yellow belly he was. Holding his revolver by the muzzle, Malcolm rode up behind him and swung as hard as he could as he passed. There was a satisfying crack and the man went down heavy.

Malcolm wanted to linger, to have his horse stomp the man until he was nothing more than red paste on the dirt road, but Elle needed him. Or he hoped she needed him, at least. She lay crumpled in the road as he approached, unmoving. As he drew closer, he saw a thin trickle of blood roll down her temple, then watched in impotent horror as the trickle became a stream.

"No. No. No." Malcolm wasn't capable of saying or thinking anything else as he watched the torrent of crimson. He slid on his knees into the dirt beside her and carefully sifted through her thick hair, now matted with blood. He had imagined running his hands through her hair when it was down, but never for something as grotesque as making sure that her skull was still intact.

An unfamiliar pressure welled up in his sinuses as he muttered to himself, and it took him a few seconds to realize the moisture channeling along the side of his nose wasn't sweat, but tears.

How had Mother done this? he thought, recalling her stricken face after she'd investigated the mysterious gunshot in the woods. Her dress had been covered with blood, and her hands in gore. She'd uttered only two words: "He's gone."

But Elle couldn't be gone. Elle was vital, and strong, and smart, and he needed her more than he'd ever needed anything. He'd once imagined that he could be happy alone forever, traveling the country and doing Pinkerton's work. Now he knew better. He could only hope it wasn't too late.

His fingers moved over a raised ridge and his stomach turned.

Please don't die, was the only thought he

could manage. But as his fingers followed the ridge, he realized that the bone showed through, white in the moonlight. Her skull was intact. He ran his fingers through her hair and his fingertips gripped something small, hard, and warm.

He pulled out the bullet and held it up to the sky in disbelief. The pellet had grazed her skull and come to a stop against several metal hairpins. Some combination of wind resistance, trajectory, and weakness of gunpowder had conspired to save her, and Malcolm thanked the Lord for whatever had made it so. Elle was still bleeding, but she was alive.

Malcolm pulled out his flask and took a quick swig to calm his nerves before pouring some over the wound so that it wouldn't fester. Her eyes fluttered open and she winced, but she was still dazed as he pulled a knife from his pocket and sawed at the ropes binding her wrists. He cut off an already torn section of her shirt, pouring whiskey onto the cloth and holding it to her wound.

"Drink this," he said, sitting her up and putting the flask to her lips. She took a pull and coughed violently, and Malcolm laughed through his tears of relief.

"I fail to see the humor in this situation,"

she said, eyeing him as he held a cloth to her bleeding wound.

"You're coughing," he said nonsensically as he blinked back moisture. "You're alive! I'm sure when next I look in a mirror, I'll find the number of gray hairs has doubled, at least, after the last few moments."

She sat up woozily and he clasped her to his chest, lifting her up onto his horse and then climbing on behind her, cradling her. He took off his jacket and draped it over her to keep her warm and away from prying eyes.

"I thought I'd lost you, and then I thought I'd lost you again. Jesus, Mary, and Joseph, I'm so glad you're alive."

Feeling the warmth of her as she trembled against him pulled at something deep within, an armor that he'd once thought invulnerable but had proven worthless against Elle.

"I thought I was going to die without telling you that I . . . I care for you," she said weakly. Her eyelids fluttered and he thought she might faint again. He'd hoped she would say something more, but given everything she'd just been though, *care* was enough for him.

"And I for you," he said as he dug a heel into his horse to get her moving. They rode up to the unconscious man in the road. The man who had almost killed Elle. Malcolm expected to feel furious, but he felt oddly cold as he released Elle and began reloading his gun. Elle's hand stayed him.

"No more killing tonight," she said through chattering teeth. "Please, let's just go. I feel like I've been trampled by a troop of elephants and my stomach hurts something awful."

Malcolm realized that in addition to nearly being kidnapped and sold into slavery and then shot, Elle had eaten very little the whole day. He didn't want to leave the man breathing, but he put away his gunpowder and spurred his horse on toward Richmond.

When they reached his accommodations, Malcolm realized that getting her situated in his quarters wouldn't be as easy as sneaking into her rooming house had been. He refused to let her go back to that hovel in her condition, though. It was late, so there weren't very many people about, but he couldn't be seen by anyone in that state: covered with blood and with a seemingly unconscious black woman in his arms. Even people who supported slavery and overlooked rape had some scruples about what was done in public.

Elle was sleeping deeply, and he shook her gently awake.

"Come now, love, you must awaken," he said as he turned a corner on the building where his room was located. He was on the first floor, which hopefully meant he could sneak her in through the window. He put her onto her feet and leaned her against the wall, although she stood of her own accord when she fully awoke.

"We're at your hotel," she said groggily. "I should go home."

Malcolm pressed a hand against her shoulder to stay her. "No, you should be taken care of. Wait here."

He reluctantly pulled his coat from around her, slipped it on, and walked into the foyer of the hotel. An old slave woman sat by the fire, darning socks. She looked up at him, took in his disheveled state, and jumped to her feet.

"Oh my Lord, what happened to you? You need me to fetch Doc Fletcher?"

"My horse got spooked by a possum and threw me," Malcolm fabricated. If word of the dead bodies in the road got around, he didn't want her making the connection. "I don't need the doctor, just some hot water for a bath, some hot food, and that needle and thread if it isn't too much of a bother."

"I'll have some boys come around with a bath basin and get you food." She put a hand to her chest. "I thought you was the devil himself when you walked in all covered in blood."

"I feel like him," he said, thinking about the myriad ways he could have led Elle away from such danger instead of straight into it. If he'd been paying better attention, if he hadn't enjoyed being pleasured in the clearing so damned much. It was too late for regrets, anyhow.

His stomach growled loudly, startling both him and the woman.

"Can you make that a double order of food?" he asked, taking advantage of his body's rudeness.

She nodded, and he turned and walked heavily toward his room. As soon as he was inside he ran to the window and hefted it up. Elle held up her arms and he grabbed her shoulders, pulling her up and inside and then holding her close against him once she was over the sash. He closed the window with one hand and then hugged her close, smelling the faint scent of roses tinged with iron.

He settled them onto the bed, which felt like extravagant goose down after a full day on the road and the stress of the last hour.

"They're bringing water for a bath, and some food. Then I'll try to sew you up."

"Thank you," she said. She reached a hand up to tentatively touch her scalp. "It might be too late for stitches."

"We'll see once you're cleaned up," he said as he kissed her ear softly. The bleeding had stopped, but red streaked her face. He drew a shaky breath.

"I cannot believe you expected me to leave you there," he said after struggling to find words that weren't *I nearly lost you, dammit.* "You think I would give you up to slavers?" Just the thought of what would have befallen Elle had he left her made him sick to his stomach.

"You promised to keep me safe from unwanted advances, not from slavers trying to sell me Down South," she said, ever prudent. "I would have forgiven you."

"A technicality," he countered. "And I would not have forgiven myself."

"Who would have passed along our findings?" she snapped. "What we're doing is more important than you and I."

"But you know what would have happened, if you went with those men," he said.

" 'Breathes there the man, with soul so dead, Who never to himself hath said, This is my own, my native land!' Do you know

317

that one?" she asked, quoting Scott at him as if the words of his countryman would make accepting such a possibility easier. "Don't patronize me, McCall. I will do whatever it takes to see the Union persevere."

Malcolm had nothing to say. She was right. Making such a sacrifice was part and parcel of being a spy, but he was unable to connect Elle with such a fate. He sighed when she leaned back and kissed his jaw. "But I'm glad you didn't leave me. I'm willing to die, but not ready. Not now."

An ache opened in his chest, something raw and heretofore unknown to him that had been unearthed by the woman in his arms.

"I don't know what I would have done if that bullet had —" His throat closed up, and he cleared it roughly.

"You were just worried about getting a reprimand," she said. "Can't go letting the best brain in the Loyal League get shot up."

"You're much more valuable than your brain," he said. "Especially to me."

She stared up at him, her dark brown eyes glossy and wide.

"I should hope so," was all she said, but her voice was thick with emotion.

A knock at the door interrupted them.

He placed her on her feet and had her stand behind the door as he opened it, keeping her out of sight as two young men carried in a large metal basin of warm water. The woman from the lobby carried in a tray laden with two heaping plates of potatoes, with bits of meat mixed in.

"Sorry for the scarcity," she said as she put the plate down. "Meat is harder to find than a needle in a bushel of cotton with this blockade going on and all these hungry soldiers passing through."

The woman handed him a needle, already strung, as well as a spool of thread and a small sachet of greasy brown paper.

"That's calendula salve, a painkiller. Stops infection, too. Let me know if you need anything else," she said as she followed the boys out. She grabbed his jacket on the way out, miming running it over a washboard before closing the door.

A confusing jumble of emotions clouded his mind as he watched the woman go. What twisted providence allowed people so subjugated to be so kind and thoughtful to the people who kept them under their boot?

Malcolm locked the door and turned to find Elle struggling out of her shirt. His shoulder felt like someone had taken a heavy stick to it, but Elle had suffered manifold more. He walked over and pulled the shirt over her head, careful not to jostle her too much as he tugged at the sleeves. The fabric that had bound her breasts was loose and jumbled, but he carefully unwound it as she stepped out of her pants.

She stepped into the basin, sinking in slowly as she adjusted to the heat and then crossing her legs, submerging as much of her body as was possible in the poor excuse for a bathtub. Malcolm watched her, noting her body's weary movements. When they had set off for home, he'd wondered if they'd have time for another round of lovemaking. Now all he wanted to do was tuck the covers under her chin and make sure she recovered.

"This is twice you've saved me now," she said as she cupped steaming water in her hand and poured it over her body. "I don't enjoy the role of damsel in distress. I'd like to switch, if you don't mind. Next time I get to save you."

"Whatever you wish." Malcolm pulled a chair over and sat beside her, an empty ceramic cup in his hand.

"I've heard of men saying they'd like to drink a lady's bathwater, but I think you might have chosen the wrong day to indulge such a desire," she said, lifting a hand and letting the water drip from her fingertips. It was already pink with blood and cloudy with dirt from the road.

He smiled at her and dipped the cup in, pouring the steaming water over her neck and shoulders.

"I'm not that parched, Elle. I'm going to wet your hair now and get the blood out."

She nodded.

She was pushing her hair out of the way when he noticed her wrists. Dark bruises encircled them and pink abrasions where the rope had rubbed her skin raw. He pulled a hand up to his lips and kissed the back of it gently before continuing to pour water over her back and shoulders.

As he washed the blood from her hair, he marveled at how different it was from his, like soft, springy lamb's wool. He carefully untangled the matted patches with his fingers and then began cleaning the wound again. Blood still seeped out, and he knew what needed to be done. He got the needle and his flask, handing the latter to Elle, but she shook her head.

"It's going to be painful," he said, as he passed the needle through a candle's flame.

"I can stand it," she said, then added quietly, "I killed a man today. I can take it."

He couldn't endorse her need for penance

— he felt no regret over the man he'd killed — but he wouldn't begrudge her it, either.

"He deserved it," he reminded her, then began his work. The needle's first pass through her flesh made him ill, but he worked quickly and cleanly, trying to make the process as painless as possible. She only winced once.

"Didn't that hurt?" he asked as he tied off the thread and snipped it. He opened the sachet of salve and smeared a dollop of it over the wound, hoping it eased the pain.

"My mama has me trained well. Even if my hair is getting pulled out by the roots, I can sit still and not move."

That sounded like torture to him, but she smiled as if remembering something fondly. Catching the puzzled look on his face, she explained, "I was the picture of tenderheadedness when I was young. I learned quickly that wiggling about wasn't to be tolerated."

Malcolm still didn't quite get it, but he nodded as if he did. He washed his hands and then brought over the food tray and handed her a plate. They ate in silence, her in the basin of cooling water and him on a chair beside her. There was one fork between them and he relinquished it, scooping up food with his fingers.

"One of these days, we'll actually eat at a

table," he said.

She smiled up at him, cheeks full of potatoes and lashes glossy.

"You're lovely," he said, running a knuckle over her shoulder because the need to touch her was so strong in him. She clasped his fingers in her hand and appraised him.

"You aren't so bad yourself."

CHAPTER 18

Elle awoke before the dawn, as she always did, no matter how her body yearned for rest. Malcolm's chest rose and fell against her back, his even breaths showing he was still deep in the thrall of sleep, and Elle wondered if he was always so late to rise. Two mornings in a row, now, she'd awoken in the arms of the man she'd resisted with every ounce of her strength and still lost her heart to. If she wasn't careful, she just might get used to it.

Her body ached and her head throbbed, but she felt safe in his embrace.

"How are you feeling?" he asked in his gravelly morning voice, the one she was discovering instantly activated her libido.

"Like someone kicked my behind up Main Street and back," she said, shifting so that her back was flush up against Malcolm's front. She absorbed the feel of him — his chest against her shoulder blades, his thighs pressing into hers, and his groin nestled against her backside.

He slipped an arm between them and cupped her ass in his hand, slowly massaging her. Elle relaxed into his touch, loving the feel of his strong fingers pressing into her. Her tight muscles loosened under his deft touch, and Elle signed at the delightful mix of pleasure and pain.

"How is it you always know how to make me feel good?" she asked, twisting so she could look back at him even though he was just a silhouette in the darkness.

He chuckled.

"It doesn't take a genius to realize that a lady who rode a horse all day might have a sore behind," he said, fingers still kneading. "Among other injuries."

He sighed as he worked, and she knew he was thinking of her brush with death. She'd forced away the thoughts of the slavers whenever they'd surfaced in the night. If she lingered on the memories of their sneering faces too long, they threatened to suffocate her, so she tamped them down. There would be a time to deal with them after the ball, after they got conformation about either the ironclads or some unknown threat.

Malcolm's thumbs rubbed the small of

her back as his long fingers worked at loosening her hip muscles. "This is just an excuse for me to touch you, you know. I'm not entirely selfless."

Elle felt little jolts of ardor tumble through her as he worked. Any guilt she felt about escaping was sanded away by his rough hands on her skin. The press of his fingertips was a wonderful reminder that she was alive and that she should make the best use of her time on this mortal coil. Her nipples tightened and moisture gathered between her legs as she willed his hands to slide slightly lower down her body.

She turned onto her back, so that she was looking up at him. He rested his head on one hand, arm bent at the elbow and pressing into the mattress. He didn't stop caressing her with the other hand, just moved it so that it roamed over her thighs and stomach, avoiding the one place she very much wanted him to touch.

"I can't stay much longer," she said, hating the thought of leaving him. She snaked her arm under the space between his armpit and the mattress and levered herself closer to him. Her hand slid up and down his back, reveling in the sculpted muscle and sinew.

His hand moved to her inner thigh, fingertips dragging along the sensitive skin. For a moment, she thought that he hadn't heard her because he simply stroked her reverently as if they had all the time in the world.

"The clothing you wore is torn and bloody, and your hat is gone. I sent a message to Timothy, your League man, asking him to send me a dress for a petite young woman. It won't arrive for a little while, I imagine."

Elle wondered what Timothy would make of that message. He was known for his discretion and didn't seem like the type to judge. For a moment the same shame that had assailed her when first they made love began to descend, but then she remembered how tenderly Malcolm had cared for her the night before. If Timothy or anyone else in the League learned of what had passed between her and Malcolm and didn't like it, they could find someone else with a steel-trap memory to assist them. She wasn't sure what their future held, but she knew now that she could not deny what there was between them, even if that made her as foolish as him.

"So you're saying you have time to make love to me?" she asked. She would see him that night at the ball, but they'd have to be on full alert, searching for definitive proof that the ironclad or some other naval project was under way. There would be no time for dalliances or the simple pleasure of being in one another's arms. And there was no guarantee of what would become of them afterward. Anything she wanted from him she'd have to take now.

She turned her head toward his chest and darted out her tongue, lapping at his small, hard nipple. She circled her tongue around the textured smoothness and then drew the nub between her teeth, gently.

Malcolm groaned, but his hand stilled on her stomach.

"You're injured," he said in a low voice. His body had gone tense and unmoving, except for his cock, which pressed against her hip expectantly. As ever, it didn't share Malcolm's concerns.

"And I need something to distract me from the pain. Consider yourself as providing medical relief," she said. She could sense his head incline toward hers in the darkness, but he did not resume his exploration of her body. She wondered if he would value his opinion of her condition over her own needs, but then his head dipped and his lips brushed against hers. At the same time, his fingers slid into the curls between her legs, searching for the slick pearl of her desire.

He teased her with abbreviated strokes of his fingertips and Elle moaned quietly at the double-edged sword of pleasure and denial.

"I *have* wanted to play doctor with you, so I'd be a fool not to jump at this opportunity." He claimed her mouth in a flurry of kisses that left her breathless. Her nails scraped down his back as his fingers worked her nub and spread the folds that held evidence of her arousal.

Her hand slipped from beneath him and down her side to grip his penis. At her touch, Malcolm made a sound that could only be described as ungainly, and Elle's core pulsated in response. She stroked him reverently, matching her tempo to each brush of his fingers over her slit. The veined thickness of his cock intrigued her, as it had during their encounter in the field. It was a contradictory organ: hard and soft, smooth and rough. The hot heaviness of it triggered some innate desire to take him within her.

As if sensing her thoughts, Malcolm slid his hand up to her stomach again, scooping her toward him so that she turned onto her side and the length of his body pressed against hers from behind once again. The head of his cock rubbed at her slick opening and they both gasped as he slowly pushed into her. Inch by slow inch, he worked himself into her, his cock forging a trail of exquisite sensation as it pushed into her depths.

"Malcolm." The word came out too loud, and she clamped her mouth. Every time he'd touched her had been delicious, but without the fear and resistance she'd felt before, his every caress was now magnified. His lips on her neck sent sparks streaking through her body, and the press of his palm against her hip left her shuddering.

He held her against his chest with one arm, keeping her body flush against his as he pumped his thick member in and out of her. She arched in his embrace, swiveling her hips to meet each of his vigorous thrusts.

"Dammit, you feel amazing," he rasped as he withdrew and then plunged into her again and again. "You *are* amazing." Each drag of Malcolm's cock against her inner walls drove her closer to completion, closer to the certainty that she would combust from sheer bliss.

Malcolm's hips pivoted and twisted as he drove into her, pulling strained animal sounds from the both of them as passion stole stealthily through their limbs. He was mindful of her injuries, but the drive behind each thrust reminded both of them that it was a gift to be alive and able to bestow pleasure upon one another. She gripped his forearm as a clamor of emotions rose within her, pushed forward by her impending climax.

"Love me, Malcolm." The words tumbled out of her mouth without thought as the pleasure enveloped her. His calloused hand slid between her legs again, pressing her closer to him, fingers circling her clit as he drove madly into her.

"Ellen," he growled reverently as he surged into her. Her world imploded into the one magnificent point of heat between her legs. She cried out as the pleasure rocked through her, nearly paralyzing her with a potent dose of adrenaline and passion. Malcolm followed suit, holding her close as he thrust uncontrollably. He withdrew at the last moment and spilled his seed on the mattress between them.

He pulled her onto his chest and they lay in sated silence. Elle drowsed, occasionally falling into a light sleep where she dreamt of the events of the previous night and the work that lay ahead of them. She dreamt of her childhood home and the plantation where she'd been born. The waking dreams were strange and random; the only constant in the vignettes was Malcolm.

A light knock at the door startled them awake, finally, and Elle hopped from the bed and took up her station behind the door. Malcolm received a wrapped package and handed it off to her immediately. The old mauve dress inside was slightly too small for her, but it would do for the day ahead. Malcolm silently helped her button it and she wondered if his thoughts aligned with hers.

If they were correct about Dix, then today could be the last day of his mission, and hers. She knew that he had only come to Senator Caffrey's mansion on a whim, and on that whim the entire axis of their lives, and perhaps that of the war, had tilted. Where would he be going after this? Where would she?

"I'll see you this evening," he said, his tone subdued. She simply nodded, unable to speak.

She noticed something around his neck then and parted his shirt to see it. She found a loop of long black thread with a mis-shapen ball of lead tied at the end.

"A reminder that you won't be lost to me so easily," he said. "And an inspiration to be as brave as you were."

Tears filled her eyes as she fingered the tiny object that had almost taken her life.

"I never cried so much before I met you, you know," she said, dashing the moisture from her cheeks.

Malcolm grinned. "You sure know how to make a man feel special," he said.

"I never laughed so much, either," she said, hugging him close.

His lips grazed hers, softly, leaving her wanting more.

"I'll find a way to communicate with you at the house," he said.

After making sure that no one was about, she slid through the window, Malcolm holding her hands to steady her as she dropped to the ground.

With one last longing glance, he shut the window and drew the curtain. She shivered in the cool morning air as she hurried toward the road that would take her to Senator Caffrey's house. Dawn tiptoed across the sky, keeping her company on her journey.

"Thought you might need a cloak, too," a voice said from behind her, and she turned to find Timothy holding out a brown wool cloak. She grabbed it and fastened it about her shoulders with shaking fingers.

"How did you know?" she asked as he fell into step beside her.

Timothy laughed. "I ain't in the Loyal

League on account of my pretty face."

"I was injured during a mission and my clothing was torn," she explained. The words seemed oddly stiff despite the fact that they were true, more or less.

"Mm-hmm," was all Timothy said. They walked in silence, but he kept glancing at her.

"What?" she finally asked when ignoring him became more awkward than whatever question he might have.

"My grandfather was an Indian, you know. Seminole tribe. If it weren't for people following their hearts, I wouldn't exist. So you don't have to worry about taking guff from me."

Elle felt exposed. It had been one thing to conjecture about Timothy's reaction from the haven of Malcolm's bed, but in the light of day it made their situation much more real, and much more frightening. Someone knew about their relationship, and once people knew something existed they could destroy it.

"Why would you tell me such a thing?" she said, letting annoyance creep into her tone.

"You got them expressive eyes, Elle. Before you knew I was watching, they were awful sad." He gave her a little pat on the back. "Don't matter what other folks think, anyhow. If that was the case, how would we keep on living knowing what most white folk think of us? Just tell me where you went and what you found out. That's the only business I'll stick my nose into."

Elle wanted to grab the little man and hug him. Instead, she recounted her story from the time she'd met Ben to her escape from the slavers.

Timothy's eyes were wide with amazement by the time she finished.

"Girl, you're luckier than a rabbit with three feet!" he said, grabbing her hand and shaking it. "But if there's something to this ironclad business, we need to be sure, and fast."

"We have to be prepared for anything tonight," she said.

They talked strategy for the rest of the walk. Her body pained her, and she didn't try to hide it. She was supposed to have been deathly ill, after all.

As they approached the property, Elle spotted Mary through one of the parlor windows. Mary turned and saw her, then stormed out of sight. Elle glanced at Timothy, who shrugged, and then Mary appeared in the yard. She approached at a quick clip, her mouth tight and her eyes narrowed.

"You look like you been rode wet and hung up to dry," she said. She plucked at Elle's hair, and Elle winced against the pain in her scalp. "Your hair look like you slept in a briar patch, too."

Timothy laughed. "That sickness that's been going around will do that to you. She well enough to work today," he said, heading for the kitchen. "Be easy with her, though."

Mary rounded on Elle. Her gaze was hard, and Elle knew something was very wrong.

"I took my leave day with Robert yesterday. I know you ain't got no kin here, so when I heard you was sick, I brought some medicine to your room," the woman said, her voice laced with accusation. "You wasn't there. Not in the afternoon and not at night. You know who else didn't show his face yesterday? The man that's been staring at you like you was the last lump of sugar in this consarned town. I had to listen to Susie moaning about it over her tea this morning. Tell me true now, Li'l Bit: Tell me you didn't give yourself to a man fighting for the South."

She'd been found out. Fear was neck and neck with the urge to cry because Mary had cared enough to check, and to call her out. She had wasted her precious time with her husband to try to help Elle, and now she'd be repaid with lies. Elle shook her head, opening and closing her mouth to show her frustration at being unable to speak. That part wasn't an act: Even if she'd been able to, she couldn't have revealed the truth about her and Malcolm. She was living a lie, and sometimes that meant disappointing people who cared for you.

Mary gave a frustrated sigh and smoothed Elle's frizzy hair down, gently this time.

"I hope you telling me the truth," she said. "I know the things they'll say to get under your skirts, if they even bother with seduction."

Elle just gave her a perplexed look and hoped that was enough.

Mary seemed to accept it.

"I was just worried, is all," she said, adjusting the ragged lace trim on Elle's sleeve. "You remind me of my daughter sometimes. She had eyes just like yours . . . Caffrey sold her down South to pay off a debt. Every time I look at you, I wonder if she gonna grow up to be as pretty as you. And I hope she won't."

Elle's stomach churned at the woman's words. She'd led a charmed life compared to most of the slaves here. Even during her time as a slave she'd been too young to understand what was going on and her master too old to do her much harm. The people here knew nothing of a benevolent master who would set them free instead of selling them for more coin. They knew struggle and pain.

The Union had to persevere.

Elle pulled Mary into an embrace, wishing she could take away some of her pain. Her friend was all wiry muscle from a lifetime of working without cease.

"Thanks, Li'l Bit," she said, and Elle now wondered if the moniker was something else that had been passed on from Mary's daughter. "I just can't wait for the day the Yanks come riding through here and rain vengeance down on these folks' heads."

She gazed at the house, where people bustled about preparing for the ball.

Elle simply nodded.

Me too, she thought grimly. Elle looked past the house, toward the rising sun, and felt that twinge of instinct that meant something important was just around the corner. Maybe Mary would get her wish sooner than she imagined.

CHAPTER 19

After Elle had gone, Malcolm called for another basin of hot water. He washed up in silence, his thoughts alternating between Elle, bloody in the road and then warm and alive in his arms, and the challenge they would face that night. Part of him wanted to stow her away safely to keep her from harm, but he knew that she would never agree to it. Besides, he needed her. He'd always preferred working alone, but the woman was a damned good detective, and the night ahead showed all signs of being challenging if they were right.

He updated the notes in his ledger after shaving, not wanting to forget anything of import that had occurred on their journey. A knock at the door as he buttoned his shirt startled him, but it was the slave woman who had been up late the night before; she held out his cleaned jacket for him to inspect.

"You must have been up late scrubbing this," he said, and she looked at him with a hint of fear in her eyes, as if he were trying to trick her into revealing something incriminating. "It must have taken ages to get all the stains out, and now you're up early working."

"Well . . . yes," she said, her brow furrowed in confusion. "I always get up early. I got to get my work done."

He slipped into the ironed and starched jacket, guilt wrapping round him as snugly as the stiff fabric. He pulled out a coin, pressing it into the woman's hand. That act felt somehow wrong, too, but he didn't know what else to do.

"No, I couldn't —" she began, but he waved her off as she tried to return it.

"I insist," he said. He dearly hoped that he was close to giving her what she needed more than a bit of coin: freedom. The politicians could deny it all they wanted, but this had become a battle not just to preserve the Union, but to decide whether slaves would be freed or not. He'd thought that's what he'd been fighting for all along, but if he were truthful, he hadn't seen slaves as more than the lot they'd been given in life. He'd thought of their general freedom, but not their individual wants and needs. Not about

340

what sustained them from day to day, or made them smile, on a basic human level. He'd considered himself to be so evolved, and then Elle had arrived. Elle who wouldn't praise him for simply doing what was right.

"Oh, there's someone here to see you," the slave woman said as she tucked the coin away. "A lady."

Malcolm had a buoyant moment in which he imagined Elle had returned. They would fall back into bed, whiling away the afternoon until it was time to attend the ball. But then he remembered that Elle wouldn't be referred to as a lady, and she wouldn't be attending the ball so much as preparing it.

Who else would visit me here?

His question was immediately answered by the sound of heeled steps and the swoosh of crinoline. Silky blue fabric stretched over a hoop skirt rounded the corner of the hall, followed by the point of a matching parasol, and finally, the entire form of Susie Caffrey.

"Well, look who the cat dragged in," she drawled, as if surprised.

"Actually, this is my hotel, so I believe you dragged yourself," he said. That she'd had the audacity to show up at his quarters astounded him. What if she'd arrived earlier and discovered Elle? But his irritation at her presence wasn't part of the role he was playing, and he quickly adjusted his tone. "Although I don't think a little pussy cat has ever had prettier quarry."

Her mouth had been teetering on a frown, but the edges pulled up into a seductive smile as she brushed passed the slave, not even acknowledging her presence. The woman made a hasty departure.

"I was sorely disappointed that you didn't come visit me yesterday," she pouted, nosily peeking past him into the room before continuing. "Daddy was busy drawing up plans in his office all day, and I was so hoping we would have gotten to spend some alone time together. No one else came by the parlor all day, not even Rufus. Just imagine what we could have gotten up to."

She ran the tip of her parasol up the inseam of his pants and he jumped, the sensation entirely unappealing. He looked down into her cold hazel eyes, at her thin lips pulled into a smile meant to seduce, and he felt something stir for her at last: pity. She was like a chasm of need, no amount of attention ever enough to fill whatever it was that was missing within. It didn't make up for her appalling behavior, but if he could spare the man who had tried to kill his love, he could sympathize with Susie.

"I'm sorry I missed what sounds like the perfect opportunity to get to know you better, but business drew me away from town for the day," he said, not acknowledging her blatant assault of his person with her parasol. "I'll try to rectify that this evening, if you'll allow it."

"Or you can rectify it now," she said, stepping forward, as if she meant to back him into his room. Malcolm held firmly in the doorway, shifting to block her passage.

"Unfortunately, these are trying times for the South, and I must attend to some urgent matters before this evening. Any rectifications will have to wait until then."

She placed her hand on his chest, and he couldn't help but compare the warmth in Elle's touch with the cold calculation in Susie's. He didn't mind aggressiveness — hell, when Elle had taken him in hand in the field, he'd popped his cork so fast that he'd wondered if her touch had even been necessary. But Susie was no Elle.

"Can't I just come in for a moment?" she pushed, with both her hand and her tone, unable to believe that he wasn't bending to her will.

"I was just leaving," he said. "I'll walk you

to your coach."

He grabbed his hat and tugged the door closed behind him. He took her arm in his and could feel her indignation in her stiff gait. As he handed her inside of the coach, she crossed her arms and fixed him with a watery gaze.

Good Lord, he thought. The man who eventually settled with this chit would be in for a treat.

"I must admit, I'm quite displeased with how this morning has unfolded," she said.

Malcolm nodded. On that they could agree. In an ideal world, he would still be in bed with Elle. "I concur. And I bid you adieu, until tonight."

"Malcolm?" Her voice rang out after him when he'd taken a few steps down the dusty sidewalk.

"You'll find that I don't appreciate being treated so unkindly," she said, her eyes overbright and her hands gripping her parasol tightly. He'd underestimated the woman's tenacity.

He walked back to her slowly, feigning confusion. "I don't believe I've treated you unkindly at all," he said. "I don't understand your implication."

"Well, I only mean to say that I'd be terribly disappointed if you were to abandon me again tonight. It's ungentlemanly to show false attentions to a woman, something a true Southern man would never do. We discuss such matters at meetings of the Vigilance Committee all the time." She batted her eyes at him as if this was a game of seduction, and Malcolm realized that for her it was.

He put on a saccharine smile and tried to reign in his temper. His lack of sleep and general agitation didn't help with either action.

"Miss Caffrey, I know you're eager to learn more about me, so I'll share a little tidbit with you right now: I don't take kindly to manipulation."

With that he turned and headed toward MacTavish's store, leaving her staring after him. He tried not to think of how he should have reacted more gently, but it didn't matter. Showing fear or acknowledging her threat with denials would not have aided him against someone like her. As he'd stepped away from the coach, he hadn't seen anger on her features, but desire. The minx probably considered their conversation foreplay.

When he arrived at the grocer's, Malcolm immediately recognized that MacTavish had either began imbibing very early in the day or was still on a tear from the night before.

"Oh, hello, Sir Reb," the wild-haired man called out as Malcolm entered the store. "What can I get you? We just received a shipment of very fine garters if you have a lady you'd like to impress."

"My lady wouldn't be impressed by garters," he said curtly, then reconsidered. Elle's fine legs in garters and silk stockings would be things of wonder. Perhaps he shouldn't be too hasty in his decision.

"Pity that. Perhaps you need this premium vellum paper. Perfect for sending and receiving correspondence of all sort." There was a glimmer of sharpness in the man's rheumy eyes, despite his demeanor.

"I'll take the paper," he said.

"Excellent choice. Here y'are," MacTavish said on a hiccup. He shook Malcolm's hand heartily. "Always good to see a Scots brother taking up the Cause. We won't let them trod over us this time!"

A woman doing her morning shopping eyed them suspiciously.

"Down with Union! Death to Lincoln!" MacTavish cried, his wink hidden to all but Malcolm.

Malcolm left the store quickly, hoping that Elle had been right to trust MacTavish. He opened the scroll of papers, finding one

346

inscribed with coded text. Roughly translated, it acknowledged the possibility of the South's having an ironclad, but was dubious that it was already near completion. They had reliable information from another source that it would take several more months for such a project to be completed, and the war would likely be over by that point anyway. In addition, without an actual location or information about the outfitting of the vessel, this information could not be acted on. It stated that the Union ship was being built as planned, and that he should return to the Capitol with all haste.

He crumpled the letter in his hand. His assessments were rarely second-guessed. For a brief moment, he wondered if they were only doubtful because the suggestion had come from Elle's hand and not his. Had Pinkerton even been shown the missive, or had it been deemed not worth the man's time?

Whatever the reason for the tepid response, he and Elle would need to furnish evidence. As much as he hoped they were wrong, he knew that there was something to the situation with Dix. He walked over to the Lancelot Inn to see if he could engineer a run-in with the frumpy engineer, but the man wasn't about. It was possible he still hadn't returned.

Malcolm sighed in frustration. His morning had been less than fruitful, and he hoped it wasn't any indication of how the night would turn out.

CHAPTER 20

The ball was in full swing. Dinner had been served, drinks had been poured, the dancing had begun, and still Elle had garnered no new information.

She'd heard officers making fun of the country boys who didn't know their right foot from their left and wouldn't know discipline if they tripped over it. She'd heard masters complaining about slaves that slipped away in the dark of night to join the contraband camps of the Union army. Word was going around that they would officially sanction Negroes wearing Union blue one day soon — the Confederate officers jeered, but in the way a man makes jest of the monster under the bed and then spends half the night unable to sleep.

A group of slaves playing fiddles stood in the corner of the ballroom, their arms moving in unison as they played a Virginia reel. The men and woman faced each other in two rows, now approaching, now retreating, now spinning each other, now stepping away. The dance reminded Elle of the war between the North and South, or perhaps of her relationship with Malcolm; the difference was that there was an order and expected outcome to the dance that Elle could never hope for in the other two.

She bustled about the room, searching for sight of Dix or even Ben, but neither of the men was about. From this vantage point she could see Malcolm, all of him now, not just his broad shoulders that stood out in any crowd. He smiled and curtsied, his body moving fluidly and gracefully. Elle looked on as he took Susie's gloved hand in his. The woman drew out the contact for a beat longer than the other dancers, who had already begun to switch partners.

Elle felt a twinge of sadness. She'd never been a very good dancer, but she still wished that it was her kicking up her skirts with Malcolm instead. Would that ever be allowed to them? One night of dancing with abandon, without worrying who saw them?

Elle sighed deeply, feeling more tired than she ever had. The encounter with the slavers had taken a higher toll than she'd realized, and the scant hour of sleep she'd grabbed afterward seemed only to have compounded her aching body's protestations. She had been working since she arrived that morning, with no quarter given when she'd nodded off while scrubbing the steps. Whatever energy reserve had been driving her was now entirely depleted. To top it off, she had yet to encounter anything of much import. She'd been so sure that something would happen at the ball that night, but Dix was nowhere to be found and everyone else spoke of inconsequential matters.

She circled the room once more, collecting empty glasses before carting them off to the kitchen, where another type of synchronized dance was going on. Slaves washing, slaves drying, slaves pouring wine and champagne, their bodies moving quickly and precisely to get the job done without bumping into one another and creating more mess to clean. The music here wasn't the strains of the violin, but Althea leading a song that shot Elle through with a pang of homesickness.

There is a balm in Gilead
To make the wounded whole;
There is a balm in Gilead
To heal the sin-sick soul.

Sometimes I feel discouraged,

351

And think my work's in vain,
But then the Holy Spirit
Revives my soul again.

The words had been sung by untold numbers of voices who had gone to their graves without tasting freedom, expecting it only in the afterlife. The bittersweet strains brought to mind the words of Frederick Douglass: *"Slaves sing most when they are most unhappy. The songs of the slave represent the sorrows of his heart."*

That unjust bargain, happiness only after death, sickened Elle. Her people deserved freedom while they walked God's green earth, and now they were closer to it than ever. Elle prayed she'd live to see the day, and perhaps to help usher it in.

As she placed her glasses down and pushed up her sleeves to avoid getting them wet, she realized that someone was staring at her. Mary. The woman had been quiet and reserved for the entire day. Elle had thought Mary was still angry with her about her absence, but then she noticed that she was behaving the same to everyone. Elle had assumed she was just worried about how the ball would turn out.

She stood wringing her hands now, and Elle went to her and laid a hand on her shoulder. Mary smiled awkwardly, and the uncertainty of it reminded Elle that Mary was so very young, and in charge of not one household, but two.

Elle raised her eyebrows, inclined her head toward Mary. She regretted the need to feign muteness with her. The woman had treated her as a friend, without knowing her status or her talent, and yet Elle had to lie to her.

Mary shook her head tightly, her actions contradicting her words. "I'm fine, Elle, just a little worried. I'm meeting Robert tonight, you see, and . . ." Mary closed her eyes, as if in duress, and then opened them. "Sometimes I feel like this load on my shoulders is too heavy to carry. Even when you know you doing right, you still feel like you doing wrong."

Elle was startled for a moment. Mary's words echoed thoughts that had plagued her for the last few days.

Mary looked around at the kitchens with sadness in her eyes; then her eyes lit on Elle's wrists and that sadness turned to anger. She gripped Elle's forearm and held up the bruised and abraded wrist between them.

"I'm not gonna ask what happened because I know you ain't gonna tell me," she

353

said, suddenly fierce. "All I'm gonna ask is that you come talk to me before you leave tonight, ya hear?" Elle nodded, although she didn't know where she would be by the end of this night if Dix ever actually showed up.

As if sensing her reticence, Mary gripped her by both hands. "I'm serious now, Elle," she said, her voice low and urgent. "Do not leave this house without seeing me first."

Something in Mary's behavior set off an alarm bell. Mary had said she was meeting Robert again. Hadn't she just seen him the night before? They usually went weeks between visits. . . .

Mary's fidgeting and nervousness, even her earlier anger, all began to fall into place. She'd seen the same restlessness in the runaways her family had given shelter to en route to Canada.

Mary was planning to escape. Her words from days before came back to Elle, that she and her husband, Robert, could help Elle if Malcolm had been harassing her.

Elle was scared now, too, for her friend. Being captured by slavers was bad enough. But being captured while escaping was something else entirely. Slaves had been running off and turning themselves over to Union forces since Butler had instituted the contraband camp at Fort Monroe. Those who tried to escape and failed were made into examples, even more so than before. The lash would become an intimate friend, if not the noose.

She hugged Mary and nodded as strongly as she could before the woman whirled away, resuming her role as caretaker of the house.

"Get those bottles opened!" she shouted at two women who stood chatting. "Y'all don't want Mistress coming in here riding our backs like the devil, do you?"

Elle left the kitchen, looking back over her shoulder at her friend. Elle knew about escape, had years and years of runaways' stories and narratives she had read collected in her mind. She could help Mary, forge her a pass that could get her past any nosy soldiers if they were stopped in the road. If she could help her friend, it would be at least one thing accomplished that night.

Trying to look as meek and unassuming as possible, Elle moved through the crowded hallway and crept up the servants' stairs. The second floor was supposed to be empty, but there was always someone who snuck away for a dalliance, or simply to get away from the heat and crowds.

She padded down the carpeted hallway,

listening at the entryway of the senator's office for a moment without entering. A fire crackled in the fireplace, but no one was about.

The room was another example of sumptuous luxury, with its high-backed couches and grand mahogany desk. Rich draperies covered the windows, and the carpets on the floor were even nicer than those in the hallway. Such finery, paid for at the small cost of human lives and dignity.

Her anger rose in her again, but she brushed it aside.

She crept over to the desk and began scanning the visible documents on its surface. It was mostly littered with invoices for the ball, showing where the senator's priorities were at the moment. Elle rifled through the papers, seeing if anything jumped out at her. There was nothing about ironclads, nothing that seemed important enough to create the buzz that had been built around the ball. She would write out a pass for Mary and then get back downstairs.

She heard footsteps before she could even reach for the quill, and rushed toward the fireplace, grabbing the poker. Maintaining it for the senator *was* part of her duties, so she hoped it wouldn't arouse suspicion.

The door opened quietly and Malcolm

slipped inside.

"What are you doing in here?" he hissed under his breath. She was about to answer, "My job," but then a giggle sounded from behind him.

"Who are you talking to, Malcolm?" Susie asked, her voice pitched low. She slid her arm through his as she stepped through the door, giving Elle a venomous smile when she spotted her. "Why am I not surprised to find you here? You're always trying to ruin my fun. Get out. Now."

Elle glanced at Malcolm, whose expression was blank.

"I said now, darkie," Susie snapped. Before giving Elle a second to clear out, she pulled Malcolm's face down to hers and kissed him.

Seeing Susie's tongue slide into his mouth, her hands cup his face, made Elle ill.

I thought I was made of sterner stuff than this, she chided herself as she dropped the poker and hurried from the room. But the last sound she heard as the door closed behind her was a feminine sound of pleasure and a low, masculine laugh. She thought of how content Malcolm had looked during the dance, how he had regarded Susie as if she were the only woman in the room. Hadn't he made Elle feel the same way?

She tried to shake the negative thoughts out of her mind, but she kept hearing Susie's moan and Malcolm's laugh. She walked down the hall on unsteady legs, angry with herself but trying to master the emotions that surged through her, threatening to pull her under.

Both she and Malcolm had jobs to do. He was doing his, and if it meant him making love to another woman, she would just have to deal with that later. She tried to push her feelings aside, to tamp them down as she usually did, but it seemed that there was no room. The part of her mind where she routinely shoved her sadness, her loneliness, and her anger had reached its maximum capacity. One final thought compounded her misery: The only person she wanted comfort from was with another woman.

She sank to her knees and felt the bitter tears come. The night was almost over, she'd no new information to help the Cause, she hadn't forged Mary's pass, and here she was crying in plain sight like a brainless twit. She was supposed to be stronger than this, smarter, but now she'd failed everyone, including herself.

"What have we here?" a familiar voice said above her. She looked up through her tear-distorted gaze to see Mr. Dix bending down with his hand outstretched. She took it and he pulled her up.

"That's the simple girl," Senator Caffrey said. Elle wanted to remind him that he didn't find her so simple that he couldn't leer at her, but she didn't. "I reckon all the goings-on of the ball have overtaxed her. She seems to be prone to crying fits like this. Don't pay her any mind."

"I have fits from time to time, though mine are a bit different," Dix said, his voice as kind as it had been when he allowed her to ride on his coach. "Come with us, girl."

"We have business to attend to," Senator Caffrey said, clearly annoyed at his compatriot's indulgence.

"We do," Mr. Dix said, unconcerned. "I'm not asking her to contribute her insights. We'll just give her a shot of brandy to calm her nerves. It's the decent thing to do."

Caffrey wasn't happy about it but didn't seem to want to argue. He slid a disdainful glare her way before entering the library.

Elle followed close behind them. She was ashamed of her brief breakdown, but it had worked in her favor. She'd been invited into a meeting with a Confederate senator and his naval engineer, and she wasn't leaving until she had gathered as much information as she could. She couldn't know if Malcolm was doing her a dishonor or not right then; she could only control what she herself did with the opportunity presented to her.

When Dix and Caffrey settled into chairs in front of the fire, she realized that they still expected her to wait on them. She poured their drinks from a half-empty decanter on a nearby sideboard and handed them off after taking a small sip under Mr. Dix's watchful eye. Then she receded into a corner as they forgot she was there and began their meeting.

"Mallory is amenable to my time table," Mr. Dix said. "The new ironclad won't be complete for some time, but it will be sailable within three months."

"Will it be able to attack?" Senator Caffrey asked.

"Oh yes," Mr. Dix said, his voice still nervous and soft. "It will be able to break this blockade wide open. After that, every advantage the North currently holds will be lost to them."

"Excellent. President Davis is going to be very happy to hear this," Caffrey said. "Now give me the specifications."

In her dark corner, Elle suppressed a fierce smile. She'd been right. On this night, she was going to help save the Union.

Chapter 21

Malcolm produced a vicious laugh at his situation as the door to the room shut. The one woman he cared about most in this world looking on as he kissed the woman who made her life hell on a daily basis. Who, for all intents and purposes, owned her. He pulled away from the kiss, hoping that Susie was satisfied. Despite his dislike for her, he felt vile pretending to enjoy dancing with and, now, kissing her. What greater blow could come to a person than realizing they had been used in such a way?

Perhaps seeing the man who claimed to care for her with his lips pressed to another woman's?

He knew that this was his work, and Elle knew that this was his work, but he would have been tempted to partake in some kind of devilry if he'd witnessed the same. It was in that moment that he knew for certain that he was truly a patriot; if his love for his country had measured an iota less, he would have left Susie and chased down the woman he truly wanted. Instead, he smiled.

"So, darling Susie, I do believe you said you were going to show me what everyone at the ball is so worked up about," he said, stepping away from her. He resisted the urge to wipe his lips, at least while she was watching.

"Is that truly why you came up here with me?" she asked. "I thought you wanted to kiss and make up after our little spat this morning."

She'd placed one of her feet up on a small velvet footstool with gold gilt legs. She ran her hands up her stockings, displaying the enticing legs encased within them.

That was the moment Malcolm knew he'd been bamboozled. He knew she'd expected his favor in return for showing him something confidential, but he hadn't expected her to lie about the files even being there. He'd become desperate when midnight neared and there had been no sign of Dix, and he'd hoped he could get the information and then evade Susie's advances. He and Elle were depending on finding the information about the ironclad that night, and if they didn't, he had no idea how they would proceed. Elle believed the Union was in danger, and he believed in her.

Susie stopped her slow, seductive journey up under her skirts.

"Now, what kind of man finds himself alone in a room with a willing and able woman and doesn't find himself up to the task?" she drawled.

One who's in love with someone else, he thought.

"Perhaps I've had a bit too much brandy," he said, ready to leave off of this route. Susie had seemed a promising vein of information, but she'd wasted his time instead. He would have to corner the senator himself. Every time he'd tried, Susie had pulled him away for another dance or a tiresome story.

"When you showed renewed interest this evening, I thought my words had shaken some common sense into you," she said. "I'm a Confederate senator's daughter, and what I want I shall have. Half the South is starving and I've yet to go without. If you think you're a finer commodity than a flank of beef, you are mistaken." She stared at him, a cruel smirk fixed to her mouth. Malcolm had known Susie was spoiled, but this was obscene.

"You cannot force a man to lie with you, Miss Caffrey," Malcolm said.

She tilted her head. "And why not? Men

do it to my sex as a matter of course. If our situations were reversed, you would call me a coquette and take what you wanted."

Malcolm sneered. "Men generally have superior physical strength that allows for such transgressions. Regardless, *I* would do no such thing."

"Superior. Physical. Strength." She drawled each word through lips curled in disdain. "Will you not change your mind?"

"I'm afraid not, Miss Caffrey."

"Pity." With that, she opened her mouth and released a heartrending scream, one of complete and paralyzing fear. She began to sob loudly, smiling at Malcolm through her tears. His blood ran cold, even though he knew she was crying wolf. Anyone else would think she was being murdered.

"Sorry, Mr. McCall. This will have to go into tomorrow's papers and be reported to the Vigilance Committee. I'm sure your superior physical strength will see you through, though."

There was a pounding of feet on carpeted wood in the hallway; then the door flew open and the room crowded with men who pulled his arms behind him and threw him to the floor.

"Oh, he said he was going to do the most terrible things to me," Susie sobbed as her father pulled her to his side and glared down at Malcolm. "He said he's for the Yanks, and he was going to help them pillage the South, starting with me!"

It was ridiculous tripe, but all the men in the room puffed their chests with instinctive protectiveness of their weeping damsel.

"Senator Caffrey, you know I wouldn't disrespect your daughter in such a way," he said. This was the second time he'd been accused of such intentions in this household, and both times he'd simply sought information.

A shined boot gave him a vicious kick to the ribs and Malcolm grunted. He curled into a ball and tucked his head into his arms to protect himself from the punishing blows.

"If you respect her so much, what were you doing alone with her in my office, son?" The senator's voice was all tightly controlled anger, his drawl abbreviated, his consonants overenunciated. "Take him to the cellar."

Malcolm was pulled to his feet. He couldn't feel fear or regret or anger. His mind was completely devoted to working a way out of this situation. As he was pushed through the door, his eyes met Elle's. She was standing pressed back against the wall, taking in the scene.

Her expression was blank, but her dark

eyes burned hot.

My Ellen, he thought. Would she believe Susie, after what she had seen earlier? Would she think him the worst of men? He ripped his gaze away from hers, lest his imprisoners make anything of it. But before he turned, he saw her pantomime clasping at a necklace. Her bullet bounced against his chest beneath his shirt as he walked, reminding him of his words.

You will not be lost to me so easily.

CHAPTER 22

Elle's heart beat out of her chest as she watched Malcolm be hustled past her.

His face was scraped and puffy, and a trickle of blood dripped from a gash over his eyebrow. She thought of how he'd tended her wounds the night before. No one would tend to him now. And if she didn't figure out a way to get him out of this, then there would be nothing to tend to. She'd heard Susie's claims echo through the hall. The punishment for rape could vary, but the punishment for treason was death.

Her body went nerveless at the thought of Malcolm swinging from a rope, all the life and joy and love gone from him.

Susie walked by then, a deviously contented look on her face. She glanced up at Elle from under wet lashes and smiled, chilling her to the bone. What had happened in that office?

The worst part of this predicament was

knowing that Malcolm's involvement with Susie had ultimately been unnecessary. Elle had sat in on a meeting that had not only confirmed her suspicions about the resurrection of the scuttled Union ironclad, but had also given her important information on the ship's date of deployment and specifications. All of this information was stored in her mind and needed to be transmitted to the Union immediately. This was too important for a missive alone: Elle wanted to deliver the message herself, and she wanted Malcolm by her side when she did.

As soon as the group of Susie's rescuers had passed, patting each other on the back for a job well done, Elle was off like a shot. She darted down the back stairs, pushing past bewildered slaves as they tried to figure out why the ball had been called to a sudden halt, throwing their well-organized work into disorder.

She searched the kitchens for Timothy, finding him in a back room with a bag of apples slung over his shoulder.

"Timothy," she whispered urgently. "Malcolm has been captured. He needs to be rescued. Can we contact MacTavish, perhaps see if he has any contacts who can help? I was right about the ironclads. I desperately need to get to Washington, and

I won't leave without him."

Timothy dropped the sack of grain and turned to her, a somber look on his face.

"MacTavish was arrested for public intoxication earlier today," he said, running a hand over his close-cropped hair. "He was wall-papered, hollering in the street like a lunatic, and they locked him up. He won't be out for a day or two."

"No," Elle said, her mind racing. "What are we to do?"

"You have to leave McCall behind, Elle," Timothy said. "Even if MacTavish was free, do you think we'd risk exposing him and the other abolitionists to free McCall? I'm sorry, but this is a war we're fighting. I'll do what I can once you've gone, but we can't risk everything over one man."

She thought of Malcolm seated on his horse, sure to be shot before he could draw his weapon but determined not to desert her nonetheless. Elle had spent her entire life doing for others, pushing aside her feelings as she used her talent to uplift her race, and now her country. But she would not forfeit this.

"I won't leave him," she said bluntly.

"Elle, you're risking everything that the Loyal League stands for to save a man that you barely know," Timothy said, confusion

369

twisting his brow. "What gives you the right?"

"My soul gives me the right," she said softly, not wanting to disappoint him any more than she had but unable to do as he wished. "My heart does, Timothy. And if you think that I can't save my man and get word to Washington both, then you have sorely underestimated me."

Mary walked into the back room then. She stepped protectively toward Elle, as if sensing the tension between them.

"What's going on in here? Li'l Bit, can you come with me?" she asked, eyeing Timothy warily. "I gotta tell you something."

Mary was escaping. The thought had been knocked from her head with all the business that had occurred above floors. She hated to reveal herself as a liar, and to place Mary in danger with this knowledge, but the woman was her last hope. Elle closed her eyes and then faced the friend she hoped would help her.

"I have to tell you something, too, Mary," she said clearly.

Mary's eyes widened, and her cheeks flushed. She took a step toward and then away from Elle, the confusion on her face like a punch in the belly.

"Elle, what are you doing?" Timothy hissed.

"Timothy, you're the one who told me to trust my instincts. Too late to renege on that now."

"You been playing a game with me this whole time?" Mary asked. The tightness from that morning had returned to her face.

"No. I'm sorry I lied, but the truth is I'm here collecting information for the Union government. I couldn't tell anyone that, even if I cared about them. Especially if I cared about them," Elle said.

"Why are you telling me now?" Mary asked hotly. She seemed torn between anger and excitement.

"Because I need your help. One of my partners has been captured." She glanced at Timothy. "If I don't save him, I think he'll hang. I have valuable information that needs to get to the Capital, and quickly. I think you're leaving tonight, and I want to leave with you."

Mary sighed.

"We all got our secrets, huh?" she asked, the anger leaving her voice. "Robert has a plan. I told you he know these rivers like the back of his hand. His latest job has been working a Confederates warship. They rely on him to do everything. He knows the ship better than the captain."

Elle nodded, anticipation building in her chest. If this was heading in the direction she thought it was heading, then the night was about to get even more interesting.

"Robert know all the signals to get the boat past the sentries and out to open sea," she continued in a hushed voice. "He got a small crew. Later tonight they're gonna steal the ship and deliver it to the Union Navy. They're gonna make stops along the river to pick up the crewman's families. I'm the last stop. He's picking me up down by Hangman's Point. Hopefully, the boys manning the blockade won't think our white flag is a trick to get their guard down."

The plan was audacious, ballsy, and so unprecedented that it just might work. And it was the only option Elle had.

"Hats off to your Robert. May I come with you?" she asked. She had known it was very likely that she would have to flee that night, although she had thought she would be doing so by land. Stealing a boat, while extreme, also simplified her plans in some ways. "I'll do anything I can to help, and I have some experience with escaping myself."

She parted her hair to show her freshly stitched wound, ignoring Mary's gasp.

372

"There are two dead slavers who learned last night that I won't be taken easily," she said.

"Lord help me," Mary said, placing a hand over her chest. "And here I thought you was this innocent little thing who needed my help."

Elle smiled. "Innocent isn't the descriptor I'd use, but I do need your help."

Mary fixed her with a stare. "Is this mess with your partner the same mess with that Rebel fella trying to molest our Susie?"

Elle took a deep breath. "He didn't try to molest her."

"How do you know?" Mary asked, all business. "Were you in the room with them? This week I've seen that man sniffing after you something fierce and then courting Miss Susie like she was a hothouse rose in the winter. Not to mention the obvious."

He's white. Elle waited for the words.

"He's a Rebel," Mary said with plain disgust. Elle almost laughed.

"And I'm mute," Elle countered. She could see that Mary was still undecided.

"It's very important for Robert, once he steals the ship, to get it into Union hands, right?"

Mary rolled her eyes at the question with an obvious answer. "Yes."

"Do you think if he got to the Hangman's Point and you weren't there he would just keep going?"

"He's my husband," Mary said. "Of course he wouldn't."

"And do you think if this had happened a week after you met that he would have left you?" Elle asked. Mary opened her mouth to counter and then shut it. Elle pressed her advantage. "You told me once that you just looked at Robert and you knew. You don't have to help me, or to understand, but I'd ask that you afford me the same respect you'd ask for yourself."

Mary laughed and shook her head.

"Now I know why you had to be mute. Smart-mouthed little sassy sue, you is," Mary said. "I'm leaving soon, with Althea and Ben. You're welcome to come, and your man if you can free him in time."

Elle looked at Timothy.

"I still got work to do here," he said. There was no judgment or sadness in his tone; that was just the way it was.

Elle gave him a long, hard hug. He smelled of a mélange of food and spices, and a hard day's sweat, and the scent made her tear up.

"Be careful," she said.

He placed a hand to her head, over where

she had revealed her stitches earlier.

"I know that you got good luck, but I hope you got good sense, too. Be safe, and make sure that man treat you right after you going to all this trouble for him. No more making cow eyes at other females just because he a detective. If I fed my wife that codswallop —"

She gave Timothy a good-natured jab and hugged him once more. "I'll write down everything I heard . . . just in case."

"And I'll send it along once that old drunkard MacTavish is out of jail. But make sure that I'm sending it along for no reason."

She nodded firmly.

"Malcolm is being held in the cellar," she said.

"How you gonna get him out?" Mary asked.

"Damned if I know now, but I will before the clock strikes midnight," Elle said. "I think right now is a good time for a game of dress-up."

Mary gave her a sharp look, not in the mood for non sequiturs.

"Tonight, my fair friend, you shall become a lady," Elle said.

As Elle and Mary tried to move through the kitchen unobserved, one of the slave women stopped them.

"Mary, what we supposed to do 'bout all these people leaving at once? Everything's getting confused, coats are lost, carriages are backed up."

In the midst of chaos, there is also opportunity.

Irritation sparked in Elle: Every second they delayed they were losing the cover this confusion would provide. But the spark was quickly smothered by shame as she took in the woman's weary face, drawn from years of servitude. If all went right, when this woman woke up the next day, Mary, Elle, and Althea would be gone, and she would still be among the enslaved, forced to deal with the loss of Mary's leadership and the fallout from the Caffreys.

Mary pleaded illness as slaves began crowding around seeking direction. It was something she had never done before, and she was then besieged by offers of home remedies and names of root women who could charm her well.

When they could finally get away from the kitchen, they snuck up the back stairs to Susie's closet.

"You're about the same size," Elle whispered as she pulled out a muted brown dress and the matching hat, which had a veil on the front that would partially obscure Mary's face.

"Why do we need that?" Mary asked as Elle thrust the pile of clothing into her hands.

"Because you're the closest thing to a white lady we've got, once you're dressed up in this finery. We're leaving by coach, with the other partygoers. No one will notice us in the traffic."

That's what Elle hoped, but she didn't need to share any doubts just then.

"You don't think we're courting enough danger tonight?" Mary demanded in hushed tones. "We was just gonna creep through the forests."

"The forests are full of drunken soldiers looking for trouble and slavers looking for money. The safest way is by the road, with Ben driving us."

They snuck out behind the house, near the stables but out of sight, where they waited for Althea. Elle had stolen a pot of ink, paper, and quill as they left, and she now sat on a fallen log and assiduously wrote down the most important details that would have to get to Pinkerton and Lincoln if she didn't.

Althea ran up to them, tears tracking down her rounded cheeks.

"Where's Ben?" Mary asked as she began removing her dress. Althea would help her dress, providing the same service Mary had provided to the women of the household for all these years. Althea began to help Mary automatically, although her hands were shaking and she sniffled.

"He . . . he changed his mind at the last minute. He said Master Dix needed him, and it would be wrong of him to leave."

Elle wanted to scream at this fresh evidence of how complex and insidious the institution of slavery was, but their personal situation had just grown much more complicated.

"Who will drive the coach?" Mary asked, turning to Elle. She seemed to enjoy relinquishing her role as commander of the house slaves, finally able to let someone else make the tough decisions.

"First, I have to get this to Timothy, then I have to get Malcolm," she said, although she had no idea where he was or how she would free him. She just knew that she would. Maybe Timothy would help her, Timothy who was only slightly taller than her. . . .

"But that doesn't answer who's going to drive," Mary snapped.

Althea stopped working and stared. "You

can talk?"

Elle carefully folded her letter and turned to face Althea.

"I can," she said, then turned to Mary. "And I will." They both looked over at her with wide eyes. "We have to figure out a meeting spot. And if you smell smoke once you're there, don't run off."

CHAPTER 23

There were only two truths for Malcolm McCall: that the Union must be preserved and that he would love Ellen Burns forever. He was sure she would have chided him for waiting until he had only hours to live to say such a thing, but she would have done it with a pleased smile. He hoped he'd have the chance to tell her, but the fact that he was manacled in Senator Caffrey's cellar didn't bode well for that outcome.

The handcuffs that bound Malcolm's wrists in front of him were much too small, and the chain that traveled from the cuffs to the floor was much too short.

"The former owner used these on his women," the senator had said as he watched one of the soldiers who had hustled Malcolm to the cellar turn the key. "I thought they'd come in handy one day, but I certainly didn't have you in mind."

Malcolm had struggled with the cuffs for

the last half hour, and now sat panting with exertion in the darkness, wrists burning and chain still secured tightly to the ground. His hands were insensate, like two dead fish at the end of his arms.

Malcolm sighed, wincing from the pain in his side where one of the lummoxes had kicked him in the ribs. He prodded it gently with his fingers: not broken, but maybe fractured.

He'd lived a good life, had helped the Union to the best of his abilities, and would die in service to his country, although the story behind his downfall was much less exciting than he'd hoped it would be. He'd been blinded by his own preconceptions of a helpless Southern belle.

He'd initially been buoyed by the look of determination on Elle's face as he passed her in the hall, but now he knew how selfish that had been. He hoped she'd fled in the confusion after his arrest and not looked back. But then he remembered the vicious beauty of her face as she sweetly said, "Maybe we should ambush them." He doubted she'd give him up without a fight, even if only for the Union.

Elle.

He tugged at his cuffs again, the pain flashing hot at his wrists and then diffusing to dull pins and needles when it reached his hands.

He wondered what she had found, and if she'd been right about the ironclad. Dix had been there in those last blurred moments as he was hustled from Senator Caffrey's office, and Elle had been close to the man's side.

The door to the cellar creaked open, the dim lighting of the hallway spilling down the cellar steps. His heart sped up with anticipation. Was it her? Where would they go after they made their escape? Would MacTavish have a safe route for them to get to Washington?

Then a burly silhouette stepped into the doorway, and Malcolm steeled himself. This was not his Elle, but that damned annoying Rufus.

"You know, I've been telling Susie for years that she was attracted to bad apples like flies to shit," Rufus said as he descended the steps with a lantern, his barrel chest puffed out even more than Malcolm thought possible.

Maybe he'll pop if I poke him hard enough, Malcolm thought wryly as Rufus set the lantern down. He suspected Rufus was thinking the same thing about him.

"Quite romantic," Malcolm answered.

"I'm sure she'll go flying into your arms now that I'm out of the way."

Rufus rolled his thick neck, the lantern light dancing in his blue eyes, making them seem molten like the fires of hell. Malcolm had been in many scrapes in his time as a spy, had been arrested before, but hunched over in this dark cellar unable to even stand up straight, he felt a new sense of vulnerability. This man wanted to hurt him and there was nothing he could do but take it. Perhaps the sick acceptance that settled upon him was what Elle had felt during their first encounter.

"I have to admit, McCall, I never took you for a man who would force himself on a woman," Rufus said. "I knew you was an uppity bastard, and a lily-livered, treasonous son of a bitch, but now I have even more reason to dislike you."

"This treason talk is getting tiresome. I'm not nor have I ever been for the North," Malcolm said, keeping his voice calm and friendly. Rufus was circling him, his eyes locked on Malcolm as he unbuttoned his coat and then tossed it aside, windmilling his arms as if testing his range of motion in his fine shirt. Malcolm didn't like that one bit. "I have plenty of friends in Richmond who will attest to that, if you want to bring me before your Vigilance Committee."

"Vigilance Committee?" Rufus laughed low and much too gleefully for Malcolm's liking. "Try the Sons of the Confederacy, boy. Don't act like you don't know what that is. We make good sport rooting out race traitors and Lincoln's lapdogs. I've suspected you for days now, listening to all the claptrap you fed Susie and the senator, and I intend to have fun with you."

Sons of the Confederacy.

Malcolm tried not to show any sign of surprise, but his blood ran cold at Rufus's words. He hadn't suspected the oaf for a second.

Malcolm had heard of the group before; Pinkertons stayed well clear of its members because they had certain predilections in their interrogation techniques. They enjoyed doling out pain, and no detective who found himself captured came out of the situation unbroken — if they managed to survive.

"I don't know if you really tried to hurt Susie," Rufus said, eyes narrowed. "Senator Caffrey can tend to that. I do know that you're a spy. Now I'm gonna hurt you and you're gonna tell me what I need to know."

In two long strides, the man had reached Malcolm and without further preamble punched him hard in the stomach. He'd known Rufus had the brute strength of a pie-fed boy, but now he felt it in his rattling ribcage. Malcolm had managed to twist away from the blow a little, but it had still knocked the wind out of him, leaving him short of breath.

"Are there any other detectives working with you here?" Rufus asked.

Malcolm's eyes were still squeezed shut, so he knew that he gave nothing away about Elle and Timothy. "I don't know what you're talking about."

Rufus clasped his hands together and raised them over his head before delivering a punishing blow to Malcolm's hunched back, sending him sprawling on the floor. He kicked out at Rufus as he fell, but the man dodged the kick and then ran in and delivered one of his own.

Malcolm drew in a sharp breath as he heard the crack in his side.

Definitely broken now.

"I ask again: Are you working with any other detectives?"

"Go to hell, Rufus. Maybe you'll find the answer you want there. Mine is still 'I don't know what you're talking about.' "

Malcolm rolled to his side and was pulled short by the chain, barely escaping a full blow to the face as Rufus swung his foot and stomped the place where Malcolm's head had just rested. The man was vicious, and if he found Elle . . .

Anger boiled up in Malcolm. He pulled his feet up under him and launched himself forward headfirst, catching Rufus right in a soft belly that had been unprepared for a blow. Rufus stumbled back and fell to his knees, arms clutched around his torso as he glared at Malcolm from across the cellar.

He struggled to his feet and Malcolm tried to gauge his attack so he could counter it, however feebly, when the sudden commotion of shouts and clattering filtered down the stairs, along with the distinct smell of smoke.

"The house is on fire!" someone shouted as they rushed past the door.

Rufus smiled then, his teeth bared and an expression of dumb superiority on his face.

"You know, I am plum tired after tonight's festivities," he said. "Since you claim you don't know nothing, I guess I have no use for you. I'll go check on the fire, though. And if anyone remembers there's a Yank in the cellar chained to the floor, it won't be me."

With that he grabbed his jacket and headed up the stairs. He shut the door behind him, leaving his flickering lantern behind, as if Malcolm would need light if the fire made its way to the cellar.

Malcolm had been in many a close call before, but the fear that gripped him now was a new specimen. Being killed by another man was one thing, and slowly roasting while chained to the floor was another. He was going to die, and painfully. He wouldn't see the end of the war. He wouldn't see Elle's beautiful face again.

No.

He gripped the chain as best he could with his nerveless hands, levered his weight at his knees, and began pulling again, using his own heft to try to dislodge the chain from the ground. His muscles strained and he felt the veins standing out on his forehead as he pushed himself to the limit.

It was futile.

The door opened again and smoke billowed into the cellar.

"Forget your lantern?" Malcolm growled, tensed for another attack.

"I'm here for nothing so useful as a lantern." Elle's low voice wrapped around him, and he knew what true elation was. "Just an idiot Scotsman who tried to plow a senator's daughter."

Her small form hurried down the steps, eyes bright, brow creased. She was dressed as a man again, in clothes that were slightly too large for her and a hat that was slightly too small. He didn't ask any questions — he was busy trying to regulate his sheer happiness at seeing her before him.

"Of course there would have to be a con-sarned lock," she snarled.

Malcolm looked on dumbfounded as she lifted the hat and shoved a hand into her thick hair. She pulled out two hairpins and then dropped to her knees before him.

"I didn't try to plow Susie. I'm sorry about the kiss —"

"You can grovel later," she said. "Hold out your hands."

She stuck the hairpins between her teeth, first flattening them and then bending up the end of one at a ninety-degree angle.

He held out his hands and she briskly set to work picking the lock. He could sense the tension in her body as she moved one hairpin back and forth through the lock, stopping occasionally.

"Where did you learn to pick locks?" he asked when he saw her screw up her face in frustration.

"Blacksmith had to come open an old lock on a door when we first moved up North, explained what he was doing as he worked and let me try it." Her reply was brisk and efficient, matching the way she worked the hairpins back and forth in the lock. Her teeth sank into her plump lower lip as she worked, and if the power of concentration had been tangible the lock would have already crumbled to dust.

God, she was magnificent when she was all business.

"I love you," he blurted out.

"Hush! I'm trying to hear the pin fall," she snapped, pressing her ear closer to the lock. She slowed her movements down even more, then with a quick flick of her wrist the shackles opened and blood coursed painfully into his hands.

She closed her eyes briefly, in relief or prayer or both, and looked up at him with glossy eyes.

"It seems, against all common sense, that I love you, too," she said. Then Malcolm's heart hurt along with the rest of him, but from overabundance. He tried to grab at her shoulders and pull her to him, but his hands weren't completely mobile and his fingers would not obey.

Instead, Elle stood and grabbed his hands, rubbing circulation into them as she pulled him toward the stairs, glancing up at the cracked door.

"Are you ready to make a daring escape,

Mr. Detective?" she asked as they climbed the steps. She turned, and because she was ahead of him they were at an even height.

"I'm at your command, Earl," he said. "All I ask for is one kiss."

He needed to touch her, to feel her mouth against his.

"You've already had a kiss tonight," she said stiffly, beginning to turn away from him. He reached for her, his hand just strong enough to maintain a grip on her arm, and pulled her back gently. Even that slight exertion sent an explosion of pain through his torso, but he wouldn't be deterred.

"That wasn't a kiss," he said. "*This* is a kiss."

His mouth slanted over hers, lips pressing firmly against hers, which were sealed tight against him. He licked at her hungrily and she opened for him on a sigh, her hand reaching up to cradle his bruised face as she met his ravenous demands. Her tongue danced with his gently, soothing him, as if she were afraid she would hurt him if she returned his ardor.

Emotion filled him for a moment, nearly overwhelmed him, and she pulled away quickly, eyes shining as if she had been affected in the same way.

"Forward march, soldier," she said, her voice a little shaky as she turned and tramped up the steps.

She paused at the door; then they both passed through into pandemonium.

CHAPTER 24

Elle's heart was thudding in her chest: Everything was happening so quickly and not quickly enough. Many of the guests had been in the process of leaving, but luckily a good number of them had stayed behind to gossip about the unsavory events of the night or in search of misplaced belongings. Elle was sure Malcolm's name would be plastered all over the scandal sheets Susie so adored reading.

They stepped into a small closet as they heard the thud of heavy footsteps approaching.

"Did Susie plan all this?" she asked. "Is she a detective for the Rebs?"

"Rufus is a spy for the Confederates," he said. "Susie is another thing entirely. She'd make a damn fine detective, though, if she could think of anything other than herself. Where are we going now?"

"I'm driving us out of here," she said,

creeping from the alcove once the coast was clear. She didn't have time to explain everything to him. They needed to escape while there was still a clamor to stop the fires.

They crept stealthily along the back hallways, empty now that everyone had run to the front to fight the flames. Soon they were out in the brisk night air, running for the stable. Elle knew that Malcolm was bristling with questions, but Mary could answer once they got to the coach.

Elle pulled the door open and commanded Malcolm into the open top cab. Both Mary and Althea jumped, recoiling from the large bloody man in a Confederate uniform.

"Here we are," Elle said briskly. "Malcolm, get on the floor and get under Mary's skirts."

"What? No!" Mary balked. "Is that why you chose this big old gown? I should of known . . ."

Elle blew out a frustrated breath. "There are several layers of fabric under your skirt. I'll let you choose which he goes under. Whatever the selection, your modesty is protected and we won't be caught."

"Elle, I'm here doing you a favor and you gonna send some white man under my skirt? Robert is gonna kill me."

"You're not doing me a favor, you're helping the Union. And what Robert doesn't know won't hurt him."

She slammed the door shut just as Malcolm asked, "Who's Robert?"

"My husband, who's saving your backside tonight and will strangle you if you try anything funny down there," Mary replied.

"I do believe Elle would beat him to the punch," Malcolm said, then groaned. "Besides, after the night I've had, I'm too exhausted to get up to much down here."

Elle climbed up onto the box and took the reins in hand. Behind her, she heard Mary giving Malcolm a summary of the plan they were undertaking. She hoped it was less impossible than it sounded.

"Come on, girl," she prodded. The horse whinnied and they began a slow trot toward the lane, away from where the crowds were clustered around the fire. The back road would be a more circuitous route, but it was safer than taking the main road, which would be even busier with people coming to put out the fire. As soon as the horse and coach pulled off of the rough track and onto the road, Elle's heart began to beat a little easier. She tried not to think ahead, or to think of the boat that would come down the river and carry them away. For now she could only think in the moment if she was to get them there safely. She had no weapon but her wit, and she hoped that was enough.

"Hold!" a voice rang out from behind them. "Hold there, boy!"

Her heart sank. She slowed the horse to a stop as a soldier on horseback galloped toward them.

"Where you going in the middle of this madness?" the soldier asked suspiciously.

"Mistress need to go home real bad," she said, jerking her head in the direction of the carriage behind her. "She was all a tizzy when that fella got arrested, and then the fire started up and she passed clean out. Her girl had to use the smelling salts on her."

The soldier glimpsed into the carriage, and Elle imagined that Mary and Althea were doing some very convincing acting because he nodded his approval.

"Careful now. This might be the spearhead of some Yankee attack on the city," he cautioned, as if they were comrades in the war. "Get your mistress home safe, boy."

"I will, sah," Elle said, already urging the horse forward. She visualized the map of Richmond as they moved forward at a cantor, recalling which roads would get them to Hangman's Point the quickest and with the least trouble.

They were moving quickly away from the mansion and down the tree-lined roads beyond when Elle heard an uproar behind them.

"Tarnation," she muttered under her breath and urged the horse on faster, the heavy carriage clattering noisily along behind her.

Maybe they haven't noticed, maybe they haven't noticed, she repeated, although she already knew what the clamor was about.

From far behind them, she heard the man's voice again.

"Halt!"

There was something in the tone of the command that made Elle's stomach flip. This would be no innocuous inquiry. If she stopped, that would be the end of them — she could feel it. Elle prodded the horse forward, lightly smacking at its flanks with the driving whip to push it faster.

"Sorry," she muttered as the horse obediently picked up speed, breaking out into a gallop. She knew that a horse pulling a carriage and four people was no match for lone riders, but she urged the horse onward, trying to gain some distance.

"Elle!" Malcolm's voice rang out from behind her. "Pull the carriage to a stop, quickly!"

Her first inclination was to ignore him, but she knew he must have a reason behind what she thought was madness, so she pulled the horse to a stop. The carriage door immediately opened, and all three inhabitants spilled out. Malcolm ran to her, pulled her from her seat, and grabbed the whip from her hand, smacking the horse.

"Yah!" The horse stood confused for a moment at its loose reins and then took off down the road, turning a bend and leaving them behind. Mary and Althea were already hustling into the cover of the trees, and Malcolm pulled Elle along after them.

Just as they were completely hidden in the shadows of the trees, a cadre of men on horses thundered by them. They passed in a loud blur of hoofbeats and dust; then only the silence of the forest surrounded them.

"It's over. We'll never make it now," Althea whispered in a voice thick with fear. "Ben said this would happen. I should have stayed with him."

"You can go back now and let me know how that goes, but I have an appointment with a steam-powered ship ready to carry me to the Promised Land," Mary said. "We got two legs, just like that horse had four, and we can get ourselves there."

She lifted the heavy skirts of her dress and began tramping through the woods. Elle felt a pang of guilt now, wishing she'd chosen something lighter.

Making their way through the thick underbrush in the dark woods was harder than Elle had imagined. They tried to move silently, but Althea and Mary were hampered by their skirts, which kept getting stuck in brambles, and Malcolm's injuries made stealth impossible. When fear or doubt crept in, Elle thought of the tired people who'd arrived at the back door of her parents' home. If they could travel, and much farther, without complaint, so could she.

"We're getting close," Mary said over her shoulder. They hadn't been walking for a very long time, but if the carriage trick had worked out, then they would have been waiting at Hangman's Point for a substantial amount of time already. She wondered if she could have found another way to get them there safely, whether she had compromised Mary's escape and Robert's plan by drawing them into her subterfuge.

Elle sighed and Malcolm took her hand. She looked up at him to find him smiling at her. Warmth flooded her, buffering her from the sharp edges of fear and doubt.

"What?" she whispered.

"I'm the one who's supposed to inspire tales of derring-do, but so far you've managed to out-adventure me at every turn. Escaping slavers, setting Confederate mansions alight, escaping via stolen river boats. Not to mention saving me from a sure death."

Elle felt sick at the thought of what had left him so beaten, and what would have happened if she hadn't set that fire and freed him.

"You saved me, too," she said.

"I always will," he said, bringing her knuckles to his lips to dust them with a kiss.

"*We* always will," she emphasized. "We bring out the best in each other. I've waited a lifetime to find someone who didn't define me by my talent or try to censor me when I said things they didn't find pleasing."

"As long as you promise not to recall every argument we have for the next fifty years, both your talent and your smart mouth are fine by me."

Fifty years? Would she really be allowed that? She looked away from him, unable to process being so happy in the middle of such a fraught situation.

"Well, let's wait until we're actually on the boat until you congratulate me on my adventuring," she said.

Up ahead, the trees were starting to thin, and more moonlight filtered through the bare branches and the last clinging leaves of the deciduous trees. Mary turned around and in the light Elle could see the woman's eyes focus on Malcolm's hand holding hers. She fought the instinct to pull her hand away, to explain that she loved him and he loved her.

Instead, she gripped his hand tighter.

"We're here," was all Mary said. "No sign of the boat yet."

"You told me your husband was a river pilot, but not how he came to work on this warship he's stealing," Malcolm said as they all tramped down to the river bank. A small rowboat waited there, and he began inspecting its soundness.

"How most black folk come to it: Some white man was too lazy to do the work he was hired for, so one of us got to do it for him," Mary said.

Malcolm paused his inspection for a moment and then shrugged.

"Can't argue with that," he said. "Did he tell you whether we should be waiting on the banks or row out and wait for him?"

"Well, he said that we shouldn't row out before we saw him because we might get sighted by another boat. That, and the currents are strong."

"Well, I'm going to push the boat out a bit and you all should get in. That way we can shove off as soon as we catch sight of the boat."

Malcolm dug his feet into the rocky shore and pushed at the boat, steadying it before helping Mary and Althea climb in.

"Ladies first," he remarked with a censuring look at Elle's trousers, and she nearly laughed. They were so close to escaping, and he was so close to her. A sense of giddiness filled her.

Then she heard a familiar sound behind her — the metallic scrape of a cocking gun — and the gratitude drained out from her.

"Fancy meeting you again," Malcolm said cheerfully as Elle turned. There, standing with his gun trained on them, was the slaver they had left in the road the night before.

CHAPTER 25

Malcolm could see that Elle was regretting two things: that she'd shown the slaver mercy and that she didn't have her gun. Her hand patted at her thigh. Her knife was likely sheathed beneath the trousers, unreachable. He was keenly regretting the loss of his sidearm as well.

The man startled as he recognized Malcolm and Elle and then trained his gun on them. "You know they have a saying for moments like this: 'What goes around comes around.' "

He looked pleased with himself, and Malcolm hoped that this would be one of the only times in his and Elle's relationship that a difference of opinion actually came to anything.

"Yes, they do have that saying," Malcolm said carefully. "But you're misapplying it here tonight. It was far more useful yesterday. I think getting killed while trying to take a person and enslave them is the exact embodiment of that phrase."

"Them boys you killed was my friends," the man said angrily. "One of them got a wife and a baby and needed the money."

"You think those black folks you're snatching don't have families?" Elle asked from behind him, her voice low and furious. "You think I *want* to have some man's blood on my hands? I have to live with the sin of killing that man because you were too lazy to make money the honest way. Instead, you decided to steal someone else's hard work. Forgive me if I don't pity you."

Malcolm casually took a few steps to the side, coming between Elle and the man, who sputtered at the challenge to his choice of vocation.

"This is just the way it is," the man said defensively. "Whites on top, darkies below. I didn't make things the way they are. And neither did Jeb or Wesley, and they dead now!"

Malcolm gazed at the man, using the logic of a child to reason on things that affected the lives of so many.

"So, if a law passed today that said rich men could snatch you off the road and force you to work for them because you're naturally beneath them, you would go willingly?"

he asked.

"Hell no," the man bit out. Malcolm stared at the man and waited for understanding of his hypocrisy to dawn on him. When a long moment had passed, Malcolm had to accept that there would be none forthcoming. This man saw himself as a person whose life held value, and for him, Elle's, Mary's, and Althea's lives did not. He probably couldn't even fathom in his wildest imaginations that their lives could have purpose beyond enslavement. It was time for a different tack.

"How much money do you think you're going to get out of this?" Malcolm asked.

"If I take them back to the senator, a few bucks. If I sell 'em myself, maybe nine hundred each for the darkies, probably more because they're all still breedable —" The man was cut off from an impatient sound in Malcolm's throat.

"No, the actual answer is zero. You're not going to get anything for these women because the senator's men would find you before you got anywhere and kill you for theft. And you're right, they'd only give you a paltry amount for returning them safely. But if you let us go, I'll give you enough money that you won't skulk along these roads preying on innocents."

Elle placed a hand on his back, censuring him.

"You got the money on you now?" the man asked, a hopeful gleam in his eyes.

"No, my belongings were taken when I was captured, but you have my word. I'm a very rich man, a rich man who wants to live. I'll have the money sent to you as soon as I make my way home."

He said the words as if they were of no consequence, but he knew it was a gamble — one that a man accustomed to getting his way or paying for it might make.

"You expect me to trust you?" the man asked, incredulous.

"Do you think the senator and his men would be more concerned with paying some poor cracker than I am? If so, you're sorely mistaken. In fact, if you bring me in to him, there's no stopping me from saying that you helped me escape."

"Why would I do that?" the man asked, taking a step back. "No one would believe a traitor like you."

"That's where you're wrong," Malcolm said, gentling his tone, making sure that he seemed like he was on the man's side. "They think we're like rats: Where you find one, there's sure to be more. And they always want to know who the others are, however unlikely the suspect. Killing a man or two besides me will really make them feel like they've got the job done right."

The man was clutching his rifle now, looking all around as if to see whether anyone had overheard the conversation.

"How much would you give me," he asked, eyes darting this way and that.

Gotcha, Malcolm thought viciously. Behind him, he could hear the stillness of the night being broken by the baritone hum of a steamship's engine. Mary's husband was approaching. They were so close to pulling this off.

"Get in the boat, Elle," he said in a low voice without turning, and continued bargaining with the man. "A thousand."

He'd been tempted to name some exorbitant amount, but that would have ringed false. Rich people didn't get that way by spending more than they had to.

"That's nothing compared to what I could get!" the man spat, tensing as if ready to spring upon Malcolm.

"One thousand and your life is an excellent bargain, I reckon. A dead man doesn't need money."

He felt the boat move behind him, heard the splash as the water accommodated the boat's new weight.

"How will I get the money?" the man asked, lowering his gun a little.

"Go to the Richmond Central bank in five days' time and ask for a wire transfer from your Uncle Walter Scott to . . . What's your name, son?"

Waves began lapping at Malcolm's boots, and the sound of the steamer was almost upon them. He began to exert some force on the dinghy with his back, pushing it slowly into the water.

"Daniel. Daniel Dumont Kingsley."

From behind them came the low, urgent shouts of the crew members of the ship, beckoning them. Malcolm didn't turn, but he saw Daniel's face go white in the moonlight. He lowered his gun and openly stared past Malcolm. The warship must have been quite a sight.

He gave the boat one final shove and hopped into it.

"Farewell, Mr. Kingsley! Your just reward shall arrive soon," he called as he settled into the middle bench and began to row.

Mary and Althea stared blankly at him, as if he were some kind of maniac. Elle gave him a fierce smile.

"The legendary Mr. McCall," she said in a low voice that warmed him from the inside out.

Then the current gripped the boat, threatening to suck them out and away from the ship that waited for them. Malcolm could spare no thought for Elle or anyone else then. It was just the burn of his shoulders and palms, and the sickening pinch of his injured ribs, as he fought the fierce strength of the water. The men on the boat urged him on from behind, giving direction when he seemed to drift off course, and finally they called, "Hold." He could feel the bulk of the ship behind him without seeing it.

A rope ladder was slung down, and he passed over Althea and then Mary to climb up the ladder in their unwieldy skirts.

"We did it," Elle murmured against his lips, slipping him a quick kiss as he bolstered her onto the ladder. He smiled, but that was when he heard the crack of the gunshot and the splash in the water next to the boat.

"I knew you didn't burn, traitor!" Rufus's angry voice rang out in the still night. And then there was another crack and another splash dangerously close to Elle.

He leapt up to where she struggled on the ladder, his hands a couple of rungs above hers and his feet a couple below. Every injury he'd accumulated cried out against the motion, but he'd accomplished his goal. His body blocked hers completely.

"Malcolm," her voice was edged with panic.

"Don't worry, lass, just climb," he said gently. "Everything will be okay. They're too far away."

This was belied by the bullet that flew past them and lodged in the hull of the boat. From above them, the rapport of rifles signaled that the men on the ship were returning fire.

"Just keep climbing. Think about all the things we have to look forward to. A long sleep in a comfortable bed after we get to Washington. A real meal together, perhaps even with utensils enough for two."

He kept on babbling as they climbed, distracting her and himself from the danger that surrounded them. The volleys stopped as they reached the ship's rail, coming into full sight of the crew of five or six men who had been giving them cover fire as they climbed.

"Thank you," he said to the men as Elle climbed up from beneath him. They looked at him suspiciously, but Mary had already explained his presence, so they moved to resume their positions.

Elle turned and gave him a bright, victorious smile. All of the night's trials faded away at the sight of her waiting for him with admiration in her eyes.

"Come on, then," she said, holding out her hands to help him aboard, and that's when he felt it. That pull, that shift, that . . . *gotcha.*

Malcolm threw up a hand to her, adrenaline and love and hope propelling him up the ladder faster than fear had. He almost ignored the motion in his peripheral vision, but instinct wouldn't allow him.

"Reb on board!" shouted a man who was emerging from belowdecks.

The look in his eyes was wild panic, and Malcolm knew then that it was too late.

Althea and Mary both screamed out their warning in unison, but the man was a quick draw. He pulled his weapon and shot, just as Malcolm threw his leg over the railing. Pain suddenly radiated in his chest, hurting even more when he saw the Elle's smile morph into a grimace of horror. He was already falling over backward, hands groping for purchase in the air, eyes on Elle the whole time. She reached out for him, and for a second he thought she had him. Then the thread of the crude necklace that she'd been holding him by snapped. Her wail began to ring out, but the wind ripped the sound from his ears as he fell into the grasping waves of the icy river.

CHAPTER 26

Malcolm was already battered, but he hit the water hard and the rushing currents made his earlier pummeling seem like a gentle caress. The icy water churned about him, pushing him down toward the bottom of the river.

NO!

He surged against the pressure of the water, fighting toward the surface, but as he propelled himself against the punishing power of the river, he realized that he didn't truly know which way was up. His mouth filled with briny liquid and he squinted against the inky darkness.

Is that the boat above?

He moved to churn toward what could have been the moon or a figment of his imagination, but got swept into a powerful current. It ripped at his clothing and sucked at his boots, spinning him about and disorienting him even more.

His chest began to ache from holding his breath, and he gasped against his will, taking in a lungful of water. Panic seized him and he thrashed about wildly, searching for anything that could give him a sign of which way to go.

There was nothing. Nothing but the black waters pressing in on him, seeking entrance at his mouth and nose.

The darkness was beginning to become a tangible thing, wrapping around him like a swaddling blanket and calming his panic as the water claimed him as its own. The sound of the boat chugging on, away from him, vibrated through that darkness. It was leaving him behind. Elle was leaving him behind.

Elle. ELLE.

She was suddenly there before him, looking down at him with those eyes that had grabbed him right from the start.

"You promised," she said sadly, reaching for him.

Something hard smacked into his chest then, river debris churned up by the boat's wake, perhaps. Malcolm couldn't begin to conjecture what it was. His body had given out — his mind was blank as the siren's call of the darkness overtook him at last.

CHAPTER 27

Elle stood rooted to the deck, the bullet hard in her palm and the black thread that held it whipping in the wind. It took her a moment to realize that the ugly sound that rose above the roar of the engine was coming from her. Timothy's hat had fallen off and her hair swirled around her face, batting at her as if trying to wake her from this nightmare.

They had made it onto the ship. Malcolm had been with her, smiling with victory, and now he wasn't. Blood had bloomed on the chest of his shirt; then he had fallen away from her into the darkness.

"I can't swim," she said in a voice that was too loud. "Who can swim? Someone has to help him —"

"We don't have time for that," one of the men said, avoiding her gaze.

She rounded on the man who had shot him, whose mouth hung open with shock as he began to understand what he had done.

Elle grabbed him by the collar of his shirt. "You. You have to go get him. It's your fault!"

But the man was already shaking his head sadly.

"I can't swim either, miss," he said, his hands covering hers, perhaps to provide comfort but more likely to stop her from throttling him. "I'm sorry, I thought he was trying to stop us. My wife and kids is down below. I thought —"

Elle collapsed to her knees, her body shaking and her eyes burning. She wanted to cry, but no tears would come. She remembered what she'd told him only the night before.

I never cried this much before I met you. She now knew it was because she hadn't understood that a person could feel so much, so strongly, before. Now she thought she'd never feel anything again.

She felt arms go around her, and she was pulled onto a pile of fabric, cradled by homespun.

"It'll be okay, Elle," Althea soothed as she ran a hand over Elle's hair as she settled her in her lap. Each drag of Althea's hand tugged painfully at the stitches, but Elle welcomed the sensation because it offset the icy coldness that was enveloping her.

Feet ran around her as the crew continued to do their job. There were still obstacles in their path and men at their heels, and who knew if the Union would accept their surrender or take it as a trick and fire on them.

Malcolm would have said something to make everyone laugh as they headed into the unknown. Instead he was down in that freezing water, cold and pale. She would never hear his laugh again, or feel his lips against hers.

"Oh, help me," she whispered raggedly. "Lord, help me."

She felt as if she were being squeezed in a vise, with no place for the excess to go. She gripped the bullet in her hand tightly and stared at the starry sky.

A heavy tread approached and then a pair of brawny legs in tan trousers blocked her view.

"Is this her, Mary?" a baritone voice asked.

"Yes, Robert." Mary's voice quavered and Elle knew that her friend fought tears.

The legs bent and Elle was face-to-face with a handsome dark-skinned man. He was young, but there was an intensity in his eyes that gave him an air of command. You felt compelled to give him your attention, and your respect.

Elle stared at him.

Help me.

"I'm sorry for your loss," he said, and she could tell that he wasn't just saying it to make her feel better. "I understand that even though that fella wore gray, he was on our side and helped my wife to get here safely. I owe him a debt of gratitude for that alone. But there are several men on this ship, and their families. I promised them I would get them out, and if I stopped to search for him I would be breaking that promise. Do you understand?"

She had said to Malcolm herself that there were more important things than just the two of them. It had been much easier to say than to put into practice.

Elle gave a jerky nod, although his words tore her in two. He mirrored her movement.

"Now, maybe —" he began, then shook his head. "Never mind. Just rest here and try to be strong, okay?"

He stood, and when he turned he held Mary close and hard, and she knew what he was thinking.

Thank God it wasn't you who was lost.

Elle closed her eyes against the couple, but that didn't stop the hot tears. She couldn't fathom that Malcolm was gone.

That she'd never hear his voice, laugh at his silliness, or burn from his touch. Grief lodged in her chest and made itself comfortable there. A quote from Dickens jumped to the forefront of her mind, terrible in the future it foreshadowed: *"The broken heart. You think you will die, but you just keep living, day after day after terrible day."*

Things were relatively quiet for some time. Elle wasn't sure if she was processing time correctly, if hours had passed or minutes. The ship slowed at one point and there was the sound of action belowdecks, but Elle could do nothing but squeeze her lips together and her eyes shut. It probably meant they were approaching the final checkpoint. Robert would provide the signal, and hopefully they would pass through to freedom or be sunk. She knew she should care more about the outcome of their journey, but she didn't have it in her. She heard the sound of soft footsteps and then Mary was beside her again, cocooning her in the warmth of an additional skirt.

"She sleeping?" she asked.

Elle felt Althea nod.

"Lord, what a night. It's all in God's hands now," Mary said, just before the sound of a canon boomed over the river.

"They're firing on us! Come get belowdecks, with the other women and children!" one of the men shouted. It was then that Elle realized that Althea was shivering with cold and that the two women were only there because of her.

She stirred and slowly got to her feet.

"You heard him," she said, making no move to follow. "You two go on."

"Li'l Bit —"

"Mary, I cannot lose anyone else tonight, please go." One of the men tugged Mary and Althea away.

The ship was going at top speed now, charging for the blockade with their white flag raised. She wanted to see this, needed to see what Malcolm couldn't.

There was movement on the Union warships, the men preparing for a fight as the Confederate ship drew closer.

Please let them believe us, she willed. *After taking Malcolm, at least give me this!*

The soldiers' features came into view, faces pale above their Union blues. They took aim but didn't fire.

Robert strode by her and moved to the prow of the ship, his deep voice booming.

"My name is Robert Grand, and I have commandeered this Confederate warship and its load of ammunition in the name of the Union. I and the other Negroes on this ship declare our freedom. We come not as contraband, but as soldiers: We wish to fight to preserve the Union, and to gain our Freedom. Please alert your captain and have him parlay with me, immediately."

These Union soldiers were astounded at seeing a black man float up to them on a stolen Union ship shouting orders, but they were not immune to the command in his voice.

"We also have classified information that needs to be directed to President Lincoln, immediately," Elle shouted in a hoarse voice. She had pulled herself to her feet and came to stand beside Robert. She still had a job to do, dammit. The Confederacy wouldn't wait for her heartache to ease.

Robert turned to look at her, a peculiar smile on his face.

"And we need a medic, posthaste," he shouted. "We have a wounded agent of the Union government on board."

Elle's head whipped in his direction.

"I know this river and I know these currents," Robert said simply. "I knew where a body would wash up, if anywhere. . . . I almost mentioned it when I spoke to you, but I didn't want to get your hopes up. Then we passed where he should have been, and I saw nothing. He wasn't there."

"Why are you telling me this?" she asked, fighting against the hope that surged in her chest. No, she wouldn't allow it. She couldn't allow for such an emotion, but Robert smiled more widely now.

"When we stole this boat, we didn't exactly have time to untie all the moorings, and several wooden posts were ripped from the dock. They trailed behind us, but not creating much drag, so we left them. Just before we passed the final guard ship, I spotted him floating alongside the ship. I don't know if he wrapped himself in the rope or got caught up in it by providence, but there he was. A couple of men fished him out, thinking he was about dead, but he's made of sterner stuff than that. Seems he decided there was something worth living for, and I doubt it's the Union."

Elle said nothing. She truly knew what it was to be mute in that moment. All of her faculties left her but the rudimentary coordination that would allow her to put one foot in front of another. She turned and made her way belowdecks.

The man who had shot Malcolm smiled and pointed her toward a cabin, and when she stepped through the door another man was cleaning the gunshot wound in Malcolm's shoulder. He'd been stripped and lay shivering beneath a pile of rough blankets and jackets.

"He's awake now, after we forced some rot gut down his throat. Bullet went clean through," the man said gruffly. "I s'pose a doctor can tell you whether he'll live or die, but I got a feeling this fella ain't the type to go down without a fight."

He ripped a strip of linen shirt and pressed it to stanch the bleeding.

"You wanna hold this? I'm gonna go check in with Captain Grand," he said, standing from his stool. Elle nodded and rushed to replace him. Her fingers shook as she held the cloth, but she pressed as hard as she could.

Malcolm's blue-gray eyes met hers, now shockingly large in his pale, drawn face.

"I . . . I p-promised I wouldn't leave you," he said through chattering teeth.

Elle raised a hand to his wet hair, a million riotous feelings fighting for supremacy.

"I remember," she said softly. "I'm glad to find that you're quite serious about keeping your word."

Hot tears streaked down her face then, and the ice that had encased her heart begin to thaw.

Malcolm gave a shuddering laugh and the sound nearly broke what little composure she had left. "So, if I tell you that I plan to love and honor you forever, no matter the hardship, would you finally believe me?"

Malcolm was growing blurry in her vision, because the tears wouldn't stop falling.

"I would," she said.

"You think the captain will marry us?" he asked blearily. "The law won't recognize it, but Mary's husband can sanctify our union."

Elle wished the doctor would arrive. Her heart was full to bursting, but she wouldn't feel any comfort until Malcolm was attended to.

"You've lost a lot of blood and been in freezing water for an extended period of time," she said. "This talk can wait."

He raised a dark brow at her, and Elle was gripped by just how pale he was.

"The cold sharpens a man's wits," he said. "I want us to get married and have wee bairns, and I can chase you around the kitchen as you cook."

Elle flooded with warmth.

"You must be delirious. Who says I'm going to be the one doing the cooking?" she asked archly. Just then a man decked out in Union blues stuck his head into the door, his eyes widening at the scene before him.

"I'm the doctor. I can take over from here,

girl," he said stiffly as he entered. He looked at her trousers and wild hair with a grimace.

"Wife," Malcolm interjected. "She's my wife, and she'll stay."

The words filled her with a warmth that was more than gratitude for the sound of Malcolm's voice.

The doctor looked even more baffled, but Elle moved out of his way and he began his examination without further discussion. She held Malcolm's hand as he was patched up, wincing for him when the doctor prodded his ribs and cleaned his contusions.

"Well, you've taken quite a beating, but you'll live," he said as he stood and collected his bag.

The doctor's words, flippant as they were, etched into her mind, her newest and most cherished memory. Elle looked down into Malcolm's eyes. They were bloodshot from the last of many deaths he had escaped that night, but to her they were beautiful.

"Malcolm, if you want me to marry you, I must insist that you leave off being abducted by hooligans, shot, and half-drowned."

"I'm not so good at fractions, but I'm fairly certain I was three-quarters drowned at the very least, Miss Elle." He lifted his head to kiss her hand, which rested on his chest. "I'll try to keep things simple, but

423

you know very well I have a taste for the dramatic."

"I suppose there is a price to be paid for all good things," she said.

The clomping of boots echoed in the tight hallway of the ship, funneling into the room just before Robert and two other men entered.

"And here are the Union operatives of whom I spoke," he said, gesturing to the two like it wasn't bizarre at all for Elle to be nearly sitting on Malcolm. "I'm sure that the information they have is sensitive, so I'll leave you to it."

Two youngish-looking Union officers stepped into the small room as Robert turned to walk back out.

"Wait!" Malcolm forced himself up to his elbows. "Captain, can you do us the honor of marrying us before you go?"

Elle's heart beat wildly in her chest and she dropped his hand. "You mean for us to be married *now*?" she asked. "You're not even wearing pants for God's sake."

"Well, yes," he said, and gave her that impish grin of his. "I'm hoping that I'm never this low again, so I'd best make use of the pity you're feeling for me right now before you go back to merely tolerating me."

Elle rolled her eyes.

Robert regarded the two of them with a surprisingly gregarious smile. "I'm not quite sure I'm vested with powers that will be recognized anywhere outside of this ship, but if these men are willing to wait . . ."

The two Union men nodded, their expressions stuck halfway between amusement and confusion.

Robert drew himself up and was back to his commanding role of captain. He looked at both of them very seriously and for such a long time that Elle nearly quailed. "You all are married."

Malcolm looked at Elle, then back at Robert. "Is that it?"

"Yes. It doesn't feel any different, does it? That comes with time," he said. "Oh! I did forget something. Kiss the bride."

With that proclamation, Malcolm reached for Elle with shaking hands. She met him halfway and leaned in for his kiss. It was weak, and he smelled of river and whiskey, but it was the best kiss Elle had ever received.

"I wish I could offer you something better," he said, and Elle gave him a gentle nudge.

"If there's something better in this world than an aggravating, too charming for his own good Scottish detective, I have not come across it in all my studies," she said, and was happy to see a bit of color rise to his pale cheeks.

The embarrassed cough of one of the Union men reminded them that they weren't alone. Elle looked up at them, then stood from the bed and shook each man's hand before he could recover from the strange scene.

Robert slipped out to handle the turnover of the ship, and the men sat down on stools, eyes locked on Elle.

"Let me tell you a little story about a big boat," she began . . .

EPILOGUE

"And that's how he convinced every woman in my knitting circle to give him a sweet and ended up sick as a dog. Little did I know that his scheming ways would be of use to our country someday."

Malcolm's mother sat across from Elle in the warm, cozy parlor of her sprawling Kentucky home. A fire crackled in the hearth and for the first time since she'd arrived, Elle felt completely comfortable.

Mrs. McCall hadn't hidden her surprise when Malcolm showed up at the front door, wounded and wan and presenting a black woman as her new daughter-in-law. There had been several awkward encounters, despite the woman's unusual open-mindedness. Things weren't perfect, but the fact that his mother was trying meant the world to Elle. The tough woman with faded red hair seemed to genuinely like her, after an initial reticence, and Elle was glad that she could say the same.

His sister, Donella, with green eyes, a shock of blond hair, and features that didn't match anyone else's in the family daguerreotype was a bit more aloof, but Elle sensed that she would come around eventually. She told herself she didn't care if the young woman ever did, but that was a lie. Realist that she was, she still hoped that Malcolm's siblings would one day treat her as one of their own. Ewan was out on Union business but was supposed to be returning from the front within the next few days.

"Elle is quite familiar with my begging for sweets, Mum," Malcolm said as he walked into the room. His playful tone warmed her soul. Several weeks had passed since his injury, and although his arm was still weak, he was regaining his weight and recovering from his fever. A terrible sickness had gripped him after his time spent in the freezing James, but he'd pulled through, proving once again that he meant to stay by her side for good.

"Ach, I don't want to know about your conjugal relations, Malcolm McCall," his mother said in her lilting accent, feigning shock, and Elle felt her cheeks burn. Malcolm hadn't been kidding when he said his father had liked a smart-mouthed woman.

"I meant her pecan pie, Mother. And that's Malcolm *Burns,* if ye don't mind," he teased, his own brogue much more apparent when he was in his mother's presence. The name McCall was useless after Rufus's revelation that he was a known quantity, so he had decided to take Elle's name as his professional moniker.

"Your father must be rolling in his grave. If he's not, he should be, leaving me with a son who shirks his own surname."

Elle sat silently, saving her sharp remarks for another time. For the moment, she was enjoying quietly watching the dynamics of her new family. After Malcolm had healed completely, they would be traveling North to meet her folks, who were also less than pleased at her choice of husband. They were excited to meet the man who had captured their daughter's heart and helped ensure Daniel's freedom, nonetheless.

And Daniel *was* free. LaValle had written her to let her know he'd been turned over to the care of the Loyal League after being rescued. Daniel hadn't responded to any of her letters himself. It hurt, but she imagined that he was much changed after whatever he'd experienced. She hoped that one day they could be bosom friends once again.

She hoped the same for the North and South, and if it was possible after the bloody war that still held the nation in thrall, it should be possible for them, too.

After visiting her parents, they would be returning to action, and they had been granted permission to work as a team.

As she watched Malcolm and his mother trade quips, hands moving expressively and eyes filled with love, Elle quietly thanked whatever higher being had bestowed her talent upon her. Growing up, it had isolated her, singling her out as someone to gawk at instead of someone to nurture. She'd had keepers instead of teachers, allies instead of friends. But in the end, her talent had led her to Malcolm, and together they had helped prevent the downfall of the Union.

While making their way to Malcolm's mother, they'd briefly stopped at the Capital to debrief Mr. Allan Pinkerton. He hadn't been given their previous missive, having been busy setting up the first secure telegraph office in the White House. After listening to their news, he immediately relayed the information to President Lincoln and set his network of detectives into action.

As Malcolm had convalesced, the South launched their ironclad, bearing down on the Union blockade and sending dozens of unfortunate men to a watery grave. But the Union had sped up the timetable on their new ironclad, and it steamed out from the Brooklyn Navy Yard to face down its Southern counterpart. Both ships were unfinished and unwieldy, but when news of the battle finally reached Malcolm and Elle it was good: The Southern ironclad was now resting at the bottom of the sea and the blockade held strong.

The front door to the house burst open suddenly and Donella stumbled in, red-faced and out of breath.

"Don, how many times have I told you not to go outside in those breeches?" Mrs. McCall chided. "This girl is going to be the death of me —"

"What's wrong, Donella?" Elle asked, reading the distress on the young woman's face. She rose from her comfortable seat. "What's happened?"

"It's Ewan," she said, holding out the smudged letter in her hand. Elle went to take it from her and was surprised when the girl threw her arms around as if she couldn't take another step without support.

My dearest McCalls . . . " Elle read aloud, then wished she hadn't begun.

431

"I know I promised to visit shortly to meet Malcolm's wife and to make sure Donella hasn't stolen all of my clothing, but I fear my furlough has been indefinitely delayed. I've had the misfortune of being captured by secessionist heathens, and I'm currently being held in one of their prisons. While not the most luxurious accommodations one could hope for, it's not so bad, although their library leaves much to be desired. Please don't worry after me. I've got food to eat and I'm not ill. You know me — I'll find a way to be of use here. I expect to be reunited with you all quite soon. In the meantime, keep me in your thoughts but know that I am well.

Your Obedient Servant, Ewan"

"No!" Mrs. McCall cried out angrily, tears falling from her eyes. "No, not Ewan. I told him not to enlist, I told him he wasn't cut out for war, but he's just as stubborn as the lot of you!"

Donella released Elle and threw herself into her mother's lap.

"Malcolm?" She was worried for everyone, but especially him. His pain was her pain, and it was etched into every aspect of his face as he approached her and hugged her close.

"He says not to worry," Malcolm said thickly, stroking her hair absently. "When he was about twelve he fell from a tree while playing with a group of boys outside. He behaved a little oddly after, but convinced all of us that he was fine. It wasn't until two days later that we realized he had broken his arm."

"How?" Elle asked, pulling back to look up at Malcolm's face. "Wasn't he in pain?"

"He was in terrible pain," Malcolm replied. "But he never wanted to give us cause to worry. Not even then, when he needed help the most."

Elle's stomach dropped.

"We'll go to him," she said. "We'll find a way to free him."

"You'll notice he didn't say *where* he was being held," Malcolm said. "That was not an accident. Dammit, Ewan!"

Malcolm held her close and Elle did the only thing she could — she held him right back. The room that had just seemed warm and inviting was now somber, the only sounds the spitting fire and the muffled sobs of the McCall women.

"I'm sorry," Elle whispered.

"I am, too," Malcolm replied in a low voice. "But I'm not the only crafty McCall.

433

If there's a way out of that place, Ewan will find it."

They shared a dour dinner after that, and Malcolm was unusually quiet when she joined him in bed.

"Do you think things will ever be put aright?" he asked. "All of this devastation, all of this loss?"

She sidled up against him beneath their warm blanket. "I don't know," she said. "I want to tell you yes, but I can't see into the future. The only thing I know for sure is that I love you, and I think I always will."

He shifted in the darkness and the warmth of his lips pressed against her brow.

"You aren't going to search that brain of yours for an appropriate quotation right now?" he asked.

She pressed into his palm as it smoothed over her body, the luxuriant caresses that signaled that the rest of the night would be spent making love, again and again.

"I did," she replied peevishly. "No one's ever written anything that captures how I feel about you. My paltry words will have to do."

"Paltry?" he asked, shaking his head. "Perfect. I love you, too."

Thoughts of the world and its struggles fell away as his lips feathered against hers and her fingers pressed into his shoulder blades. They were together, and that meant they could weather everything to come.

ACKNOWLEDGMENTS

First, I'd like to thank Esi Sogah, Michelle Forde, and the entire Kensington team for believing in this book and, just as importantly, for always letting me know that. Working with all of you is incredibly fulfilling!

I'd also like to thank Victoria Adams for loving Malcolm and Elle so much and inspiring a certain chapter in this book (you know which one).

My wonderful, tireless, and incredible agent, Courtney Miller-Callahan, for always knowing what to say, for being a fellow GIF lover, and for just being a damned awesome human being.

Katana, Derek, and Krista: my Brooklyn writing Squad and the best critique group I'll ever encounter.

My raptors, for always pushing me forward with their gentle, yet razor-sharp raptor claws. You guys complete me, like various animal genes in a genetically modified dinosaur DNA strand.

My husband, Nicolas: Je t'aime, même quand je suis trop occupé pour faire le lessive. Pleins de bisous!

Beverly Jenkins, for clearing the path for writers like me and for tirelessly representing POC in historical romance — and American history.

Finally, thanks to Ta-Nehisi and the Golden Horde/Black Republicans, for creating a space where I could lurk and grow into a historical romance author.

AUTHOR'S NOTE

I wasn't supposed to write this book. When I first became serious about my writing, I decided that, although I loved reading historical romance, I'd best stay away from it. It would lead to too many feelings to untangle, too much unfairness to wrap up with a happy ending, given the kind of heroes and heroines I enjoy writing. Eventually, as I learned more about the history I'd never been taught in the classroom — beyond the simplified stories of George Washington Carver loving peanuts and Rosa Parks being tired — I realized it was important that more people write about the experiences of POC and marginalized people in historical settings, and that I'd like to be one of those people. But I'd never write about THAT.

The Civil War, that is. It's still an open wound in this country — is it even history, really, when the effects of it still vibrate beneath the surface of American life? Too fraught. Too hard. Too draining.

But, it seems that once I decide something is off limits, it's destined to happen. (I also told myself I wasn't interested in dating French men, so you can already guess my husband's nationality.) The more I learned about American history, the more I saw it as the staging ground for stories just as entertaining and epic as the Regency dukes and viscounts romance readers swoon for. I also saw the possibility of extending the tropes of the Civil War beyond "brother fighting brother" and "swooning Southern belle," two categories that conveniently left out a whole swath of people, generally of a darker hue.

Many things fed into the ideas that formed this book, but first and foremost was Ta-Nehisi Coates's blog on *The Atlantic,* where he discussed the Civil War and its relation to American society in a series of blog posts spanning the end of 2008 until 2014. The blog posts, as well as the contributions of the commentariat that would come to be known as The Horde, deeply influenced my decision to write historical romance and to write specifically about the Civil War.

Many of the characters in this book are based, in part, on real-life historical figures.

Elle is based on Mary Bowser, a former slave with an eidetic memory who was placed in Jefferson Davis's White House to funnel information to the Union. Malcolm is based on Timothy Webster, one of Pinkerton's top detectives during the war. Mary's husband, Robert Grand, is based on Robert Smalls, a slave who was a brilliant river pilot and used this to his advantage. After stealing a Confederate war ship and codes, he led an illustrious career, which I will hopefully get to share with you later in this series.

SELECTED BIBLIOGRAPHY

The following is a selection of the books used to research this novel:

Brock, Sallie A. *Richmond during the War.* New York: G. W. Carleton & Co., 1867.

Douglass, Frederick. *Narrative of the Life of Frederick Douglass.* Boston: The Anti Slavery Office, 1845.

Jordan, Robert Paul. *The Civil War.* Washington, DC: National Geographic Society, 1969.

Lause, Mark A. *A Secret Society History of the Civil War.* Champaign, IL: University of Illinois Press, 2011.

McPherson, James M. *Battle Cry of Freedom.* New York: Oxford University Press, 2003.

Pinkerton, Allan. *The Spy of the Rebellion: being a true history of the spy system of the United States Army during the late rebellion, revealing many secrets of the war hitherto not made public.* New York: G. W. Carleton & Co., 1883.

Pratt, Fletcher. *The Civil War in Pictures.* Garden City, NY: Garden City Books, 1955.

Van Doren Stern, Philip. *Secret Missions of the Civil War.* Westport, CT: Praeger, 1959.

■ ■ ■ ■

A READING GROUP GUIDE: AN EXTRAORDINARY UNION

ALYSSA COLE

■ ■ ■ ■

ABOUT THIS GUIDE

The suggested questions are included to enhance your group's reading of Alyssa Cole's *An Extraordinary Union*.

DISCUSSION QUESTIONS

1. The lives of African-Americans during the Civil War are often presented as a single story: slaves who either escaped or were liberated by Union troops. Did the historically accurate portrayals in this book make you rethink some of the history you learned in school?

2. Elle is part of a society of African-Americans who aided the Union throughout the Civil War. Do you know of any African-American spies for the Union outside of Harriet Tubman?

3. Historically, the idea of the Southern belle has been seen as something to strive for. How does this *An Extraordinary Union*'s depiction of this archetype, based on several stories from the historical record, conflict with other pop culture representations?

4. Elle is reluctant to give in to her feelings for Malcolm because of the structure of society. Although consensual interracial relationships did exist at the time, discuss some things Elle would have had to take into consideration.

5. Malcolm's relationship with his father colors much of his feelings about love. How does he overcome his hesitancy?

ABOUT THE AUTHOR

Alyssa Cole's is a science editor, pop culture nerd, and romance junkie who recently moved to the Caribbean and occasionally returns to her fast-paced NYC life. When she's not busy writing, traveling, and learning French, she can be found watching anime with her real-life romance hero or tending to her herd of pets.

The employees of Thorndike Press hope you have enjoyed this Large Print book. All our Thorndike, Wheeler, and Kennebec Large Print titles are designed for easy reading, and all our books are made to last. Other Thorndike Press Large Print books are available at your library, through selected bookstores, or directly from us.

For information about titles, please call:
  (800) 223-1244

or visit our website at:
  gale.com/thorndike

To share your comments, please write:
  Publisher
  Thorndike Press
  10 Water St., Suite 310
  Waterville, ME 04901